TADEUSZ KONWICKI

The Anthropos-Specter-Beast

TRANSLATED FROM THE POLISH BY
GEORGE AND AUDREY KORWIN-RODZISZEWSKI

S.G. PHILLIPS/ *New York*

Library of Congress Cataloging in Publication Data

Konwicki, Tadeusz.
The Anthropos-Specter-Beast.

Translation of Zwierzoczlekoupior.
SUMMARY: Amid warnings of the earth's end Peter encounters the
Anthropos-Specter-Beast and travels with the Investigator Dog on mysterious
trips into the Universe.
[1. Fantasy] I. Heller, Julek. II. Title.
PZ7.K83554An   [Fic]   77-13500

The
Anthropos-
Specter-
Beast

The Anthropos-Specter-Beast

This book is not meant for obedient sons and daughters and they will not benefit from reading it. It is simply not worth their while. Rebellious ones are quite another matter. They will find quite a lot of useful ideas and examples in this amazing story, and a good deal of sympathy and understanding for themselves..

My name is Peter, because I was born in a year when everybody named their daughters Agatha and their sons Peter. My father works at the Aeronautical Institute, although he always wanted to be a musician. I must make it clear that he is not an astronaut or a supersonic test pilot, but something in an office with computers. I suppose that he spends his time adding and subtracting and dividing and multiplying. I never ask him about it, because he becomes very irritable. My mother does the same things as other mothers—cleaning, cooking, sometimes a bit of washing, and she is always worrying. When she is alone she pulls out an easel and starts painting. Well, I hope that gives you a picture of our household. It is not easy to be an obedient son with such parents.

But I have suddenly remembered that we have Miss Sophie living with us. I see her occasionally, when she is going into the bathroom, or into the kitchen for an apple, because she is dieting. At the dinner table she prods and picks with her fork at an empty plate and I am afraid that one day she will be forced to pounce on the dish of potatoes in a rage of hunger. She never speaks to us. I suppose she despises us. Miss Sophie is my older sister and is in the sixth form, where they teach the new experimental syllabus, so that even father could not help her with her mathematics. In any case, she never asks for help.

The first thing I can remember ever seeing or hearing was television. Since then I have seen one or two thousand films unsuitable for children. I am not saying this in order to show off.

The fact is that I know everything. I do not much care about watching films, but what am I to do? I find it hard to get to sleep and usually stay awake until about eleven, and so, whether I am interested or not, I sit in front of the television set to save myself from going off my head with boredom.

Besides finding it hard to sleep, I have another trouble. I cannot stand other children, especially the younger ones and the ones of my own age. I could get on with the older ones perhaps, but they do not want me, so I am left with Father and Mother. My father feels that he has to be a good parent and tries to pretend that he likes playing with me, but he soon gets irritable and then flies into a temper. With Mum it is different—she enjoys playing, but it is still not the same.

So I have to manage by myself. I have read all the books we have in our home, even *The Household Doctor*, although the horrible illustrations put me off. I read the encyclopedia easily.

I am still afraid that some silly person will be thinking that I am showing off all the time, but I don't care. If you really want to know, I don't care about anything. I am telling you this because it is important to my story, and it is a story that will make your hair stand on end and have you screaming for your mother, and you won't be able to sleep all night.

The whole point is that, owing to the unfortunate circumstances of my life, I know all that there is to be known. The world has no riddles for me. I would not even mind quietly dying, for what more can I look forward to now?

Perhaps you do not want to believe what I am telling you. You may think that I am in reality some sort of disillusioned journalist or businessman, but no—I am Peter, in the second form at school and trying to be clever enough to hide what I know.

But first I must tell you about two things that happened to me. The first is rather private. Last autumn I fell in love. To think that only a year ago the only films that could regularly put me to sleep were the ones about love! It is quite painful for me to write about this, but I speak what I feel and I can see no reason for hiding this rather dreadful episode in my life.

I met her in a nearby courtyard, where she was playing the

"elastic game" with some friends. This game was a new craze. Two of the girls had a circle of elastic passed around and stretched tightly between their thin legs, while the girl in question jumped between and over the two strands in some sort of pattern. It was actually her jeans that I first admired. I had never seen any like them before, so I stood and stared at them. And then she stopped playing her game for a moment to get her breath. She saw me, brushed a strand of hair from her face, and tossed her head angrily or haughtily. I suddenly felt a strange burning feeling. My mother was waiting for the soda siphon that I was bringing from the store, but I could not move a single step from the spot and I stood like that until it was dusk.

I will not tell the whole story, it is too painful. Everybody knew that she had a boyfriend in the next street, the son of some Hungarian or Peruvian diplomat—a small, dark chap, nothing remarkable. Everybody knew about it—all the children in the neighborhood, about three hundred kids altogether—all except me. Like an idiot, I did not know a thing. Of course you can guess the end of it. One day I saw them walking together in the next street, licking huge ice-cream cones, although the cold weather had already begun and no decent children were any longer eating ice cream. Everything became clear to me and the cold steel of reality struck me to the heart.

From that moment I knew that the world is a pitiless place. I lost whatever illusions I had. I took a clean sheet of paper from my writing pad and began to draw a picture of them walking along that fatal street. At first I wanted to make them look ridiculous. I added a big nose and masses of freckles to her face (I purposely do not mention her name) and then drew this Hungarian or Peruvian fellow as small as a Pekinese. Afterward I felt a bit uneasy. I will not be revengeful, I thought. It is not their fault; it is the cruelty of life that is to blame. So I drew them as they really are.

While I was drawing them I felt a compulsion, which I could not resist, to swear that never, never again, to the end of my life, would I ever again love anyone. Then it occurred to me that it would be easier to keep my oath if my affections were turned to something quite different. So I told myself that I would look out of the window, and whatever object my eyes first fell upon, that object I would love to my last breath. So I looked out very cautiously, but there was nothing to be seen—that is, there was nothing unusual. There was the familiar street, deserted at this time of day, and near the monument of some educationalist, an acacia tree struggling in the wintry wind. I waited for a long time, for some reason, until I realized that I was looking at the very acacia tree that there had been such a row about in the spring, when an old man with a saw came and began to cut off one of its four main branches. All the neighbors in our street joined together in protest and somebody phoned the police. But the fat sergeant did not know how to deal with the old man, who went on sawing quite unmoved. It turned out later that, far from being a vandal, he was a friend of the educationalist and that this one branch that was rotten needed to be removed in order to save the tree.

Well, I realized that the acacia tree I was looking at was destined as the object of my affections and I was even filled with a kind of joy. A tree is beautiful, especially in springtime, and it is also something solid and reliable. And, of course, an acacia tree will not make a fool of itself with some Hungarian or Peruvian fellow.

From that day on I often looked out of the window at my tree. At the start of winter it went to sleep, but I see that it is now waking up and the brown buds are showing.

"What is he looking at, standing there?" my father would ask, usually with irritation in his voice, whenever he saw me staring out of the window.

"He must be bored," my mother answered calmly.

"Bored? I was never bored at his age," said my father.

He may be right. I understand what he means, but things are different nowadays. Father believed in fairies and storks bringing babies when he was a child, and on St. Nicholas' Eve he used to put his shoe by the hearth to be filled with presents, whereas I enjoy the advantages of modern science and can read about mathematical games and theory, about gravitational fields and matter and antimatter and universal chaos.

[8]

It all makes me feel sad. I can see no sense in my father getting up at six in the morning and traveling by train somewhere to his computer, or my mother dabbing away for hours at a piece of canvas with a tuft of hairs, or in Miss Sophie's grim determination to keep her weight down, or in the dozens of horrible years that I still have to live in this world.

So I am bored. I feel terribly bored from early morning until late at night, every minute and every single moment. I endure the dreariness quietly and hide my suffering, because everybody finds fault with me. Other boys get punished for the usual reasons—for breaking a window or being late or being rude—but I am punished just for being fed up, which hurts nobody but me. What is there to say, after all? I suspect that many people suffer in the same way. Some are well aware of their affliction, others just feel a sort of blank dullness and that's about all. It is a waste of breath talking about it, so I promise not to mention this subject again.

One day, when I came home from school, I kept on looking at the three-branched acacia by the monument. The whole house was utterly quiet. Our neighbors do not begin to make a noise until about eleven at night. I was looking at the faint mist of green that shrouded my precious tree and thinking that in a few days' time it would thicken and brighten and burst into leaf under the ruffling of the spring breeze. I vowed that I would never let any more hooligans climb its trunk or carve any stupid nonsense on its delicate bark.

Suddenly the telephone rang, but since I did not want to speak to anyone, I remained standing by the window. But the caller would not give up and the phone went on ringing; in the end I took off the receiver.

"Is that Peter?" I heard the awful voice of our she-monster, Cecilia.

"I suppose so," I replied.

"You always answer in that imbecile sort of way."

I was silent.

"I can't hear what you are saying," shouted Cecilia.

"I am not saying anything."

"Impudence!"

"But honestly, I have not spoken a word," I said.

"I'll deal with you one of these days, you'll see. You are getting far too conceited."

"I am not at all—"

"Be quiet! I have no intention of arguing with you. Is your mother in?"

"No."

"Is your father there?"

"He's not in either."

"Why not?"

"Because he is not back from work yet."

Cecilia was silent. Maybe she was reviewing my reply for signs of insolence. I could clearly hear her angry breathing.

"Oh, really!" she shouted, "very well then!" and she banged down the receiver with such a crash that the telephone tinkled in complaint and then crackled and heaved a sort of sigh.

There is no need, after that, to tell you what Cecilia is like, but I will tell you what she *looks* like, because it is rather important. She is my mother's friend, and she must really be an old maid, although she often talks a lot about a husband who died years ago, at the time when Miss Sophie was born, it seems. She is tall and thin, with short hair. Her strange, darting eyes are full of anger, and her rather small face, with its high color, reminds one of faces in old portrait paintings. Cecilia is sure that she resembles a famous painter called Van Gogh, but she looks more like Judas in the picture called "The Last Supper." She is possessed by some sort of demon. Everybody knows this, but they try to soften the truth, and that is why my mother speaks of her as "our charming she-monster."

I returned to the window, feeling annoyed. A few boys were riding their bicycles and a man was leaning out of his car window and shouting at them. Passersby hurried along the pavement in coats far too thin for this spring chilliness. They must have been sorry that they had let themselves be taken in by the weather forecast of the day before, which had promised a heatwave. The thought that today's television programs were a complete bore was making me feel still more irritated, when the doorbell sounded.

[10]

I went into the hall without hurrying and opened the door. A huge Great Dane, taller than me, stood there motionless, not even moving his tail and staring at me with big eyes lit with a bluish gleam, but no whites showing. He stood there, feet apart and chest as broad as a bear. Feeling a bit disappointed, I was about to slam the door when he quite unexpectedly asked, in a deep, slightly hoarse voice:

"Are your parents in?"

"No, they are not," I replied, completely flabbergasted.

"That's fine," he remarked, pushing past me into the hall and brushing me unceremoniously with his hard, ribbed flanks.

"What do you want?" I stammered.

"It's all right, my friend," he said, making for the living room.

From dog habit he sniffed the furniture, and even began to raise his leg against the television table but thought better of it. When he had sized everything up he said: "You have a nice place here, but it's rather cold."

"They have turned off the central heating," I said.

He came close to me and scrutinized me a while in silence. His soft, black lips dripped a little with saliva, which faintly impaired his dignity.

"You are reminded, I think," he said, "of certain books, in which sensitive children, who are misunderstood by their families and friends, are visited at night by animals or by some splendid hero. Am I right?"

"Well, I'm listening," I said.

"Don't make ironical remarks, my friend." His black lips curled with distaste. "I do not go about comforting a lot of silly children. I am the Investigator Dog. I repeat that: I am the Investigator Dog."

For a moment I felt rather scared. After all, he was a very big dog. He must have weighed at least a hundred and fifty pounds and even as he stood quite still, the huge muscles swelled under his rust-brown coat. I tried to smile.

"Have you nothing to say?" he asked, in a voice so deep that the panes in the window trembled. "Perhaps you think that I am mad?"

My thoughts were in disorder, but I did wonder if he had been inoculated against rabies. "Why not?" I managed to say. "It *is* possible."

"What is possible?" he asked suspiciously.

"Well, investigating," I said—"discovering things."

"You're right, friend, it can be done. I have been keeping a watchful eye on you for some time now. You can be my partner if you like. What do you say?"

He was so taken up with his idea that he did not notice my lack of enthusiasm. He pulled up two armchairs facing each other and settled himself heavily in one of them, ordering me to sit in the other.

"But what are we going to do?" I asked.

"Don't ask questions. Everything will be clear eventually."

I saw how, as he sat on his rump, his hind legs kept slipping off the cushions when he tried to cover his lean belly with his paw, and I wanted to laugh, but he looked at me fixedly, now showing the whites of his chestnut-brown eyes.

"Are you ready?" he asked quietly.

"Yes, I'm ready," I said, but I felt uneasy.

"Very well then, my friend."

We looked with increasing intensity into each other's eyes, and gradually the windows behind the dog's head lost their outline, becoming just blurred patches of light which imperceptibly faded away. In the enormous silence I could hear a distant sound of water, the sort of splashing sound that could be made by boys wading across a shallow river. It became completely dark and I was suddenly afraid that I had become blind. I wanted to jump from my chair and shout for help, but just then I felt, rather than saw, a faint but growing light like early dawn.

I began to make out menacing shapes that strained toward me, but they turned out to be alder trees growing freely and luxuriantly. Soon I could see the sky, thinly fleeced with clouds, and hear the sound of a river running over boulders.

I was sitting on a narrow slope beside a riverbank. Around me grew grass longer and thicker than any I had ever seen before, flowers of every color, ribbon-like creepers entangled in thick trees and the yellow-green trails of a plant with small whitish flower cones that may have been wild hops.

A cold breath rose from the river, so I climbed to a low rise of ground and found myself in a small meadow overgrown with weeds whose flowers were like heads of white cotton. I saw a strange, very green valley. Behind me and the river an oak forest rose into the sky. In front of me a gentle hillside was topped by the edge of a pine forest, and a church tower above the red roofs of a dozen or so houses. It seemed that there was a railway line, because I noticed a horizontal plume of gray smoke and the hoarse scream of an engine drifted down to the river. The valley ended on my right in a line of white stone, where a distant town shimmered in the hot air. To my left, the valley enclosed a big park with poplar trees half concealing a honey-colored building that seemed to me to be an old manor house.

I heard a deep voice. "Well, what do you think of it, at first sight?"

The Great Dane was crouched in the long grass, panting. A dribble of saliva hung from his mouth.

"Where are we?" I asked in a small voice.

"Somewhere in the universe, my friend."

"I seem to know this valley," I said.

The dog looked at me quizzically, with eyes half shut. "Perhaps you have been here on holiday."

"We go to the seaside for holidays because the iodine in the air is good for me. I was very ill some time ago."

I saw now that several cows were grazing under a clump of alders, and some boys—cowherds, perhaps—were throwing stones into the river, which was half in shadow, for the sun was already dropping over the distant town. The light shining obliquely on the unshadowed bank was tinged with intense redness. There was a sound of someone singing a long-drawn-out kind of tune in a throaty voice. I felt rather uneasy—in fact I felt frightened.

"What shall we do now? Shall we go back?" I asked.

The dog stood up and stretched himself and yawned. "Where?" he asked.

"Home."

"I must show you something first," he said. And he set off, padding across the field. I trampled a molehill flat with my foot, and on its warm surface I drew a rough sketch of the valley and the road that led back. The dog stopped and looked around at me distrustfully.

"What are you messing about with there?" he asked.

"Nothing. I've found a fresh molehill, that's all."

A plume of smoke rose again behind the red roofs of the village as the train started off again after a short stop. But it was a funny sort of train, not like any that I had ever seen before. It reminded me of the trains in illustrations in old children's books.

We were still crossing the field when a large bird rose up suddenly from a tuft of grass and flew with a heavy flapping of wings toward the edge of a pinewood where it struggled over a big sandy cliff. The Great Dane chased it and then turned back and started rooting about in the mintgrass, whose scent made him sneeze. But he could not find the bird's nest. He joined me, looking rather sheepish.

"Have you ever been here before?" I asked.

"Yes, of course. I know every path and track," he said.

"Why did you bring me along with you this time?" I asked.

The huge beast considered for a while and then answered, rather unwillingly, "You will see later. Be a little more patient, my friend."

We were crossing a country road when, from out of a wild rosebush there staggered a large chicken with disheveled wings, brown stains on its breast feathers, and grains of corn or barley sticking to its dirty beak. Although its eyelids drooped and it moved about unsteadily, it managed, oddly enough, to keep to the road.

"Here's Chippy," said the dog, in a tone of disgust. "There is a brewery behind the big house and he feeds there on a heap of barley pressings. Disgusting!"

Chippy was singing something, although it was not so much singing as a kind of fuddled squawk that he uttered at intervals, as though he were hot or tired of walking. He passed us without seeing us.

"Keep away from him," said the dog in a low voice. "He is a notorious rascal. You will be hearing more of him."

We were soon standing before a big iron gate, through which we could see a gravel path leading to a big golden-colored house. There was someone sitting on the lawn under a striped umbrella, reading a newspaper.

"This gate is always padlocked," said the dog in a low voice. "Let us try around the other side."

We moved along a tall fence of rusted iron railings. Lilac bushes and trails of jasmine obstructed the view as we waded through brown grass almost as tall as half-grown corn. The dog disappeared from sight now and again in this strange growth. A bird with a long tail flew over our heads. I guessed that it must have been a pheasant, because gardens like this could only be inhabited by pheasants.

Suddenly the dog halted and pricked his ears.

"What is the matter?" I asked.

"Be quiet," he hissed, twisting the skin on his back to drive away the flies. "Something is going to happen."

He stood there motionless for a while, amid a subdued whining of mosquitoes, while a bird sang in the lilac bushes. I had never heard a nightingale, but only a nightingale could have sung as this bird did.

Suddenly there was a rustling in the undergrowth and a small

[15]

white hoop rolled toward the railings from the midst of some hazel bushes, bounced back from the low brickwork, and fell to the ground among the bare stalks of last spring's cowslips.

I looked at the dog. He raised his paw to signal me to keep quiet. There was a sound of quick, light steps as someone pushed through the bushes and the foliage swayed here and there. I realized that there was somebody looking for the hoop, which had been fashioned out of a peeled hazel twig.

Suddenly a little girl appeared, dressed all in white—white dress, white ribbon in her hair, white socks and shoes, and holding a white hazel wand. She stooped to pick up the hoop. I thought that I knew this game. I must have read about and even seen pictures of the game of hoop-la, in which your partner throws the ring to you and you must catch it on your cross-stick, an implement that looks like a small sword.

As she picked up the hoop, the little girl saw us standing there, motionless behind the railings. She froze instantly, looking at us with amazement. I could see that she wanted to run away, but something held her rooted to the ground. For a moment I thought that it was the sight of the Investigator Dog's eyes upon her.

Someone called from the side of the big house. "Eva!"

She opened her mouth. The red sunlight rested on her head, moving slowly to pick out her white ribbon.

"Eva! Where are you?"

She looked in the direction of the voice, but could not move a single step. A bell sounded from a distant church on the hill.

"Eva!"

There was a sound of someone making his way toward us through the bushes, and a boy burst out from the dark foliage. He was oddly dressed in the sort of knickerbockers buttoned below the knees that nobody nowadays ever wears. And I had never seen striped socks or a pullover like those he wore. He was holding a stick made from a peeled hazel wand.

I felt very hot and suddenly realized that my leg, which was resting on the brickwork that supported the railings, was beginning to tremble violently, so violently that it seemed to be trying to shake itself free of my body. For the boy in knickerbockers seemed to be me—to be really me, as I remembered seeing myself when I looked in a mirror. It was then I who stood, dressed like that, glowering darkly at myself standing there with the Investigator Dog on the other side of the railings.

"Eva," said the other boy, "are they bothering you?"

She shook her head, and the red light of the setting sun slid from her hair.

"Go back indoors," he said, "it's cold here," and he pulled her by the arm and pushed her toward the bushes, and when she had disappeared he came to the railings.

"I don't want to see you here again—ever. Do you understand? Because next time I will bring my gun with me." Then he, too, disappeared into the shrubbery.

"He is the exact image of me," I said, gulping.

"Do you think so?" said the Investigator Dog. There was an odd note in his voice. "Perhaps you are maligning one of you. I don't see any resemblance."

"No, it's true," I said. The impression was so strong that I began to break out in a sweat.

"Rubbish!" The dog tried to pass it off. "You must be tired. Perhaps you are just imagining things."

"Who is she?"

"He keeps her captive in this house. You have seen how the gate is fastened with a large padlock."

"But why is he keeping her captive?"

"Because . . . He is simply holding her prisoner."

"She has such long hair," I said, "it reaches to her waist. I have never seen such hair."

"Quite so. And it is you who are going to set her free, my friend."

"Me?" I said.

"Yes, you."

"But where are we?"

Dusk was approaching and dampness began to rise from the cool ground. From not far away there came a murmur of running water.

"Well, it's time to go back home," said the Investigator Dog.

He sat, and fixed his eyes upon my face. His pupils expanded and flickered with a blue light and his brow knitted into enormous wrinkles, as though he were making some great mental effort.

We stayed like this, motionless, for a while. Somewhere in the grass a cricket was chirping, and there was a voice far away chanting like a muezzin calling the faithful to prayer. I became suddenly aware of other eyes, at the dog's back, that stared at me persistently, and a crooked shadow lurking behind the cracked trunk of an old poplar.

I was going to speak, but the dog spoke first. "Dammit!" he swore. "There must be something wrong. Let's try again."

As he spoke, the skulking shadow suddenly lengthened and began to bound in great leaps toward the river. I caught a glimpse of a tawny flank striped with black and a long sinewy tail.

"Look," I said, "there's a cat that looks very much like a tiger."

The Investigator Dog did not bother to turn his head. He shrugged his huge shoulders. "That's Fela," he said, "the tigress. No decent creature will have anything to do with her."

"Where did she spring from?"

"Be patient, you will soon know everything. We must go back." He fixed his eyes on me, ignoring the mosquitoes that settled on him.

"Your attention is wandering. You cannot concentrate," he grumbled in a drowsy voice. "We must return to our world. It is already late. They are waiting there for both of us." His voice became softer and slower. It was growing dark. And then night descended, perfectly black and silent. . . .

The doorbell sounded repeatedly. I got up from my armchair. An April rain was falling, mixed with sleet. The dog was no longer to be seen, only a few traces of mud on the chair pulled up against mine. As the doorbell was becoming increasingly threatening and impatient I opened the door, and there stood my mother, Cecilia, and Miss Sophie with a briefcase. My father stood on the stairs, and all four were furious.

"What are you up to?" shouted my father. "We've been ringing for about half an hour."

"Sorry," I said, "I didn't hear."

"He didn't hear!" My father turned to the others and flung out his arm.

"He must have been up to something," said Cecilia. "I'm telling you, I can read the guilt in his eyes."

"I wasn't in," I said.

"What did I say?" cried Cecilia in triumph, and her voice shook all the windows up and down the seven-story stairwell.

"It's true. I've only just come back."

"Wait a minute," said my mother," you've just come back, and we've been standing here since twenty past two and we haven't seen you."

"I can't help it," I said.

"Then tell us where you've been," Cecilia said with a cunning smile.

I did not want to lie or make a lot of empty excuses, and besides, they were all still standing outside the door, so I told the truth:

"Well, it was simply that a dog called, a huge Great Dane, who seems to be an investigator. He suggested that we should take a trip out into the Universe. We visited a planet very much like the earth, but it was rather more beautiful. I met a girl there, who played hoop-la with a boy who looked exactly like me."

"No doubt the dog spoke with a human voice," said my father scoffingly.

"Yes, he spoke very well."

"You didn't meet a tiger, by any chance?" asked Cecilia, with a meaningful look at my mother.

"Yes, I did. But how did you know? Only it was a tigress, not a tiger."

"If you ask me, you have no idea how to bring up children!" exclaimed Cecilia. "If he were mine I would give him a good thrashing. Such laziness! He doesn't even make any effort to tell lies properly. He doesn't care a fig for any of you, my dears."

She pushed past me, just as the dog had done earlier, and they all came into the hall, criticizing me as they took off their coats.

"You exaggerate, Cecilia," my mother was saying in self-defense. "He's simply got a taste for fantasy."

"They say that writing pays well," said my father. "I read in the papers that a sixteen-year-old English girl earned a hundred thousand pounds with her first book."

"But have you read her book?" challenged Cecilia, "because I have."

"No, I haven't read it."

"She's very unkind about her parents—she makes them out to be awful monsters."

"But for all that, a hundred thousand pounds is a hundred thousand pounds," said my mother philosophically.

"Well!" shouted Cecilia, so shrilly that the gas heater automatically ignited in the bathroom. "If it had been me I'd have thrashed the life out of such a child."

"But seeing that you have no children," remarked my father, "what you say seems to be rather theoretical."

"You're a fool. It's no use talking to you," said Cecilia. And still quarreling, they passed into the room where the two chairs were still facing each other. Just at that moment it began to hail with hailstones as large as marbles. Miss Sophie locked herself in her room and switched on her radio to some deafening pop music.

My mother set the table for dinner and began to warm up something in the kitchen while still taking part in the conversation. On the other side of the wall a baby started to cry, alarmed by Cecilia's voice. I sat by the window and watched Cecilia from the corner of my eye. I liked her actually, especially in her fits of fury.

"I rang you up two hours ago," she said eventually, calming down, "it was this idiot who answered."

"You mean Peter?" asked my father amiably.

"This time I meant Peter. But you yourself are no better than an idiot."

Father changed the subject and asked, "What's the news today? I haven't read the papers yet."

"So you don't know?"

"Not yet," said my father meekly, "but I expect now I shall soon hear it all in detail."

"It's in all the papers, but I heard it in the BBC news broadcast too "

I decided to play up to her, and asked, "What's the BBC, Aunt Cecilia?"

"The BBC is the English broadcasting station, where your aunt used to work during the war," she answered with dignity.

"Do not interrupt with silly questions," said my father, anxious to hear the news.

"Why are you picking on the boy?" asked Cecilia. "He will grow up to be proud of his aunt."

Mum served the meal and they started calling Miss Sophie, whose room was reverberating with the strains of teen-age pop.

"Is this gravy? Meat with fat gravy?" cried Cecilia.

"Yes, it is," said my mother, "my menfolk like it."

"They are idiots," replied Cecilia. "Civilized people eat their steaks grilled. Take this rubbish off my plate at once."

"Idiot" was Cecilia's favorite word and was applied to everyone. I was used to it and it did not bother me, but my father, who was given to standing on his dignity, found it more difficult to bear. His face would turn red, but he did not dare to protest.

Finally Cecilia began to eat, and it must be said that she was certainly a hearty eater. Miss Sophie appeared, sat down at the table like a sleepwalker, and began picking about among the vegetables on her plate as if she were looking for a hidden pearl.

"Cecilia, my dear," said my father mildly.

"What is it?" she asked.

"I thought you had some sensational news."

"Indeed I have." She stopped eating and her eyes gleamed triumphantly. "My dears, the earth is going to collide with a comet on the eighth of May!"

Silence fell.

"That gives us less than a month," said father at last.

"Yes, it will be on St. Stanislas' Day."

[21]

"But we have no one in our family with their name day then," said my mother dubiously.

Cecilia dropped the hand holding her fork upon the table and made a vase of catkins jump. "How can you put up with such a nitwit?" she asked.

Father's face assumed a vague expression.

"The biggest comet in history," Cecilia continued, "is going to collide with our globe. Do you understand?"

"A cosmic cataclysm," whispered father.

"You are right," said Cecilia. "In other words, the end of the world."

"Heaven help us!" cried my mother, terrified. "Perhaps I ought to get in some flour and sugar and salt."

Cecilia fixed her with a glare and my mother dwindled under her gaze until she seemed no size at all. Cecilia, brimming with contempt, continued her meal.

"They have predicted the end of the world so many times already," began my father cautiously.

"That's the best proof that it's going to happen."

"But after so many millions of years?"

"Well, it was bound to come some time."

"But why just now?" asked my mother.

"I don't give a damn," muttered Miss Sophie, who had managed to play with her food for five whole minutes without swallowing a single morsel.

Silence fell again. A shaft of sunlight shone through the windows. Some well-fed pigeons were cooing on the window ledge.

Cecilia began to give us a very complicated lecture on the nonexistence of God. People, she said, had invented him, and human imagination gave him a sort of reality, but he was powerless. You are not asked to understand this argument, for I do not understand it either. Aunt Cecilia has very original views and is a rationalist, which means that she is the intellectual type of old spinster who thinks that the human mind is everything. She never admits that she is an old spinster. She regards herself only as an independent, self-reliant rationalist, who stands head and shoulders above the idiot mob, by which she means everyone but herself. As my father tried to look ironical, Cecilia added some remark about man originating from woman, and to say that God created woman from Adam's rib was a downright lie. It was absolutely the other way round. Man was an inefficient variant, a mere bungled copy of a woman. My father grew red in the face, and in order to prove her point she began to whisper in his ear so that the children could not hear, and my father's face grew even redder.

It took Aunt Cecilia a long time to make her departure because she was always remembering another thing that she had to say. When the door had finally shut behind her we could hear her scolding our self-important caretaker about something.

My father stayed sunk in thought for a while, and then he asked, "Well, what do you think of it?"

"It has seemed like the end of world for some time," my mother observed.

"We shall soon find out," said my father, who then shut himself in his study with a batch of newspapers, while my mother began washing up. A friend of Miss Sophie's arrived. The two girls whispered at the door for a while, and then Miss Sophie disappeared. I felt very bored. I went into Miss Sophie's room, a kind of cubicle with half a window. There were picture cutouts from magazines on the walls. In one of them was a trendy teenage model, looking so thin one might have thought her deformed. Miss Sophie did not like her, and I know why. Photographs of actors and pop stars were fastened to the wall with pushpins. All over the room, lying, hanging, or standing, all kinds of mementoes were scattered about—an old horseshoe, empty scent bottles, and the like.

I knew where to find what I wanted. I lifted the mattress. Miss Sophie's diary was in its usual place. She is terribly sensitive and she would have killed me if she had known. But I get fed up with reading ordinary fiction. Miss Sophie's diary was about real life.

I opened it where I had last left off reading, a few weeks ago. The pages were all heavily decorated with doodles and drawings.

"It is spring at last;" Miss Sophie had written. "The winter has been dragging on as if it would never end. It has been unendurable torture to see him every day, to constantly rub shoulders with him, and even to meet him after school, and always to have to pretend to be indifferent. But I shall never speak to him again. He is just a plain villain. What did he see in her? He ought to be ashamed of himself.

"The days are getting longer. Clouds as white as snow sail across the blue skies, and the breeze brings a breath of spring, the scent of nature coming to life. Everything is becoming bright and full of hope. But I think of my fate and go on crying late into the night. I have dear, kind parents and a dear little brother. I am healthy and have all that I want, but in spite of all this I can see no sense in continuing to live. I can find no purpose in life, nothing but emptiness and disillusion. I feel a constant urge to go to the bank of the Vistula and throw myself into its troubled waters. I think that this is what I shall do. It is the only solution."

At this point on the page there were a few stains. They were tear marks, tears actually wept by Miss Sophie. Beneath her mask of cold indifference, she was suffering agony. I knew the boy she was talking about. His name was Gagatek, a big, glum sort of fellow, who lived in the next block and never said hello to anyone, not even to my father. At one time, before he jilted her, he would ring up Miss Sophie quite often. I could always recognize his hoarse voice and awkward speech. For some reason I suddenly felt very sorry for Miss Sophie. The slimming business must have been exhausting, and then on top of that there was her unrequited love for that miserable wretch. I even felt tears rising in my own eyes, although I did not like the bit about "a dear little brother." I was not "little" and I was not "dear." I was just her brother.

At that moment my father came out of his study and I had to put the diary back in its place.

"Yes, my dear," he said to Mum, who came out of the kitchen, "earthquakes, cyclones, floods, sunspots of unprecedented intensity, and this comet or huge meteor rushing toward the earth."

"So it is the end of the world, after all?" asked Mum quietly.

"Well, you can't expect them to say so in so many words.

They're afraid of causing a panic. But I can see clearly what it all means."

"What shall we do, then?"

"At least we shall not have to go and buy that new summer jacket for me."

"Are you out of your mind? What will you wear when the warm weather comes?"

"It isn't worth it. There's no point in buying a jacket to wear just for three weeks," said my father.

"Goodness, how frightening it is!" my mother whispered.

"I don't see anything frightening about it. It's all the same to me. Maybe it's just as well."

"You would like the world to collapse because you have trouble at your office? And what about our children?"

"We can do nothing to stop it. Whenever the end of the world comes, there will be children who will have to witness it."

"You are a poor sort of father!" said my mother.

I opened the door. They stopped talking instantly and looked embarrassed. My father began to scratch his eyebrows nervously, and for once my mother did not tell him to stop it. "Shall I make you some custard cream, my poor little Peterkin?" she asked.

"What were you talking about so loudly?"

"Your father has problems at work. He is a bit overwrought," my mother lied quickly.

"I heard you saying something about a comet."

"You must have misheard. That stupid Aunt Cecilia said a lot of silly things. It was enough to upset a child."

My father smiled ironically and was silent. I knew that he, like me, dreamed of the end of the world.

Later in the evening, before going to sleep, I listened to their subdued voices. My father sounded irritated and Mum sighed a great deal. Outside a strong wind was blowing, the fierce kind of wind that fells trees and blows roofs off—a herald, probably, of the end that was upon us. I deliberately did not look at the newspapers—although they tempted me, lying open all over the place—because I was afraid of being disappointed.

I had read some time back about a meteor that, according to

certain scientists, could cause a cataclysm if it passed near the earth. It is well known that sometimes a scientist will try to make a name for himself by publishing information that has not been thoroughly checked or properly considered. The popular press always pounces on this sort of thing. But I, with my profound knowledge, especially of science, cannot read such stuff without a smile of pity. So perhaps it was better not to look at the newspapers or to read details of this news unless I was prepared to calculate its probability on paper, as was my usual habit. For I wanted the forecast to come true. I don't think I need to explain the reason to you. You know by now my attitude to life, and about my terrible boredom—which I recall having promised never to mention again.

I had some practical reasons, too, for my wish. My parents had become quite old. My mother would be forty next year and my father must have been already about forty-three years old. Sometimes I wonder why they want to go on living. They say, of course, that they live for their children, but that must be just an excuse.

I remember Aunt Cecilia saying about them that they were a "loving couple." This disgusted and annoyed me. How can people be in love when they are nearly forty? I put up with books in which the loving pair are eighteen or nineteen—or twenty at the most, but that is the limit. For a man of twenty-seven love is indecent. If the hero or heroine is as old as this, or older, I throw such books behind the sofa after I have read a few pages.

But to return again to motives. Because of Gagatek, Miss Sophie wanted to throw herself into the Vistula. I should think that the end of the world would be handy for her too.

Looking at the actual situation, that silly girl in jeans who played the "elastic game" and her diplomat's son from Peru or Hungary would have the fright of their lives when the earth was about to blow to pieces under their feet. She would be sorry. She would cry bitterly and swear that she would give anything to change things back as they were. But it would be too late. As for him, I have nothing to say about him. I despised him. But when the moment came, the greatest pleasure for me would be to watch Cecilia's face. I was sure that it would be quite blank. Can you imagine how her eyes would stare? The end of the world would have its pleasant side.

You must be surprised that I make no mention of my school or of settling accounts with my teachers. It is simply because I have nothing against them. I even admire them. For a modest salary they are willing to work hard teaching what they can to dunderheads, nitwits, stammerers, sissies, laggards, blubberers, good-for-nothings, toadies, loafers, and hooligans. I could make a longer list of names, but you are too young to read them.

The neighbors upstairs became active. Something that sounded like an outsize cabinet fell with a terrific thud and there was a clumping of heavy boots. A chair creaked and a radio started up full blast. I realized from all this that it was about eleven o'clock. There's certainly something to be said for the end of the world, I thought, and then I fell asleep.

Of course I dreamed, as usual. I must explain that I am not the oversensitive type of boy who has strange, beautiful, poetic dreams, full of scents and colors. My dreams are generally nightmarish, full of torment and fear. The things that I see are mere shreds and bits and colorless fragments, cruel glimpses forgotten soon after waking and making very little sense. Even Professor Freud, and the other psychologists and interpreters of dreams, would have some trouble in making anything of mine.

On this particular night, however, I dreamed a good child's dream, a sensible, logical dream with an interesting ending.

I was in a huge square, facing a tall skyscraper, in the midst of a big, swaying crowd that was gazing at the western sky behind the building. The hum of human voices grew into a sort of hysterical wailing. The sky turned a horrible yellow color, and black clouds began to roll up from the north and south. A strong wind started to blow, bringing a sound of thunder from the distance. A shaft of lightning struck and something seemed to have happened in the middle of the square. Maybe the earth had cracked open, or a flood burst up between the paving stones, or a flow of lava. I could not tell, because the crowd was so thick. People began to scatter in all directions, shrieking dreadfully. I started running too, straight ahead.

I must have gone into the skyscraper, because I suddenly saw what seemed like huge corridors, or maybe they were long halls, with tall columns. Someone was lying in wait for me in the shadows of the colonnade. I was running as fast as I could. There was a rumble of collapsing walls behind me, the whine of a cosmic wind, and the cries of thousands of people. A little girl, all in white, was running beside me. A boy in knickerbockers, the one from the mansion in the green valley, was pulling her by the hand. I wanted to help her, but the boy dragged her away from me. They were running faster than I was, for I was already losing my strength to the point where I could scarcely raise my feet from the marble floor. We ran on through many changing surroundings. I even remember that there was a park, or perhaps it was a zoo, full of panic-stricken animals.

We entered an empty railway station, with the tracks all pulled up and entangled. The little girl in white and the boy from the golden house were climbing into an odd-looking airplane that was standing on its tail. It immediately gave a jump and took off vertically, leaving me desperately shouting after them. I may have been crying too, but I am not sure, because it was in a dream.

I awoke soaking with sweat. My fear melted away like night shadows in the familiar, reflected light of the street lamp. In fact, I had had a dreadful fright, although there was nothing particularly interesting in my dream. I suspect that dreams are hints of some great mystery that the human race is going to take a long time to solve.

In the morning, before going to school, I soothed my mind by reading some of a minor work by a Russian scientist, Professor Cyril G. Samoyedov, entitled *Ourselves and the Universe*. It is not bad on the whole, although maybe rather naïve in parts.

My mother was starting a new painting, one which captured very strongly the atmosphere in our household. There were elements of catastrophe in it, expressed in abstract form, and I think that this striking picture was very significant, in the light of what followed.

I had hardly left home when I came face to face with signs of panic. Our swollen-headed caretaker was standing in the stairway with a map of the heavens open in his hand, looking very excited and explaining something to one of the tenants. An old woman in the middle of the courtyard was looking at the sky through a piece of smoked glass. Workmen, who had been repairing the road during the last few days, were sitting on the curb looking very depressed.

The tension could also be felt at school. None of the teachers would allow anyone to ask questions, and pupils who wanted to be excused were afraid to raise their hands. The lessons were hurried through as if the staff wanted to get rid of us as soon as possible.

After school I wandered about the streets. I felt rather pleased that everyone seemed afraid but me. I noticed the timid way in which passersby looked at each other's faces, and how, without knowing it, they drew their heads into their shoulders, hunched and watchful, as though fearing an unexpected blow, or thunder, or the rumble of a collapsing world.

An abnormally fat boy ran across the street, trembling beneath his clothes like a jelly. We called him Buffalo.

"Have you heard about the comet?" he cried, while he was still some distance away.

"Yes," I said.

"It's all a hullabaloo about nothing, don't you think?" he shouted as he hurtled like a bombshell into a self-service grocery. All the neighbors were sorry for Buffalo's parents. They were both small and thin and had a haunted look in their eyes. Why such a freak of nature should have been born to them, of all people, was a mystery. Buffalo stuffed himself all day long. Their cupboard and their refrigerator were kept padlocked, but Buffalo, puffing and blowing and groaning with greed, always managed to break the lock and wolf all the food, down to the last crumb. Some people said that there were even the marks of teeth on their furniture, but I do not believe that.

[29]

A day or so later, on my way home, I passed through a nearby courtyard where there stood a statue of a stag. It was just an ordinary stag with antlers, put there apparently by some sports-men who maybe felt that they owed something to the animals they had hunted.

The scene before me would at one time have shaken me, but now I stopped for a while, simply out of boredom, and looked without any special feeling at the girl with the jeans (still I will not say her name). She was wearing the same jeans, but now they were rather worn, and she was playing the "elastic game" with her girl friends. You are, of course, expecting me to tell you that the Hungarian or Peruvian boyfriend appeared the next moment, and that is what I thought would happen. But he did not show up at all, and as I stood there I began to wonder if I had imagined everything that had gone before. Maybe they had never walked together along the street, licking ice-cream cones.

She stopped playing and bent down to adjust her shoe, and then pretended to be looking at the windows of a red house covered with a straggling vine, leafless at this time of year. But I knew that she had noticed me and was watching me. Then she said something to her companions, and the idiotic girls first began to giggle and then laughed until they choked. They would stop for a minute and pull themselves together before bursting out again into a sort of hideous neighing. I tried to pretend that I was waiting for somebody, and I even turned my back on them.

What, indeed, did I care about her, jumping there on her silly legs, and not even really knowing what lay in store for her in three weeks' time? I would have liked to be nearby when the time came. I would not have tried to help her, not even if she knelt to me. But, who knows? Maybe in the end I would have allowed myself to be placated. It would make no sense anyway, and besides, I had made up my mind long ago. It was too late now.

I passed on in the direction of our courtyard, thinking that I would go out into the street once more to see how the acacia tree was faring. Then I saw the Great Dane sitting on the stone steps in front of the entrance to our staircase, licking his huge flank.

"Hello, my friend," he said, his voice even deeper than I had heard it before. "I rang your bell, but nobody came to the door."

"I didn't think that you'd ever show up again," I said.

"I had some work to do at home. Would you like to come along today?"

"Where?" I asked.

"Don't be a simpleton—where we went before."

"I haven't had my dinner yet."

"If you don't want to come, that's OK by me. I'm not asking a favor."

"Well . . . all right. I'll come for a little while."

"I can't spare a lot of time, either," said the dog.

At that moment Buffalo's parents passed by, laden with huge string bags stuffed with provisions. His mother had a dogged, resentful look on her face, which was not surprising.

Then, "Do you hear?" she said angrily to her husband. "The dog is speaking to that boy in a human voice."

"Have you nothing more important to worry about?" said Buffalo's father dispiritedly.

The dog followed them with compassionate eyes as they passed. He must have known about their misfortune. A drop of saliva fell on the cement step. It was funny that he did not know how ridiculous he looked.

"Well then?" he said, suddenly rousing himself from his musing.

"We could go into the attic. Hardly anybody ever goes there."

"All right," he agreed, "I don't mind."

It took us quite a time to climb the stairs, because the attic was on the eighth floor.

"What do you think about the comet?" I asked, when we were about halfway up.

He stopped for a moment, with his big tongue hanging so far out that it almost touched the stone floor.

"Do you believe in reincarnation?" he asked quietly.

I was silent, taken aback by his question, and he must have thought that I did not understand the meaning of the word. "Reincarnation is a kind of migration of the soul," he said, "Someone dies and his soul, his being, passes on to become someone else. You understand?"

"Life passed on eternally," I said, "a kind of immortality. I read about all that some time ago, when I was small."

The dog's face darkened. His eyes, the color of chestnuts freshly deburred, fixed on me in a hostile stare.

"You don't believe in reincarnation, then?"

"One can't believe in everything," I said. "Anyhow, what were you in your last incarnation?"

The Investigator Dog shifted his weight from one foot to the other and continued the climb upward.

"I was a lord," he said casually.

"Do you mean that they called you 'lord'?"

"I was an ordinary English lord. I hope that something of that life has left its mark on me."

"But what is your real name?"

"Sebastian."

I was silent, feeling rather abashed. I could see clearly now that I was dealing with a snob.

We reached the attic. It was dark and quiet, and there was an acrid smell of dust and cobwebs that irritated one's nose.

"Well, how about this?" I asked.

"It'll do. Let's sit here by the wall, where there's a little light."

Sebastian's feet slipped on some old newspapers and he swore rather roughly. It occurred to me that he must have come from a somewhat questionable background.

"Can you see me?" asked Sebastian.

"Yes," I said, sitting down. "I can see the spittle hanging on your lower lip."

He wiped it away quickly with his big paw.

"Do you know," I said, "it seems to me that I have seen that valley before."

He smiled slightly. "Don't ask any questions now," he said. "One day you will understand everything. Are you ready for the journey?"

"Yes, I am ready," I said.

The Investigator Dog and I were standing in an old gateway. The plaster was peeling from the walls, the wood in the gate was rotting, and there were flagstones missing in the stone pavement. We were in the midst of a stream of people who were pouring out into a sunny street. Somewhere from a courtyard came the sound of loud music. I could see lights flashing in electric signs and a big colored poster above a brightly lit entrance to a very small old cinema. People were coming out at the end of a show.

"Where are we?" I asked.

Sebastian moved in toward the wall for fear of getting his paws trodden on. "Damn!" he said. "We have gone a bit off course. We have got into the town."

"What do we do now?" I asked.

"It doesn't matter. You must see the town as well. You will find it useful for the sequel to the story."

We came out into the street, which was full of small shops with windows full of cheap goods, tiny cafés, and shabby cinemas. Depressed-looking horses clip-clopped along, pulling faded, dirty cabs. People in rather odd clothes were hurrying along the sunny pavements.

"I know the way," said Sebastian. "Let us turn here. It will be shorter."

A bell began to toll with the heavy, pounding rhythm of bells in big churches, and then another joined in, slowly and languidly, on a different note, filled with sadness that died away upon air that was hazed with light. In front of us lay a small open space, a sort of garden. A crowd of small, gilded domes rose on the left, topped by the double crosses of the Orthodox Church. It was from here that the melancholy tolling came. On the right-hand side of the square was an old Roman Catholic Church, housing the second bell that was calling worshippers to the late afternoon service.

Sebastian proceeded at a gentle trot, but I could scarcely keep up with him. We passed through a narrow, twisting lane, lined with wooden, single-story houses, some painted and some the weathered gray of old timber. A few houses stood upright, others leaned sideways or forwards with windows and doors awry. We passed a garden overshadowed by a steep, shingled roof with a lopsided turret surmounted by a rusty crescent. Sebastian glanced at me, and I nodded to show that I recognized the building as a humble little Muslim mosque.

The lane ended and we were confronted by the kind of village road that can be seen in old pictures—sandy, with deep ruts made by wooden cartwheels. Soon this road divided and there, under a wayside cross that stood at the fork, lay an old acquaintance, Chippy the chicken, prone amid the weeds.

He raised his white, blind-looking eyelids.

"Where are you off to, lads?" he croaked.

"Don't answer him, or we shall never get rid of him," growled Sebastian, quickening his pace.

"Wait a minute, I am coming with you," and Chippy began to stagger to his feet.

"Hurry," urged Sebastian," don't waste time on him. It will soon be evening, and we still have a good part of the way to go."

I stole a backward look. Chippy steadied himself against the rough tree trunk that formed the upright of the cross and called after us in an ear-splitting voice, "Lend me fifty groschen or I will put a curse on you. Niggardly skinflints, misers, stuck-up money-grubbers! I will put such a curse on you that it will shrivel you up!"

We turned left again. The road dropped as it approached a river flowing quietly between two lines of alders. Then we climbed upward, still sensing the nearness of the river from the coolness and the muddy smell of water.

"I saw them in my dreams," I said, speaking with effort because of weariness.

"Who?" asked Sebastian.

"The girl in white and him."

Sebastian quickened his pace without a word.

We crossed meadows covered in a haze of white fluff like thistledown and could already see the golden-colored house.

This time Sebastian made a wide circle and approached the park from the rear. The brewery hummed somewhere behind us. The fence here was very dilapidated, with missing iron railings replaced haphazardly by wooden boards.

With his paw, Sebastian pressed in one of the boards, which was already heavily scratched. He must have been here many times—when, and why, I still did not know.

We pushed through a thicket of raspberry canes on the other side of the fence. There was a sound of grasshoppers singing in the summer heat. Spiders had spun whole curtains of cobwebs. As we forced our way through this tangle of plants and cobwebs, Sebastian began to sniff. He rubbed his nose with his paw, but it was not much help. The scent of raspberries was too strong, and in the end he had to stop and sneeze in order to clear the unfamiliar smell from his nose.

"Ugh, dammit!" he said between sneezes. "I suffer from hay fever. In spring and early summer, when everything sheds its pollen, I even have to go to bed. Well, two more sneezes—ah-tishoo! Ah-tish-oo!"

Though he had been in his previous incarnation an English lord, he had of course no handkerchief, so he wiped his nose in some nettles and then swore fiercely.

"Psst! Quiet!" he hissed, although I had been standing perfectly still all the time. "And mind your feet. There may be traps or snares about here."

A bird flew from a nearby tree in the direction of the setting sun, so that I could not be sure whether it was a crow or a rook or even a pheasant. In any case it was a big bird, and with the sun behind it, it looked quite black. At that moment there was a single muffled shot. Dark feathers scattered from the bird's plumage and it began to fly in an odd, lopsided way, and then dropped. Something flopped behind the raspberry bushes and there was a beating noise in the grass.

"That's him," said Sebastian softly—and I knew at once whom

he meant. "Quietly, friend, or there will be trouble."

We moved over to the back of the house. I noticed an old moss-covered wellhead with a big winch and broken steps leading to a rickety wooden porch with broken windows. This was the north side of the house, where the sun never penetrated. Old close-grown chestnut trees obscured the sun with their dense foliage and there was not a single blade of grass to be seen on the black ground.

"Will you risk it, friend?" asked Sebastian softly.

"Uh-uh," I answered.

The skin on the Investigator Dog's back was twitching as though plagued by mosquitoes, but it was simply nerves. "Straight ahead, then," he growled in English, nudging me with his ribs.

We reached the little porch in a few leaps.

"What did you say just then?" I asked, gasping with the effort.

"Oh, nothing important. The English just came to my lips. Come on, let's waste no more time."

We advanced cautiously into a sort of big, dark hall. Sebastian must have been feeling for a door, because I could hear his head bumping against the wall. Then there was a creaking noise and we saw before us a square room with an altar and candles. It was probably the family chapel. The straw matting on the floor was covered with green tomatoes. Baskets full of early apples stood on the sills of the stained-glass windows.

Noiselessly we reached the half-open door on the other side of the chapel and entered a big drawing room. A huge chandelier hung from the ceiling with blood-red crystal drops that shimmered ceaselessly as if stirred by the breath of some giant hidden in one of the dark corners. A small cat slept on a mahogany piano. It must have just seen a big dog in its dreams, because, with eyes still closed, its ears moved and it bared its thin fangs.

We passed on into a study that smelled of tobacco smoke and lavender. On the walls hung old photographs, barometers, a collection of Finnish knives and silver-mounted shotguns. I saw in a glass jar standing on the writing desk a bunch of multicolored feathers, maybe from birds shot in the park. Beside the jar a book on anatomy lay open, showing the horrible picture of a man without his skin. A ring had been drawn with a red crayon around the exposed heart, and in the margin against it a large exclamation mark. Across the book lay a white stick of the kind used in the game of hoop-la.

Sebastian, also, regarded the open book and the white stick with horror.

"She is near—in the next room," he said, in a strangled voice.

I could see how deeply he was disturbed. His smooth, shining skin twitched rapidly all over his body, as though he were trying to pull it over his head, like a sweater. His muzzle quivered in an odd sort of way and his left eye winked continuously. His behavior was a new mystery to me.

Sebastian approached the door unsteadily and put his nose to it, first pushing cautiously and then pressing harder. At last he must have got it slightly ajar, for he applied his eye at a level just above the handle. He stood like that for some time, trembling convulsively with one paw raised, looking as if he were gently touching a precious object.

All this time the tumultuous cries of swallows could be heard outside the windows.

I touched Sebastian's back. "What can you see?" I whispered. But he would not let me take his place, and only pressed his great head harder and harder against the oak panel. I began to hear, in the early evening calm, between the bursts of swallows' chatter, a faint sound like a melody played on a single string. The dog's whole body shivered.

I bent down and put my head under his warm muzzle and looked through the chink. Here is the sight that we both saw that day, an hour before sunset.

The girl in white was sitting in a rocking chair. She wore the same white dress and socks and shoes, and the same ribbon in her dark hair. No time had passed between our sight of her at the fence and this present moment, no Cecilia had visited, there was no school, no warning of the world's end. It seemed that we had never parted from sight of her, except for the few moments that it had taken her to run here to her room.

Flickers of light from some unseen source shone on the walls. The girl—her name was Eva—had dark, almost black hair. I could clearly see it as she bent her head and then held some pieces of glass, or slides, up to the light. Her eyes were greenish, beneath very dark brows. Her whole face, including her mouth, had a gypsyish, Eastern look. The girls in my father's school must have had such faces. He was born somewhere in the east of the country and was always pining for the scenes of his childhood.

The soft tune come to an end and Eva, without taking her eyes off the slides, groped with her free hand for the wooden roof of a little Swiss chalet that stood on the shelf. She lifted the roof—for a moment we could see small objects and a diminutive staircase— and then she replaced it. The music began again, and I realized that the little wooden house was a music box.

My leg was becoming numb from crouching against the door. I wanted to move my foot because of the pins and needles that started when I stirred; but I stumbled, or maybe Sebastian tripped me; anyhow, we both tumbled noisily into the room.

Eva jumped from her armchair. Sebastian tried to get to his feet, but his big paws slipped and skidded on the polished floor, and he looked more comical every second, as he mumbled desperately: "I most sincerely beg your pardon. We meant well, that is to say, we are in possession of certain facts, and because of that, my colleague and I are anxious to help—yes, that is the right word—simply to help—or rather, if it becomes necessary, to bring help. In other words, to assist in the restoration of freedom."

He would probably have gone on stumbling and skidding about all night, but he eventually collapsed and began to pretend that he felt more comfortable like that. Eva stood before us with a finger on her lips.

"Nobody can free me," she said softly, with a sigh. "Nobody will ever succeed. Retep will kill everyone who tries."

"*Who* will kill everyone?" I asked, my voice choking. She looked at me, but I am not sure that she saw me.

"He will. Retep will," she repeated in a whisper. "Oh, if only my parents were still alive!"

A round teardrop slid from her long lashes, a strange teardrop

[38]

that reflected the green of the chestnut trees beyond the window, the blue sky, and the red of the setting sun.

Sebastian began suddenly to make suffocating noises, wrinkling and rubbing his black muzzle with his paws. "Allow me—let us run away together—for ever. I know the way . . . on another planet . . . to better and kinder people—"

"No, we cannot go today. Another day, maybe. There is something very important that I must recover first, my most precious keepsake."

"I beseech you!" cried Sebastian in a shaking voice. "Tomorrow may be too late. Let us run away. Everything is ready for the journey."

"Do not talk about it, I implore you. I cannot go. Not today." And another tear rolled down from each eye. I felt a salty taste in my throat.

"He is coming now, I can hear him. He will shoot you." Her voice was almost inaudible with despair, as she pushed us toward the door.

"We will come back," said Sebastian. "But is there still any hope?"

"Yes, I will go on waiting. Good-bye, my champions," she said.

Dazzled, indeed disturbed, we found ourselves back on the dark veranda with the broken windows. The sound of high-pitched, plaintive singing came from the river, or perhaps from the big forests still farther away, or the meadow grass as high as corn that I imagined surrounding the valley, haunted by will-o'-the-wisps at night.

The dull sound of a gunshot came from nearby, perhaps from around the angle of the house.

"Hurry, my friend!" said Sebastian.

We ran, leaping with all our might, toward the raspberry patch. The close air, full of early evening scents, enveloped us as we pushed on headlong for the railings.

Sebastian growled suddenly. I was about to ask him what the trouble was, but at that very moment I felt as though some beast had caught my leg between his jaws. The teeth snapped tight, clenching harder and harder. I turned around with a cry, but there was no one behind me. Only the raspberry canes still moved, where I had brushed my way through them. I parted the grass to look at my left leg and foot, which were hidden in the tall growth. Two iron jaws, clamped on my leg, gnawed it as though it were asparagus.

Sebastian looked at me, his own eyes full of pain.

"I am caught in a snare," I said, uncertainly.

"That is a trap, which is much worse."

"What about you?" I asked.

"I am the one who is snared. It is a trifle, by comparison, but my legs are useless. If only you could move over nearer and help me."

"It is all very well for you to talk about your legs. This trap will soon have bitten my leg through."

Sebastian was silent for a while and then he said, "Well, this is the end. We shall have to surrender."

"What do you mean?" I asked.

"We shall have to call for help, then Retep will come, and then . . ."

He stopped and stared at the sky. He looked as though he was about to start howling at the white face of the moon that was already hanging over the roof of the house.

"And what will happen then?" I asked.

"He will shoot us."

"He will do that?"

"Yes, just simply shoot us. Remember that I warned you. I don't mind. I am prepared for my end. I am fed up with life. If the end is now, well, that's that."

"But after all, this is a game," I said "What are you talking about? Has the heat of the sun affected you?"

"This is no game. The game is back home," said Sebastian cheerlessly. "There is no return from this place."

"But we returned before," I said.

"Because I know the secret. But this time we shall not be so fortunate. There's the risk, my friend."

There was a rustle nearby. Someone was making his way with difficulty through the prickly canes.

"Have courage. Hold up your head and die with dignity," said Sebastian. "Good-bye, comrade!"

We gazed, fascinated, into the bushes. Slowly a gray head emerged, topped by a sunburnt face with a greenish-white moustache, and then the whole body of a small old man in a collarless shirt, jeans, and huge boots soled with pieces of old tire.

"Now I've caught yer," he said, speaking in a singsong East Polish dialect.

"He means that we are in trouble," said Sebastian, interpreting. The old man nodded his gray head.

"You must let us go free," I said in an authoritative voice. "We are in a great hurry. We are strangers here."

"I can't let you go," he said, in his rather plaintive, rising-and-falling accents. "Now you're trapped, you'll have to suffer for it," and he smiled at us kindly.

"Old man," said Sebastian solemnly, "would you have our young blood on your conscience in your declining years?"

"Listen to him! What a crafty *sabaka* it is," said the old man slowly, in deep amazement. "When you're in trouble you can speak human-like. No, my leverets, I can't let you go. Master Retep is wicked, yes, very wicked 'e is. If anyone gets in here it's *anumlik* for him."

Sebastian was in no hurry to translate the dialect words but, of course, I could guess that *sabaka* meant something like "cur" and that *anumlik* could only be something disastrous, like "it's curtains for him."

The old man sat on a tree stump overgrown with fungus and began to roll a cigarette on the lid of a box in which he kept his tobacco and paper. Carefully licking the edges of the cigarette paper, he said reflectively:

"Now our poor Vin, poor orphan lad that he is, with no father or mother to his name, he vanished one day. It seems he vanished forever, as though he was unhappy with us, as though we treated him badly. But both of us, both me and my old woman, we worked hard from dawn till dusk so that we could give him a good education, the brute. Even the priest gave him lessons and took an interest in him. But he always looked down on the way we lived and wanted a different sort of life. And so one day he ran

[41]

away, and we don't know where he is or what he's doing."

"He's probably making life hell for somebody else," said Sebastian gloomily.

The old man lit his neatly rolled cigarette and sighed. "Could be," he said, "so touchy he was, you couldn't go near him. But he liked tormenting others real cruel. The tears would run down his face and he would curse the wicked world and himself as well, and then, with the tears still on his face, he would set about doing harm to his neighbors, the cursed *haman*. Where did he get such a nature from?"

"Perhaps it was from his grandparents," Sebastian suggested cautiously.

"That's a lie you're telling, my leveret. It's we who are his grandparents. Well—I'm sorry for you two, very sorry. And specially for you." He pointed a tobacco-stained finger at Sebastian. "Such a fine, big animal. And purebred too, eh? That collar alone must be worth a good bit. Somebody must have spent a fortune on you. And now what are you doing? Gallivanting in other people's gardens, that's what you're doing."

"We could make some inquiries about Vincent for you," I said offhandedly.

"What are you? Holiday-makers?"

"Yes. We come from a big city."

"From the biggest one?"

"Yes, it is the biggest."

"And you haven't met our Vincent?"

"Not yet. But we could try to find him."

"You will have to go looking for him among the most important people because our Vincent is ambitious. And he's proud too, God knows."

"But before we can begin looking for him, we have got to get out of this place."

The old man wagged his forefinger at me good-humoredly. "You're a cunning fellow, you are. But if I let you go, Master Retep will send me packing."

"This is the only safe way out. We can slip through here without making a noise, and nobody will know," I said.

"Tell me, why has your face got so red? You're not by any chance lying to me, my young leveret?"

"Well, if you don't believe me—" I said indignantly.

"I can see that you are as proud as our Vincent," he said, and coming closer he knelt with difficulty in front of me. "You won't deceive an old man?"

"Why should we?" I asked. "We are as keen as you are."

He heaved a resigned sort of sigh and opened the jaws of the trap.

"Be off with you then, my leverets," he said, when we were freed. But he seemed sorry to let us go. He was especially slow in releasing Sebastian, and kept muttering to himself and grumbling, as he ran his hand along the dog's lean flank. He just did not want to part with such a splendid animal.

It took us no more than a second to get to the fence. The old man was upset at our haste.

"Hold on a minute, you ungrateful pair of *hamans*. What's the hurry? Let's have a talk about this and that." But we were already on the other side of the railings.

A breeze stirred in the trees. It was the night wind that blows suddenly in the early evening, bending branches and shaking the leaves. The red beams of the setting sun played over the wet windblown grass like squirrels.

We ran, until we were out of breath, along the road that led across the fields to the river.

"We've made it!" I said, filling my lungs with pine-scented air.

But Sebastian was silent. With his head down, he seemed to be sniffing the moss at the roadside. I slapped his side, which felt as hard as a washboard. "What's the matter, Sebastian?" I asked.

He turned his head, blinking his dark eyes, which were filled with tears.

"I'm sorry," he said in English, "everything's fine."

"Sebastian, what *is* the matter? When we were in the house you were shaking like jelly. I could see how you were hardly able to stand on your feet."

Sebastian started forward again, placing his paws heavily in the ruts full of loose gray sand.

[43]

"It's nothing, my friend. I've somehow come unstuck. It must be my unlucky day." And that was all that I could get out of him.

The sun was sinking behind the horizon and we plodded on in the twilight. The air had two layers, it seemed, a warm one and a cold one, like a pond on a swelteringly sunny day. An object rose from under a wild rosebush and I recognized, against the fading aluminum light of the sky, a messy-looking beak stuck with barleycorns.

"Hi, you, smart guys!" croaked Chippy. "Do you want a fight?"

Sebastian pretended to ignore the attempt to pick a quarrel, and Chippy followed us along the edge of the road.

"Maybe you don't like it here, then?" he cried, trying to suppress his disgusting hiccups. "Maybe you think you are doing us a favor by coming here?"

Becasue we were silent, he turned to somebody or something that was scuffling nearby in the tall grass.

"Look at these two geezers, Fela," he said. "By the way they are hurrying you'd think that they'd been invited out to supper. Stuck-up rubbish! Tin-pot gentry!"

This idiotic expression finally annoyed me. "You'd better go and wash your snotty beak in the river," I said.

Chippy was speechless. He spread his miserable wings, stood for a while stock-still, and then began to flap for all he was worth, while emitting positively ear-piercing squawks: "They insulted us, Fela. You heard them! They used rude words. They insulted us, that's what they did—quiet, honest, hardworking folk who live here."

Sebastian, still silent, started running toward the river, and because I knew that he must have a reason for running, I, too, began to sprint.

"Hold it, you city scum," shouted Chippy, "I'll teach you a lesson that will last you for the rest of your life. Stop! Wait a minute! My feet are hurting me. Stop, drat you, or I'll curse you to eternity."

His shrieks collapsed into lamentations, as we ran on toward the river, which welcomed us with its cool murmurings. On we plunged into the rapidly falling darkness, so fragrant with mint, so full of invisible bats that could become entangled in one's hair, and of the sound of cicadas. It was darkness like the darkness remembered from fairy tales.

And then the thought came to me. Actually, it is one that lurks in my mind all the time. If sometimes it seems not to be there, it is only because I am distracted by other things. It is like a continually present and pervasive anxiety. I must stress again the fact that I am a rationalist, which means that I believe only in human intellect or reason. But, although I am the most rational of rationalists, I see that there is a place for superstition and even welcome it. Only those rationalists who are beginners, and therefore over-keen, are as eager as believers to mock at superstition. Believers, in fact, cannot see the snags. They explain everything in terms of the powers of good and evil. A rationalist has to look for scientific explanations when he is faced with strange phenomena. And science sooner or later will show every superstition to be actually reasonable, and then it will be established as a natural fact.

What I am really talking about is the Anthropos-Specter-Beast. He is everything that is not understood in nature and mankind. He is the Unknown itself. No one has ever seen him, but everyone is well acquainted with him, with his habits and his strange ways—though this does not mean he can become so familiar that they are no longer afraid of him. The most sensitive of us could even describe his nature and, perhaps, his appearance also, although I do not think that his appearance is of great importance.

You may think that I am talking about some creature that I have invented, but it is not so. I have only discovered him—that is to say, I have proved his existence scientifically, and now I am giving you a proper analytical description of him, that is all. For my part, I have not yet been able to make up my mind about him.

When and where does he make himself known? He is always present in those strange moments that we remember for the rest of our life. He is present in our sudden awakening from sleep in the late afternoon, when we see through the window a red sun setting and hear the loud twittering of sparrows squabbling in the road, and feel the first puff of evening air that fills the curtain. For a moment everything seems strange and frightening, as if we had just entered the world for the first time. In that moment the Anthropos-Specter-Beast is very near.

He is boldest of all in our dreams, where he lies in wait for us in every shadow and molests us, torments, hunts, and even kills us, and then when we turn over in bed, trying to shake off the terror and stop the thumping of our heart, he departs unwillingly, lingeringly and vindictively, and leaves us with a strong uneasy presentiment of his return.

There are times when the Beast attacks openly, sometimes in broad daylight and in the presence of other people. He will suddenly come upon you when you are ill, when your mind does not know where to take refuge and wants only to escape, no matter where. He will catch you in a café, in an airplane, during a film. You must have sometimes seen people in a cinema with an air of desperation, pushing their way along a row of seats when the film is only halfway through. They are people who, for no apparent reason, have felt the presence of the Beast, and that is why, leaving their sanity and common sense and all that they have been taught behind them, they flee like panic-stricken animals.

It seems to me that our senses, on the whole, make us feel safe in the world and protect us against the Anthropos-Specter-Beast; and that it might one day be proved that the prime importance we give to the senses is not justified and that they will be seen to be only an accidental complex of functions.

Consider the fact that the Beast attacks us when our senses are paralyzed in some way—by dreams or illness, or by some other external condition.

Miss Sophie once said to me: "There is some chewing gum on the shelf in my room. You can have it." Of course I knew that she did not touch chewing gum, because she is slimming and is very particular about keeping to the rules. But she knew that I was very fond of going into her room. What drew me, I did not know; the urge was irresistible.

It was late in the evening and I could not be bothered to switch on the light, so I made my way in the darkness along a passage to her room, and went to the shelves. I can swear that I am not the slightest bit afraid of the dark. Darkness is no more than absence of light. But during this visit to Miss Sophie's room I was on the verge of having a fit. The Anthropos-Specter-Beast was everywhere—in the hall doorway, in the corridor, in the bookshelves, in the air, in my breathing, in every corner of my mind.

I returned with the chewing gum, trembling and wet with sweat, but firmly resolved to follow up the discovery that I had made. It had become plain to me that it takes no more than one sense to be out of action—in this case it was the sense of sight—to encourage the attacker. I may not have made myself very clear. It is a difficult subject. I am the only creature who has the courage to face up to this problem, which everyone else conceals by silence, or by a pretense that everything is going splendidly. I can easily tell the people who fight without success. They are the ones who, when they are listening to you, smile in the wrong places. Their eyes seem suddenly to be confronted with an abyss, and fill with pain. These are the people who are given to fidgeting in their seats and then suddenly get up and leave unexpectedly. They go about their daily tasks absentmindedly, doing things from habit, and it is they who will, for no apparent reason, ring you up in the middle of the night just to ask how things are.

I imagine that many of us can, in the end, no longer bear to be beset in this way or to continue with this game, which is like some sort of senseless duel. That is why they take their own lives, and the rest of us, when we read the news of their death, will say: "He was a strange sort of man, not quite all there. There was something odd about him."

What this nightmarish game, this terrifying duel, is all about, I do not yet know. I am on the track, but I cannot quite explain it.

From what regions of the universe does this Beast come—if he does, indeed, come from some edge of space? And what is he up to?

I may still be able to unravel the mystery, and with your help I will do all I can. If you find some parts of my story too difficult to understand, go back to the first page and start again.

In the end we found ourselves back on the staircase by the front door of our flat.

"We drifted a bit off course again," said Sebastian, "Do you mind?"

"Mind what?" I asked.

"Just generally," said the Investigator Dog, looking at the dusty window.

"No. Why should I?"

"We are friends, then?"

"Yes."

"Forever?"

He stood with his flank toward me, but I could see that he listened very intently to my replies.

"Forever," I said.

I wanted to ask him something that had troubled me from the very beginning, but he must have read my mind because he moved off down the stairs, saying: "I will drop in to see you."

"When?" I asked.

He hesitated for a moment. "I don't know yet. Maybe tomorrow, maybe the day after. One day."

I listened for a while to his padding footsteps and heard him sneeze once or twice as he went out at the entrance, then I rang our doorbell. For a time nobody answered the door, until at last Miss Sophie appeared with a new and very odd hair-style.

"Where have you been?" she asked. "It's long past dinner time."

As usual, she did not wait for me to answer. She was only interested in what she said herself. She went into her own room, banging the door.

My father, mother, and Cecilia were sitting in front of the television set watching a program about the cold-drawing of tubes at a steelworks. They were all three silent, even Cecilia, so I sat down in a chair.

"You will be able to manage," said Cecilia at last, in a voice so loud that a notice appeared on the screen apologizing for a temporary fault. "You think that you wouldn't succeed? You with your luck?"

"My dear Cecilia," said my father wryly, "where is this luck that you are talking about?"

"Do not underestimate your good fortune. It is asking for trouble. You have a wonderful wife, promising children, and good friends."

My father pulled a face, as though this were too much.

"Well, am I not right?" asked Cecilia. But he just waved her question away with his hand in a resigned sort of way.

"Do you know, you really are stupid." Cecilia raised her voice, and the hall door opened by itself. "You'll come up against it one day, and then you'll see. Fate will punish you for your pride and ingratitude."

"What pride?" asked my father in a suffering voice.

A technician on the screen proceeded to explain the cold-drawing procedure. My mother had all the time been silently busy with her sketchbook.

"Dad," I said in a low voice. He looked up.

"What does *anumlik* mean?"

"Anumlik? In my part of the world it meant 'the end, the finish'—like saying 'amen'."

"And what does *haman* mean?"

"A haman is a lout or brute, or something like that. How did you come to meet these words?"

I had no time to answer, because Cecilia butted in. Of course my father was an ignoramus, she said, not to know that Haman was a character in the Bible, an oppressor of the Jews. My father

[49]

started to say something about 'back in the East where he came from,' but Cecilia did not want to hear anything about the East and went off on a tirade about primitive ignorance and superstition until my father said that he was sick of everything.

The truth of the matter was that my father had been dismissed from his job. In other words, he had been sacked. He described the wrong that had been done to him in a voice full of hurt pride and anger. It seems that he could not get along with his boss, who would not accept new developments in the field of mathematics.

But I know the real reason for the quarrel. My father's boss was a supporter of Sempiterna, which is a rather poor football team. I said "supporter," but he did more than support: he was crazy about Sempiterna. He went to every game they played, however far from home. He often traveled with the team to other towns and came home full of bitterness and fury, because they usually lost. It was not easy to understand why he was so devoted to them. They were just a feeble provincial team. But perhaps that was his reason—the fact that they were a local, home-bred bunch.

My father despised Sempiterna; he also went to every game, but only to enjoy their humiliation. Because he had played football in his youth and knew the game, he supported another team that he had seen by chance and liked. So every Monday an argument flared up over Saturday's game, and in the end it went too far. Sempiterna was about to drop out of the league, and his boss even accused my father of casting spells. It is not easy for two people to work together in such a situation. My mother did not know about this true reason. She thought that it was the mathematical issue and looked on my father as a champion of scientific thought.

Miss Sophie came in wearing a dress not much longer than a medium-sized waistcoat. "Mother, I am going out," she said.

"All right," said my mother mechanically, "but don't stay out too late, as you usually do."

My father looked gloomily at the unfinished painting of universal doom that my mother had been working on for several days. "Why should one get so upset about all this?" he said. "It'll find its own solution."

"Do you mean the meteor?" asked Cecilia.

"My dear, it's not a meteor, it's a comet."

"It makes no difference. Not to us, at least. I am prepared for anything. It is only people without imagination who are afraid of the collision."

"Are you really not afraid?" asked my mother.

"Have you ever heard of the anti-universe? The negative universe?"

"No. What is that?"

Cecilia looked at my mother with slightly narrowed eyes— very brown eyes, full of little specks of light, like icicles. "Do you know what a negative is in photography?"

"Of course I do. What is white in the photograph is black in the negative."

"Well, it is the same with our negative universe."

"But what has the universe to do with photography?" asked my father.

"*You* don't understand either," attacked Cecilia.

"Of course I do," he answered, without sounding very much as if he meant it. "I read about it somewhere. But if you ask me, there are even more theories about the origin of the universe than there are about slimming."

"Which means that you think that the anti-universe theory is rubbish?"

"I wouldn't put it as crudely as that. But I don't like it. On the whole it is rather below your intellectual level."

"How do you know what is below my intellectual level? A man who spends the whole day watching television has no right to air his opinions among cultivated people. I am wasting my time. I have so much to do, and here he is annoying me with his ignorant remarks."

Cecilia's face was gradually getting redder and redder, until it looked as though someone had spread it with tomato sauce. She stood up briskly, smoothed down her immaculately clean and well-pressed dress, cast a fleeting glance at her legs, which were noted for their perfect shape, wrapped an expensive scarf that she had bought in England around her neck, and went out, all the time saying withering things to my father. My mother followed her to the hall door, trying to calm her.

I am quite certain that you have not understood a single word of this conversation between my father and mother and Cecilia. I must admit that the subject is a very difficult one. My father's point of view did not surprise me, but I knew what Cecilia was trying to say. And what she meant was not at all as silly as it may seem. I will explain it to you later.

The truth is that there is always a sort of curious sense in Cecilia's madness. If I tell you that Cecilia is a vegetarian and that she takes a shower three times a day and practices yoga exercises, and if I add that she was born under the sign of Taurus and that none of her husbands could stand her for longer than six months, you will understand for yourself that her opinions must be treated with respect. I have said only a little about her and her interesting life. I hope that you will get to know her better later and that quite a few of you will have your eyes opened very wide at the many-sidedness of human nature.

"She is quite mad," said my father, when my mother came back into the room, "does she have to come here ten times a day?"

"In actual fact, she has a heart of gold," said my mother, without conviction. "When one gets to know her better one finds out the kind of person she is."

"Where did you meet her?"

"Waiting in a queue for butter. I've told you, haven't I?"

"You told me that she was one of your school friends."

"A school friend?" said my mother, surprised.

"You told me so a hundred times."

My mother stood in the middle of the room, thinking.

"Well, is she a friend from your schooldays or a friend from the butter queue? For goodness' sake, make up your mind!" said my father, getting into a temper but still keeping an eye on the television screen. The picture had just changed and was showing a rolling process for rails or some such thing. My mother's eyelids began to flutter as if she were a sleeper suddenly awakening.

"We have twenty-four thousand zlotys in our savings book.

[52]

With luck that will see us through to the end of the year," she said softly.

My father's tone became quieter. "I shall be pretty low myself by then in people's eyes," he said.

"Well, others manage somehow, and so shall we."

"Yes, but remember that we have two children. We have lived for years as though we were still poor students, always believing that the good times lay ahead. And look at us now, beginning to turn gray, feeling the first twinges of advancing years, and with more and more worries and no prospects."

"I am only anxious that things should not get worse," sighed my mother.

My father stared for a while at the never-ending procession of rails and then muttered vindictively: "I wish that comet really would hit this damned world of ours."

I did not take any part in this conversation. After all, what good would it have done if I had explained that it was an asteroid or minor planet, and not a comet or a meteor, that was hurtling toward the earth, for God alone truly knows what any of them are. Some scientists maintain that a comet is a cloud of rarefied gas particles, others that it is something else. As for meteors, millions of them fall upon the earth without any major effect. But an asteroid is a heavenly body of much greater size. My father and I could both count on its desired effect. He was just talking though, and the truth is that really he must have been afraid of such a cosmic catastrophe. As for me, it was the only way out. When I thought sometimes that I would one day have to earn my living and perhaps even bring up children—those selfish, pitiless horrors—it made me shiver, and at that moment I was ready to jump into the deepest river I could find.

I ate a little, although I had no appetite. My father went out to seek the advice of his friends, my mother pulled out the easel with her pessimistic abstract painting, and I was left to suffer the hopeless passage of time creeping on until evening.

So I went into Miss Sophie's room. From her window one could see the whole red brick wing of the block. There were neighbors hanging around in all the flats. Some old women were looking out into the courtyard, keeping an eye on grandchildren. Somewhere a man was quarreling with his wife. There was a girl making faces at herself in a mirror. A crippled child was tapping a finger against the side of a fish tank, ignorant of a fish's dislike of vibration.

I watched all these people behind windowpanes that reflected the spring clouds, and I wondered what they thought about this asteroid and the end of the world, or at any rate what they made of their own lives and fates.

As I watched, I suddenly began to yearn for the green valley with the murmuring river, the big house that I called the Golden House, though what was golden about it was whitewash that had yellowed with time. I yearned too for the strange town and the evening sound of bells, for the tall bushes of wild cumin and for the air lying in layers of warm and cold, like water in a heated pond, and I understood for the first time in my life what longing really is. For until then I had never had reason to feel it.

Neither my mother nor Miss Sophie ever showed that they longed for anything. My father was the only one who had any reason for yearning, for he had memories of places where he was born and brought up, far away in another country.

My eyes filled with tears. I felt that I was somehow finer and nobler than other people and that nobody understood me. Then a strange kind of bliss or sweetness flowed from my heart and through my whole body, and I reached with my hand under the mattress where Miss Sophie's diary lay.

I opened the book at the last entry:

"From morning till night," Miss Sophie had written, "everybody talks about this frightful comet that will soon be colliding with the earth. Mother and Dad are very upset, and only my young brother, who maybe does not understand anything yet, is enjoying himself. I am afraid that I am not kind to him. I shall have to mend my ways. But the truth is that I have neither time nor thought to give to these domestic problems.

"Am I afraid to die? There was a time when I wanted to die. When I was younger I would sit for hours by the river imagining my own death: the funeral, the grief of my family, friends, teachers—and *His* despair. There, it has happened again. I am speaking of Him, although I have promised myself never to mention Him again.

"Actually I am concerned about the problem of death. When I think about my end, I realize with surprise that I do not care. I do not care about anything—even *Him!*"

Here was something that I had never been able to understand—I mean that Miss Sophie in her everyday life was quite different from the Miss Sophie who wrote the diary.

As I was thinking about it I heard a thumping sound in the yard and looked out of the window. A fellow was kicking a ball against the end wall of the neighboring block, practicing shots with his left foot. It was Gagatek himself, the mysterious "Him," spelled with a capital letter, of Miss Sophie's diary.

I thought for a bit that I would draw a skull and crossbones beneath the last line of the diary and then I did not feel like doing it. I pushed the silly book back under the mattress, taking no care to replace it exactly where I had found it.

Somebody started letting out dreadful, ear-piercing shrieks. I thought that at the least somebody had got himself pinned against the wall by a car backing into the courtyard. But it was only Buffalo's mother. She was leaning from her open window with a plastic egg box in her outstretched hand, and her shrieks rose sky-high. The egg box was half eaten—one could see where bites had been taken out of it. Her undersized husband, in a neat sweater and the latest-style spectacles, stood at her side with his head clutched desperately in his hands, as though he were about to unscrew it and hurl it after his fleeing son. Buffalo was running as fast as his legs would carry him, diagonally across the courtyard toward our street. Some neighbors came out to see what was happening, and I too decided to take an after-lunch stroll.

A small party of men were drinking together on our staircase, passing a dark-green bottle from hand to hand.

"To the comet!" said one of them, taking a long pull at the bottle. "Would you like a drop, lad?"

I recognized him as a man who was given to feasting by the

dustbins in the company of an old lady and another man, who was a cripple. The dustbins in our courtyard stand in an out-of-the-way corner, by a low wall. This man liked me, but he liked our rubbish buckets better and would even snatch them from me before I could reach the dustbins and search carefully through them.

It was this same fellow who now handed the bottle to one of his comrades and burst into tears. A third member of the party, quite a young man, started singing a popular song, which ran:

"In a year, in a day, in a little while,
Our lives will reach their end . . ."

The others joined in:

"In a year, in a day, in a little while . . ."

I left them drinking gloomily by a cold radiator, preparing themselves to meet the cosmic disaster.

Buffalo was sitting on the low stone wall, under the acacia, picking green shoots off my tree and chewing them sadly.

"I'll teach you to pick those leaves!" I said, as I got near him. "Do you want me to kick you?"

Bufallo drew his head into his shoulders in submission. Although he is my own age, Buffalo is taller than I am by half a head. When he is standing he looks like a letter "A"—that is to say, his head is small and below it he gets fatter and fatter. He wears shorts and his purplish calves are an irresistible target for sticks and catapults.

"What d'you mean?" he asked, trying to bluster. "Is it your tree?"

"Yes, it is. It has been mine since last winter. Remember that, because I won't tell you again!"

He lowered his head and looked up, scowling and sniffing. I followed his gaze and felt suddenly hot. There, returning home, maybe from a walk, was the girl whose name I will not say. She was holding a leash in her hand as thick as a good-sized stick. Her face had the expression that people wear when they do not want to see anyone. I was afraid that Buffalo might notice that I was looking at her.

I said in an offhand voice: "I like the jeans, don't you?"

"What jeans? Where?" said Buffalo, rousing himself.

"I said she is wearing nice jeans," I answered.

"Oh, yes. Her father travels all over the world."

"How do you know?"

"Because she is in my form at school."

I settled myself on the wall. The little girl in jeans had already disappeared into the doorway. For some reason I felt rather sorry for Buffalo.

"Did you get a hiding at home?" I asked.

He sniffed and said apathetically, "No, I ran away."

"What was it about?"

Buffalo flapped his hand, looking more and more gloomy.

"You must have nicked something," I said.

"Yes, I did," he admitted, after a short silence.

"And that was what all that row was about?"

"Yes, but this time it was the vitamin rations."

"What vitamin rations?"

"For the end of the world, of course."

"And you gobbled up everything?"

"The whole lot," said Buffalo dismally.

"You're bragging. There must be something left."

"No, there's nothing left. I've even eaten the container," said Buffalo firmly, in a hoarse voice.

I was silent. A pigeon settled on the head of the statue on the monument, ruffled its feathers and then began to preen the rather shabby plumage on its breast.

"I am always hungry," said Buffalo. "Is it my fault?"

"Is she good in class?" I asked.

"Is who?"

"The girl in jeans?"

Buffalo sniffed a bit more. "Yes, she's all right."

"Have you been to her house?"

"Whose house?"

"How thick you are! I'm talking about the girl in jeans."

[57]

Buffalo thought about the question for a while and I began to feel on edge, without knowing why.

"No, I haven't," he said at last—"you know, I'm already counting the days until the comet comes."

"Why's that?"

'Because I would like to see it hit my folks. And specially I would like to see it hit my old man's car. That car is at the bottom of all the trouble. They are always stinting the family to pay for it, and letting me go hungry. It's not me who's to blame."

"I can give you a piece of chewing gum."

"You're not kidding?"

I gave him a piece that I had had around for about six months. I do not even remember what Miss Sophie gave it to me for. Buffalo began to chew furiously, with half-closed eyes.

"It's grand stuff," he said. That was his favorite expression when he was pleased with anything.

"I suppose she has a dog?" I asked.

"Who has a dog?"

"That girl, of course. Didn't you see that she had a leash?"

"Yes, I suppose so."

"What kind of dog?"

"Why are you so stuck on her?"

"I am not stuck on her," I said. "I'm just asking. One has to talk about something."

"It would be better to play at something."

"What shall we play at?"

"Well, partisans, for instance. I'll be the commander," said Buffalo.

"Why you?"

"Why should you mind? I've always wanted to be the commander, more than anything I can think of." He stopped chewing and looked at me so beseechingly, with his little eyes watering in his chubby face, that it affected me.

"Are you really so keen?" I asked.

"Yes, terribly. Everyone in the block has been commander except me. It won't hurt you to do me a favor."

I actually did not mind at all. I'd never joined in games like cops and robbers. Usually I would be irritated when somebody said: "Let's have some fun." There is something silly about it. It may be all right for children to say it, but when some old lady says "It was great fun," I really feel sorry for her.

At this moment Buffalo's father came out of the courtyard door carrying a respectable-looking but ancient briefcase. He pretended that he did not see his son and went on along our street toward the town center. He must have been rather ashamed of Buffalo.

"Well, what's it going to be?" asked Buffalo.

"Do you know which is her flat?" I asked.

"Whose?"

"Oh Lord! That girl in your class."

"It's nearby. In the next block."

"Come on, we'll call out under her window."

"What for? It's better to play at partisans."

"Oh, all right," I said.

"But I'll be commander," said Buffalo.

"OK, you can be commander."

"Let's take the Gestapo by surprise." He ran off along the street, in the direction that his father had taken, trotting ponderously, his haunches shaking slightly, looking like a mountain on the move, while I for some reason followed obediently behind him.

At the end of our street stand the ruins of the house destroyed in the Second World War, quite famous ruins which we've even learned about at school. As far back as I can remember they always wanted to clear it away, but it's still there. At one time parts of the wall were quite high, with gaping windows with moss on their ledges. In the end, the structure collapsed and became just a pile of bricks, full of secret nooks and hiding places. If you looked you could find remains of wall plaster and signs of the house's former life: nail holes in the walls, words scratched by children, even fly marks, not to mention stoves, ovens, drain pipes, and door handles.

"Take them on the left flank!" hissed Buffalo, puffing as we climbed the piles of bricks, "keep covered—follow me!"

"You owe me something in return for being commander," I said.

"What?"

"Well—something," I said with hesitation. "When there is a chance, will you help me with something? Agreed?"

"Agreed," said Buffalo. "Advance! Attack!"

He began to creep toward Mr. Josef's car-repair shop. Behind the ruins, in what may once have been a backyard, we crouched by a break in the wall and peered over.

A small concrete space lay before us, full of cars. Some, with crumpled roofs and bodies and broken windows, had been pushed to the sides, and others, in running order—and some of them even new—were tightly packed in the middle.

At the edge of the yard Buffalo's father stood hesitantly, his ancient briefcase pressed to his side. His gaze followed Mr. Josef, who, perspiring and blank-eyed, was endlessly shifting cars from one place to another. His concentration and the noise of engines starting and revving up made the whole operation seem awe-inspiringly professional. Each time that Mr. Josef passed close to him, Buffalo's father called plaintively: "Mr. Josef, you did say that you would have it ready by six!"

But Mr. Josef had no time for anything but the work at hand. He jumped into cars and out of them like a maniac, surged forward about three yards with tires screeching, and then hurtled into another car and drove that one, also screeching, into the empty space.

"But, Mr. Josef, it was after all supposed to be ready by six. I specially asked you," lamented Buffalo's father.

Buffalo gloated over the scene, his face slightly thinned by cruelty, with the odd result that he actually became rather good-looking.

Just then a fresh car entered the melee. The young lady who emerged from it did not look at all like a motorist. Before she had time to take off her white gloves, Mr. Josef was at her side, one moment lifting the hood, the next moment loosening nuts. His pale eyes became suddenly animated and he began chattering, giggling, and whistling.

Buffalo's father protested monotonously: "After all, Mr. Josef, I was here first."

Buffalo raised himself on one knee and picked up a large brick.

"Down with the bourgeoisie!" he shouted hoarsely, and with a mighty heave he hurled his missile at a blue Fiat standing quietly amid the throng of cars. There was a clang of brick upon metal. Buffalo's father jumped and began to peer in all directions. Mr. Josef did not notice anything, because he was nimbly insinuating himself under the lady's car.

Buffalo took my chewing gum from his mouth and stuck it on the belt that held his trousers up, and then he selected a much bigger brick.

This time the impact sounded like a grenade exploding down a well. Buffalo's father uttered an appalling yell and rushed to the blue Fiat. He began to run his hands over the body like a surgeon examining a patient.

"Mr. Josef," he cried, "there are dents and scratches that were not on this car before!" Then he lost all control and shrieked, "I am going to call the police!"

Mr. Josef crawled from under the lady's car and rose slowly to his feet. "What scratches? What dents? It's the way the light falls," he said stolidly. "It's an optical illusion."

At that moment a third brick found its mark. Buffalo's father stepped aside neatly and straightway turned in our direction.

"It's him! It's him!" he cried. "Don't run away. I can see you. It's him! Assassin! One of these nights he will kill us in our beds!"

But we were already far away, running along our street, under the trees in their mist of green. Buffalo, still breathing heavily, was already chewing my gum again.

"I feel much better," he said, "it's grand stuff."

I must say that I did not feel too comfortable about this frolic of Buffalo's. I had played only a passive part and had done no more than let Buffalo take advantage of my ignorance. In fact I rather despised his exploit. After all, his father had put all his savings into that car and thrift like his deserves respect.

Buffalo must have sensed how I felt about it, because he

stopped under the acacia tree, sat on the wall, and began to pull silly faces. I mean that he tried to arrange his face to look as if he did not care about anything or anybody. I sat next to him and stared at the tree that I had wanted to love just to spite everybody. The acacia was swaying slightly in a northerly, or rather a northwesterly direction, which brought with it a scent of newness and change.

"You know, I hate my folks at home," Buffalo said at last, but without his usual assurance, "how about you?"

I did not answer because I did not want to discuss such a subject. A fellow with a beard came by, carrying on his back a wooden trestle with a wheel and banging monotonously on a tin with an iron rod as his eyes searched the tall rows of closed windows. I guessed that he was a knife grinder who had wandered from somewhere into our street.

"And I hate my old man most of all," said Buffalo softly. "He lives and breathes for that car. He even gets up at night to look through its windows to see whether anyone has pinched anything. He never takes us out, because he is afraid that something might happen to it. Don't you think I'm in the right?" he ended, picking at a stone in the wall as he tried to justify himself.

"We were supposed to be playing partisans," I said, dodging his question.

"We've already played it," he muttered despondently, "besides, I've had enough."

"Don't you feel a fool?" I said. "Did you want to show off to me?"

"No—and I don't care what I did or what you think."

We were silent for a while.

"Let's make a dash for the baker's in the other street," suggested Buffalo suddenly.

"Silly idea," I said.

"Gosh, there's such a lovely smell there. I could sniff it for hours."

"Gosh," I said, mimicking his way of speaking.

"It's true. A nice warm smell of fresh crusty bread. And another smell of cream cakes, just a bit overdone perhaps, or flavored with vanilla. You can't think how I love smells like that—" and he actually quivered with pleasure—"are you coming?"

"No."

"Well, good-bye then!"

"Good-bye."

And he ran off at a heavy trot, without noticing my look of mocking amusement at the way his fat calves shook. I thought that, after all, Buffalo must be happy. He had a passion that made his life worth living. And yet there he was, like the rest of us, waiting for the comet. It all seemed very odd.

I went in at our courtyard gate. Miss Sophie appeared at the other end of the yard with one of her friends, but as soon as she noticed me she hid herself from view behind a wall. She is ashamed of us. When she is with her friends, whether male or female, she always pretends not to notice us. But there was one time, when she was still small, when Dad broke his arm and had to walk about with it held out in front of him in a white plaster cast that looked like a bundle of washing. Miss Sophie was not ashamed of him then. She was even proud that he had broken his arm, because all the other children envied her, and whenever he appeared in the doorway she would call out, on her own accord, "Dad, Dad," and run toward him. They say that she even kissed him on his cheek, but I do not believe that.

Sebastian was sitting on the concrete steps in front of our stairway. He looked uncomfortable with his back against the wall and guarded his belly with one paw, out of modesty, as usual.

"Hello, my friend, how are things going?" His bass voice was not perfectly under control and there was a sort of faint hospital smell about him.

"Is anything wrong?" I asked.

"No, nothing. I just dropped by. I hope that it is not a bad time."

I noticed that he was swaying slightly. He blinked his eyes desperately, as if trying to clear away a mist, or to re-focus.

"Are you not feeling well, Sebastian?" I asked.

He smiled ruefully and two trails of saliva fell one after the other from his curled lips.

"Not feeling well? What rubbish! Lend me two zlotys, friend, until tomorrow, or rather until after tomorrow."

"I haven't any money. Not even in my savings box," I said, and then I suddenly remembered that my father had lost his job and there wouldn't be any money.

At this moment Miss Sophie passed by. "Fine company you keep!" she snapped.

Sebastian stared after her blankly.

"She's not bad," he said, "where did you meet her?"

"She is my sister."

"Oh, I'm sorry." He leaned his side against our door. "You know, I swallowed some valerian drops and everything seems to be going round and round."

"Are you crazy? Only cats take valerian drops."

"I didn't know," he sighed, and looked for a place where he could lie down. "I don't mind. The main thing is that it makes you forget everything."

"But, Sebastian, you were a lord, after all, at one time."

"Yes, a lord and a traveler. A famous traveler," said Sebastian, and dropped down upon the steps.

"Sebastian, what *is* the matter with you? I always thought of you as the most sensible dog on earth."

He twisted his lip in an ironical smile. "Everyone has his bad moments, my friend."

"Perhaps you are not happy with your masters?"

"They are all right. One can live with them."

"What is it, then?"

"It's my heart. That's all I can tell you. Nothing more. Can you part with a two-zloty piece until tomorrow?"

"But I told you that I have no money!"

"Yes, you did." He tried to rise from the cold concrete. The sky was beginning to darken, with gathering clouds, and small flakes of snow were starting to fall.

"Where is this asteroid, this one light in my future, and my only consolation?"

I was surprised at his use of the astronomical term. "How do you know that it is an asteroid?" I asked.

"I know everything, my friend. That is my misfortune."

Just then our caretaker came out, still sleepy from his afternoon nap, and therefore irritable.

"Off with you!" he cried, and tried to kick Sebastian, who drew back clumsily.

"Is this the place for a chat? I'm sure he hasn't been vaccinated against rabies."

"His master is an important official," I said.

"Official or not, these steps are a pedestrian passageway, not a place to lie about in," said the caretaker in a milder tone but still slightly annoyed.

"Don't argue with him," said Sebastian in a low voice, "he is a rough sort of fellow. I know him." He drowsily lifted his foot for a moment, then changed his mind and left it in the air.

The caretaker became angry. "What did he say? What is the great lumping creature talking about?"

"Oh, nothing. It's only his stomach rumbling," I said, "he can eat five pounds of bones at one go."

"Good-bye, my friend," said Sebastian, heaving himself up and going off toward the gate.

"When will you call for me?" I asked. "You know what I mean?"

"Perhaps tomorrow, perhaps the day after—some day—if we survive that long." He disappeared in the shadow of the gateway. A flock of sparrows suddenly descended upon a piece of greasy paper and began to squabble, chirping noisily. The thin wafers of springtime snow were gradually ceasing to fall.

Everything seemed abnormal somehow. Everybody was waiting for the comet: my father and Cecilia and Miss Sophie, the dull-witted Buffalo—even Sebastian, who in a previous incarnation had been a lord and a great traveler. Everybody was fed up and felt rather sick. Who, after all, wanted the unwarming sun to go on rising day after day, or was anxious that workmen should get up and go to their heavy labor, or that children should continue to suffer at their desks, or that patients in hospitals should go on bearing their pain?

Later, when I went to bed, I thought about it all for a long time before falling asleep. Shadows of branches leapt about on the walls like ghosts. The television set crackled continuously. The town looked strangely quiet and empty, except for the wind that rushed along the streets and stormed at windows.

Mum was always telling me: "You are too small." Other people too made me aware of my size. But I knew that it was not so simple as that. After all, my mother and Cecilia sometimes said of my father: "He is nothing but an overgrown boy," and my father and mother spoke of Miss Sophie as "a big child." My father would quite often wink in the direction of Cecilia as if to say: "She is absolutely childish." Something must have got mixed up.

Perhaps we are all children to some extent: old retired people and elderly gentlemen with paunches, energetic people in their prime, rebellious youths, as well as we ourselves, the real children who embody pure and essential childhood.

Then there was the fact that my father had lost his job. He put a brave face on it, but it had made him very nervous. Even late into the night, as I lay in my bed, I could hear subdued whispers and sighs. But this may have been drafts skirmishing about the apartment.

One can imagine my father's anxiety. He is afraid that one day there will be no money. Nothing for the rent, for the telephone, the television, for clothes, and maybe even for food. And this state of affairs could continue until no one knows when. I think, though, that what makes him most afraid is the loss of his position, not so much in the world as a whole as in this town, and among his office friends who live on the block. His habits and routine too have fallen away from him, with all the peace and security that he felt in them.

[66]

I saw, then, that I was in a very strange and difficult situation. My father dismissed from his job, I myself going on mysterious journeys and told that I am to free an unhappy little girl dressed all in white, and Sebastian, the Investigator Dog, plotting incomprehensible escapades. Altogether I had lost any pleasure in living, and now, to crown everything, here was this asteroid heading straight for earth and straight for those of us who were incapable of collecting our thoughts.

I pitied my mother most of all. You may have got the impression that she is a good soul, a sort of domestic hen with a heart of gold, or a Cinderella with gray threads in her hair and innocent eyes. I deliberately drew this picture of her in order to throw my father, Cecilia, and Miss Sophie in sharper relief. But the facts are actually quite different, and whether or not you want to hear it I must give a true picture of my mother. It will be much easier for me to describe her now, at night, with the terrible spring wind blowing, the television crackling, and the streetlights creaking outside.

My mother has golden hair. I know that this sounds commonplace, but it is true, and I cannot help it. Or rather it gives a golden effect, for really the color is a deep one, that of a dark kind of gold in which red lights gleam. But I dare say that each hair is slightly different in color from the rest, for I have found some that were very dark, some medium-dark, and others so pale that they're almost transparent. It is altogether beautiful hair. It is slightly curling or waving, which is unfortunate at a time when straight hair is in fashion. My mother tried to straighten her hair on curlers, but the results did not please her. Some time ago Cecilia brought her as a present some special fluid for straightening hair, and then it was all right for a few months.

As for her face, I almost dare not describe it in case you do not believe me. Oval-shaped but not too long, with a beautiful forehead and without a single wrinkle. Well, maybe I am exaggerating a little. A tiny, unimportant wrinkle may appear perhaps, but only when she smiles. After all, everyone is bound to have wrinkles when they smile. Her eyes are usually blue, and usually a very pure blue, but sometimes a slightly greenish color appears in them and at other times they look as though the irises are sprinkled with sepia. Her nose is small, straight for the most part and slightly turned up at the end. Her mouth is very mobile, with white teeth. It looks as if she has just eaten something nice, like a crisp cake or a mint.

And then, her general appearance: small, very slim, always looking faintly tanned, even in winter. And how beautifully she walks, very straight, with her head thrown back a little, and short, firm steps. The sight of her as she walks seems to be not unpleasing to others, for they all watch her in the yard whenever she goes out or in.

Of course you have the right to suspect that I am boasting, but in that case I must tell you—reluctantly, because it proves the truth of what I am saying—that a lot of men turn around to look at her in the street, old and young, soldiers and civilians, bosses and workmen. There was one old man who bumped his head against a lamppost while he was staring after her, and lost his hat.

But why must I make apologies? My mother is so beautiful that I think she is wasted on us—that is, on my father and Miss Sophie and even on me. And that's a fact.

I simply wanted to go to sleep, but all sorts of thoughts still strayed in and out of my mind. I will not tell you any more about them except that they were private thoughts, and that when I wanted to think about my acacia tree the idiotic girl in jeans kept on coming into my mind, perhaps because she was Buffalo's classmate and I had been playing that afternoon with him.

At last, when I was finally sinking into a warm, velvety dream, I thought that I was somebody else, I did not know who, and I felt that I was touching with my hand a lumpy hollow which gave me a blissful, tingling sort of feeling. But with the last shred of consciousness I was terrified by the finality of my illness and the approach of death.

And then I had another dream. I was standing on the platform of that railway station full of tangled rails, from which Eva, the little girl in white, took off into the sky in a strange sort of airplane or rocket with that hateful Retep. I dashed forward in my dream, stumbling over torn-up rails, the air above me vibrating and heavy with smoke. I went on, walking now, for a long time in the oblique, dense, almost horizontal light that precedes sunset, and suddenly saw a lead-blue bay and a small town lying among dark-green dome-shaped trees, the church with a squat, square Gothic tower and red-tiled roof, and other houses with red roofs. I walked along the high shore of the bay, leaving the town behind me, looking back all the time, gazing until my eyes filled with tears, at this little place, and saying to myself over and over again how beautiful it was, and that one should so fill one's eyes with such beauty that one remembers it always, to the end of one's life, because this was the true beauty that can cause pain impossible to explain.

I came to a branch road, or maybe a crossroads, where there was a wayside shrine to the Blessed Virgin. Beneath the feet of the Virgin, pink-cheeked and red-lipped in her sea-blue mantle over a white robe, were glass jars and bottles full of wild flowers—poppies, cornflowers, clover, mullein, mallow, lupins, briar roses, and white yarrow flowers.

From the side road, which was rather dim and mysterious and looked like a poplar alley, emerged Retep in his ridiculous plus fours. He had his airgun but was leaning on it as if it were a walking stick.

I wanted to run away, but then he smiled and I noticed that he was rather good-looking and attractive.

"You see how long I had to wait," he said.

I wanted to speak, but could not. He put his hand on my shoulder and I hunched myself, because I thought that he wanted to get a hold on me, but he only meant it as a friendly embrace.

"I know," he said, "you had to wait for the comet. But now we shall be together forever."

We came to a narrow peninsula, like a sort of sandy road half-submerged in greenish water, or maybe it was a sandbar. And then suddenly we were in a warm, sunny wood. I recognized

[69]

some of the trees. They were not the kind that grow by the sea, but sycamores, larches, mountain ashes, alders, birches, pines, aspens, shady maples, young or dwarf oaks, and the like, all of which I knew by sight, even if I did not remember their names. Some quite large birds flew up from the tall grass. They were cinnamon-brown with purplish breasts. I wondered if they were grouse, but grouse are bigger, and I began to feel a bit scared of them, but Retep pressed my arm, perhaps aware of my fear, and said: "I was always longing for your company, too, but it was not possible until now."

And all the time the mighty sea was roaring nearby. It felt as if the wood was enclosed in a warm air bubble, submerged deep down, on the seabed.

There were many kinds of plants, giving the impression that they had been deliberately brought together there. I saw the familiar Virgin's tears, with tiny hearts suspended on thin stalks, the hairy mint, fool's parsley with spiky fruit that brings beautiful dreams and oblivion.

Retep tugged at my arm. "It's here. We have found the spot at last," he said. Little trees, bent by the wind, parted in front of us and I could see yellow sand dunes covered with silvery, razor-sharp grass. We stood, sweating, on a sun-drenched hillock buffeted by a strong, salty, seaweed-smelling wind.

A huge, wide beach lay below us. Great white-crested waves broke over a shelf of sand, wetting the feet of some people who stood looking out to sea and shouting indistinctly. My heart began to beat hard. I realized that they were my family: my mother with a colored parasol in her hand, Miss Sophie draped in a towel to hide her plumpness, my father with a newspaper in his hand, and Cecilia red in the face. Well out from the shore, partly hidden by big waves, two slight creatures seemed to be drowning, engulfed in the welter of water. One was dressed in white, with dark hair streaming. The other wore blue jeans, their color deepened by the water. The two girls held each other's hand as they struggled with the waves. But I could not tell whether they were trying to swim out to sea, or—urged on by the watchers— were fighting, without success, to swim back to land. Whichever it was, they were receding before our eyes.

There are plenty of over-clever grown-ups who will tell you that this dream is of no significance, because Freud, the expert on dreams, says ... because this, because that! I would not bother you with silly dreams if there were not some very deep meaning in them. I do not like dreams myself, and I do not care for people who always tell you what they dreamt last night. But these dreams of mine are connected with the various strange adventures which lay ahead of me.

When I awoke the next morning I did not think about dreams or anything like that, but only about one very practical matter. Miss Sophie had evidently got out of bed on the wrong side, because she was in a very bad temper. Even my mother kept out of her way. My father lay in bed, gazing blankly at the ceiling, because he no longer had to go to work. So I could set out for school without my books, with no one to bother me. Just outside our gate I bought a paper and sat down under the acacia tree, which was by now beginning to get on my nerves.

I opened the paper and began to read the last pages. Meanwhile Buffalo ran out and rushed off to school, taking large bites at something that he held under his jacket. Then the caretaker appeared and the roadmen looked at him and jerked their thumbs at him, making the gesture of someone downing a drink, and the caretaker saw them and wagged his head at them angrily. Then Buffalo's father came down and carefully examined his Fiat. He ran his fingers delicately over some scratches, looked at them against the light, polished the headlamps, switched on the window wipers, prodded the tires, rubbed some marks from the coachwork with his elbow, and finally went off to work on foot. Several people went in and out of our courtyard entrance and dogs of all breeds and sizes were running about their business.

I read the advertisements in the newspaper. Somebody wanted to sell a hundredweight of Indian ink for ball-point pens, someone else had a plot of land, with farm buildings for sale, another offered a pair of budgerigars. There was an advertisement for the next-of-kin of someone who had died. But, apart from cars, advertisements were mostly for domestic help. The people advertising competed with one another in offering marvelous working conditions. One would-be employer stated that there would be plenty of time for watching her new twenty-three-inch television. I was scanning the page idly and without much interest, when I suddenly came upon the following advertisement:

> Leader of film unit working on the film *Spaceflight to Andromeda* is looking for suitable boy actors, aged 11 and 12. Apply 13 Wspolna Street, 9th floor. . . .

You can read the advertisement a second time, if you wish. I read it perhaps seventeen times. It was definitely suspicious—too good to be true. The comet was the only explanation for it.

I thought of the fact that, at that very moment, at least a hundred thousand boys in our town were reading that advertisement, or maybe even more, because undersized fourteen- and fifteen-year-olds would also have a chance of passing as twelve-year-olds. Of course, at least half of them have no need to seek employment and half of the remaining half would be afraid to play truant and would go to school faithfully until the end of term. But the rest, a mere twenty-five thousand competitors, would take the risk.

I suddenly felt scared and, shaking with fear or excitement (it could have been either), I rushed into town. I did not even notice that there was someone running beside me the whole way, until I heard a voice saying: "Are you playing truant?"

"No, I'm going on business."

I stopped for a moment. Sebastian put out his huge red tongue. It was as wide as a soldier's uniform belt. His eyes were haggard and had a strange, sidelong look.

"You wouldn't like to pay a quick visit to—you know where?"

"I haven't got time."

"Perhaps you no longer want to go there?"

"No. Why shouldn't I wish to go there? I do want to."

"Then perhaps you are afraid?"

"There is something that I have to do. It is something very important."

"But we could call in for a minute."

"For a minute?"

"Well, yes, just for a quick look. Would you like that?"

"Yes, but I have no time."

"Why are you dithering, my friend? Coming back, I could drop you right at the place you are going to. We always get shifted off course."

"Well, perhaps, on those conditions," I said hesitatingly.

"Then let us not waste any more time," said Sebastian in a thick voice. I saw again the skin along his ribs beginning to shiver. This seemed to me to be somehow significant.

"Come over here, to the side," he said, "we will have the wind behind us."

We sat beside the telephone booth. I could see, over Sebastian's shoulders, a pair of legs fidgeting behind the glass.

"Ready?" asked Sebastian, his deep voice quivering.

"OK."

We had scarcely looked into the pupils of each other's eyes when we were already far away from the universe of asteroids, polluted moons, and ageing planets, infinitely far away from sorrows, pain, and despair.

We had drifted terrifyingly off course, as usual. We stood beside a church, in a graveled yard, beside a weather-beaten wooden cross, the kind that was erected as a memorial of a plague. The church was wooden, rather newer than the cross, shingle-roofed, and full of lights; from within a tremulous choir intoned plaintively: "From pestilence, hunger, fire, and war, good Lord, deliver us!" while incense rose up in a cloud from the nave, obscuring the rays of the dying sun. For the sun was in the western sky, as it had been before—as though it would never actually set. But we could not see it through the thick spruce trees, and everything was illuminated by the strong glow of sunset.

In front of us, just beyond the churchyard full of what looked like wartime graves, a whole valley spread out as if it were contained in a huge, inverted green felt hat.

I studied this valley intently, trying to imprint it on my memory so that I could draw it later. There was a steep, thickly wooded slope and below it a railway track like the four strings of a mandolin, on which a sort of trolley was running, operated by two men who strenuously manipulated a bar or lever, as if they were pumping. Several houses, quiet as if drowsing in the early dusk, topped the railway embankment. Beyond them stretched very dark fields, as far as the black line of the river, with the tiny lights of fires showing where travelers were camping. On the far side of the river rose a steep bank, still russet-red from the afterglow of the sunset, with young dwarf oaks waiting motionless for night to fall. Most notable of all were the birds. Huge dense flocks wheeled darkly over the valley, uttering strident cries—the usual evening ritual or play of common jackdaws. Under the eaves of the church, swallows darted in and out of their mud nests and the flowerpots attached with wire that some kindly sacristan had hung there for their use.

Sebastian and I, without a word, ran down the stony path to the big house hidden in the trees. Some creature was running abreast of us, obliterated by the dark tree trunks. We ran faster than legs could carry us, as if on wings, until, out of breath, we halted amid some white ruins—white walls with broken edges showing the ancient bricks of which they were built. Brambles and small birch trees grew between the walls and there were thickets of tall nettles full of darting birds.

"Who is it?" I asked, curious about the creature that ran beside us. It was the tigress Fela. She halted, trying with a rheumatic paw to brush something from her sad face.

"What place is this?" I asked.

"It used to be a hospital. It was destroyed by artillery fire in the First World War," said Sebastian. "Children play at cowboys and Indians here and pick blackberries, and the dead haunt here at night."

Fela began to cry out softly, limping on her forepaws. She was a very miserable animal. The lower rims of her eyes were encrusted with the yellow stains of tears, and she had lost the whiskers on one side of her face. Toothless and with molting flanks and pitiful tail, she had obviously had a hard life.

"Is Retep at home?" asked Sebastian. Fela nodded her poor head and began to yelp again, like a small puppy. Sebastian hesitated, trying to control the trembling throughout his great body, as he added: "And what about her? Eva, I mean—little Eva?"

The tigress nodded and scratched the turf submissively with paws only half furnished with claws.

"I will repay you when I am able," said Sebastian in a low voice, "but keep an eye on everything."

Fela flung herself on her side and watched us with desperate sadness as we moved away.

"Don't forget that we have only come for a quick look around," I said.

"Perhaps you don't want to come here again?" asked Sebastian.

"It isn't that. I am looking for a job. My father has been dismissed from the Institute."

"My master has his troubles too. Life is like that nowadays, my friend."

We entered the park, this time from a different side; but here also there was a raspberry patch festooned with cobwebs, and with large berries on which pale green caterpillars crawled. In the thicket beyond, a crowd of small birds fluttered and twittered unseen.

Even at this distance from the house we could hear music. We crept nearer, parting the tall grasses already wet with dew, until we could see the big lawn in front of the house, which was not really so very golden after all. The plaster had peeled off in a few places and the pillars of the porch had warped as if they could no longer support the triangular roof.

On the round lawn, which was surrounded by a gravel path, stood a table covered with a white cloth. A Gramophone with a huge rusty horn stood on the table. There were glasses filled with a pink drink and a big flask of what looked like dark pond water, but was really freshly brewed mead, into which people were dipping peeled cucumber halves.

Sebastian began to tremble again. He could see what I too saw: children dancing in time to the raucous yet muffled music, some gentlemen in checked suits eating cucumbers with mead, and ladies in long dresses full of pleats and folds chattering gaily. I felt an odd sensation when I saw also the little girl, Eva, whom we had to set free.

All these people, assembled for their meal, looked as if they were standing in a big pond of tea. But it was only because of the glow of the setting sun.

"Hands up!"—the sharp order came from behind us—"Don't move, or I'll shoot."

I turned my head carefully, and saw Retep with a gun trained upon us. He was smiling unpleasantly.

"A nice look round we've had!" I muttered. But Sebastian wore the blank look of an ordinary, obedient, not very intelligent dog.

A silver-haired old man, standing on one side in the raspberry patch, was smiling too, but his smile was kind and understanding. "So you've got yourselves caught," he said in a slow, singsong voice. "didn't I say they'd catch it!"

"Get up!" said Retep, cocking his gun.

I raised myself from the wet grass. Sebastian continued to act stupid and blinked his eyes.

"Get up!" repeated Retep. Sebastian, groaning, raised himself onto his feet.

Then a lady carrying a parasol came over from the table with the Gramophone.

"What is happening, Retep?" she called. "Who is it? Is it someone from the post office? Perhaps it's a telegram from Papa."

"No, it's some layabouts. I must teach them a lesson."

"What kind of a getup is the boy wearing?" asked Retep's mother. "How did he get dressed like this? He can't be a local."

"They must be holiday-makers, ma'am. I've chased them out before," said the old man, still smiling.

"They are always loitering about here," said Retep. "I'm sure that they are looking to see what they can steal."

"You know why we came here," I said suddenly. "You know very well."

He began to laugh, a forced and somehow unnatural laugh. "You see, Mama, how insolent they are! This time I will not let them off. Konstanty, bring me the gloves."

The old man scratched the back of his head. "Would it be them leather gloves you want?" he asked.

"Yes. And be quick about it."

The Gramophone stopped playing. A few guests were looking curiously in our direction. The wretched Chippy crawled out from some shrubs on his sticks of legs, hiccuping vulgarly and trying to raise his white eyelids. His beak, as usual, was stuck with soaked barley grains.

The tall lady with the parasol cried hysterically: "Retep, my child, I forbid you!"

"Don't be afraid, Mama," said Retep softly. I felt very uneasy.

"My son, how did you come to be so cruel? Who is it that you take after? Set them free at once!"

"No, this time they won't get off so easily," said Retep, slowly and with relish.

Some of the guests approached and asked what was happening. I noticed Eva behind them. I thought that she was crying, because she held her hands to her cheeks. But when our eyes met, she tried to smile and raised one hand, closing it and then opening it again, as if waving, saying good-bye, or making some hesitant request.

Then Konstanty reappeared with two pairs of boxing gloves slung over his shoulder.

"It seems I've brought a present for the holiday-makers," he said genially, probably thinking that the gloves were a gift for myself and Sebastian, who was acting as if he was the stupidest Great Dane in existence.

"What's up?" asked one man in English, twitching his upper lip, adorned with a moustache as thin as an eyebrow.

Retep threw a pair of gloves at me. They fell at my feet, in a patch of dark clover. "Put them on," he said, "unless you're afraid to."

A stork flew almost soundlessly across the brilliant western sky. Eva caught at a branch of elder that swayed in the evening breeze, so that only the edges of the dark green leaves showed between her slender fingers.

I picked up the gloves, new ones made of dark leather, and put them on, tucking the laces under the cuffs. They creaked as if they were stuffed with horsehair or seaweed.

"Shall we begin?" asked Retep.

"I won't allow it!" his mother cried. "I cannot bear such brutality. It would be better if you were to have a croquet match, or something."

"This is the age of the sportsman, dear lady," said one of the guests. "Times are different. It's grit and toughness that counts today."

"But it is absurd to fight like this, for no reason," said Retep's mother.

"Well, are you ready?" asked Retep.

"Yes, I'm ready," I said.

He approached me and we began aiming blows, feinting and parrying and keeping at arm's length. Then he retreated to the middle of the ring and took up a boxing attitude, a rather odd stance, like that of boxers in old pictures. I raised my fists and approached him. He began to dance about, taking small steps, with his eyes all the time fixed on mine, so that I felt uneasy and blinked a little.

"Guard the lower part of your body," muttered Sebastian.

I instinctively lowered my elbows, and at that moment Retep struck me a direct blow on the forehead. I stumbled backward, trying to dodge him. A sort of sigh or murmur of approval rose from the spectators.

The corners of Retep's mouth curled in a slight smile that was neither ironical nor superior. He wanted a fight and was enjoying it.

"Try to get him first," growled Sebastian. "Hit him with your left—your *left!*" That is exactly what I wanted to do, but he dodged me and I hurtled headfirst into the cobwebbed raspberry bushes.

"Ha ha! There he is, picking raspberries," chanted Konstanty. "There are some more berries to your left."

I returned to my place. I was already growing angry at all this:

the good-humored old man's cackling, the gaping guests and Retep's springy footwork. But before I had time to gather my wits he advanced upon me and struck me a series of blows in the pit of my stomach. Luckily my stomach was empty, and it rumbled slightly. I struck out instinctively in defense and then heard a dull thudding sound; I saw that Retep had fallen on his back. I must have hit him without knowing what I was doing, almost by accident.

"Oh!" gasped the guests.

"Finish him off! He's reeling. His eyes are all misted over," advised Sebastian in a hoarse whisper.

"Stop, boys, that's enough!" cried Retep's mother. "This is not the way to behave in front of guests." She tried to catch her son's arm, but he was already dancing on the spot, dangling his arms in line with his body, trying to relax his muscles.

"Please go away, Mama," he said jerkily, "don't interfere."

I saw tears in his eyes and he clenched his teeth until the muscles of his jaws stood out like tennis balls. Konstanty cackled, imitating Retep's movements.

Retep attacked me violently. I jumped back, but he did not give me a second to offer any defense. He was crowding me most of the time, raining blows steadily on the front and side of my head and on my arms and ribs. But I gave as good as I got. Retep's cheeks became redder and a dark-red trickle appeared beneath his nose.

"Heavens, the blood!" cried his mother. "He will kill Retep! Stop, I order you!"

"I'm the one who's going to do the killing," wheezed Retep, launching himself bodily upon me.

"If you don't get the other fellow, he'll get you," chanted Chippy. From the corner of my eye I saw him spreading his miserable wings belligerently.

"This is a good show! Look at them, wrestling like a couple of young porkers," chuckled Konstanty. He too had tears in his eyes, but they were tears of good-natured merriment.

We broke apart for a moment. I was beginning to gasp and found it increasingly difficult to snatch any air.

"Finish him off with an uppercut," Sebastian hissed with

excitement. I wanted to do just that, but I heard the beginning of that muffled bang, like the sound of an exploded puff-ball. I heard only the start of the sound—the rest was drowned in a strange noise. I thought that at some time during the fight I must have struck my head against a tree trunk. I tried to turn to look at Retep but could see only the darkening sky, and that was spinning around and around. I felt something rough on my forehead. Sebastian's worried eyes and deeply wrinkled brow were close to mine and he was licking me.

"It was an accidental blow," he growled as he licked my forehead, "sheer bad luck."

"What happened? What's the matter?" I asked dazedly. "Has he given up?"

Sebastian waved a paw stuck with bits of moss. "You have lost, my friend. One blow like that and you were finished."

"What are you saying? I'm still ready to go on. Where is he?"

I tried to rise. Through a dancing haze I saw the guests moving away and Retep, with his mother wiping his nose with a handkerchief.

Then something warm and delicate, like a butterfly's wing warmed by the sun, touched my cheek. It was Eva.

"Thank you," she said, putting something into my hand, from which the glove had slipped. I saw her dark hair, with the red lights in it, her big eyes, like the eyes pictured in ikons, and her trembling mouth.

"Save me, I implore you, or I shall die," she said, and then she vanished. Sebastian, with saliva dripping from lips that had a bitter curl to them, helped me to my feet.

"Sebastian," I said, "I am in a hurry. You remember that I was going into town on business."

"Wait a minute—in any case it doesn't matter now."

Suddenly in the dark sky I saw a falling star. I know that falling stars are only meteorites, but when they slide down the sky, singly or in bright showers, and fade upon the horizon, they can help us to gain our wishes.

We came back home again to our town and our everyday life, standing in the middle of the road in sleet and rain and an icy wind. Window wipers were beating desperately backwards and forwards and drivers were tooting at us angrily. I pulled Sebastian onto the pavement.

"For once, you see, I have got us back without straying off course," said Sebastian. "Here you are, Wspolna Street—dead on target!"

"My ear is burning dreadfully. It feels as if someone had hung a heavy weight on it."

"It does look rather swollen, but that'll soon pass. You stopped an accidental blow, just a simple swing to the head."

"A fine look around we had!"

"Don't give up, my friend. The next time we'll cut him up. But you need a bit of training. I'll teach you a few tricks."

"It's all very well for you to talk now. When we were there you acted just plain stupid."

Sebastian looked dejected. His large eyes, that were almost too beautiful for an animal, filled with reproach. He did not trouble to shake off the drops of rain that slid from his forehead and along his black nose.

"What could I do?" he said at last. "Does anybody treat me seriously? But what's the use of talking about that?"

"She gave me something," I said.

"Who did?" Sebastian pricked his ears.

"Who do you think? The King of England's daughter?"

"Why do you flare up so quickly?" Sebastian shifted his weight from one paw to the other. I could have sworn that he blushed, but of course, dogs can't blush. But the expression of his face had quite changed, to something that one could certainly call the equivalent of blushing.

"Have you still got it?" he asked. "You didn't lose it?"

[81]

I opened my burning hand. There, lying in the palm, was an old railway ticket, slightly worn, as if it had been carried in a pocket during a long journey.

"A railway ticket," he said at last, in a shaking voice.

"Yes, Vienna to Warsaw."

"No, the other way round. It's from Warsaw to Vienna."

"Same thing. But look, the date has been rubbed off."

"Anyway, it must be old. See how old-fashioned the lettering is."

"Why did she give it to me?"

Sebastian was silent for a while and then he said, in a low voice: "Perhaps it was so that you should remember."

"Remember what?"

"That she is waiting."

A man in a raincoat deliberately jostled the dripping Sebastian as he passed. "Found a fine place for a chat, haven't you?" he said angrily.

The rain stopped. A dust-cart came along the street. The men began to drag out the metal dustbins from a nearby gateway, emptying them into the big container with a deafening din.

"Give it to me," said Sebastian.

"You'd soon lose it."

"No, I wouldn't. Gentleman's word!"

"You've nowhere to put it."

"I'll put it under my collar."

"I'd better keep it. I can always show it to you."

"But don't lose it, my friend."

"Why are you so anxious about it?"

"I must go back. I only came out for a few minutes to buy some papers."

"Good-bye, then!"

"Do you feel better now?" asked Sebastian.

"Go on, or you'll freeze to the pavement," I said.

"Shall I come again?"

"Of course."

"Tomorrow, maybe?"

"All right. Tomorrow!"

"You know, I have come to like you," he said, and then stopped. He wanted to say something else; I felt that it was something that he had already prepared in his mind. But he turned away and ran at a heavy trot along the street, dodging the passersby.

I had no difficulty in finding 13 Wspolna Street. A lot of people were rushing in and out of the entrance door and several cars were parked in front of the house. Notice boards pointed the way to a corridor full of doors. One was marked CASHIER'S OFFICE, another MAKE-UP, and another DIRECTOR. A crowd of men were milling about in one big room, and there were ladies banging away at typewriters. A big, dark man was writing or drawing something on a piece of cardboard that hung on the wall.

I stood there for some time, until a thin, almost transparent young man, with ears like wings, stopped in front of me.

"What do you want, youngster?" he asked. His voice sounded friendly, but he looked as though he could pounce at any moment.

"I have come about the advertisement."

"You would like to act in the film?"

He scrutinized me so unrelentingly that I was afraid there was something on my face.

"Yes, I could play one of the parts," I said.

"Have you a parent along with you?"

"Which parent?"

"Father or mother. We must have their consent."

"I'm an orphan," I said. I was annoyed, because I don't like telling unnecessary lies.

"Well then, you have a guardian, or there is some other adult."

"I have nobody, truly I haven't."

He hesitated a moment, gazing at me sadly. "Well, I don't

know," he said at last, and then "Brush!" he called, to someone in the next room.

A typical suburban ruffian came out, with broken blood vessels on his nose that looked like a collection of hieroglyphics.

"What is it, Niko?" he asked. "Have you got a new boy?"

"This is the director of photography," said the young man, who was known as Pale Niko. He presented me. "He's got no parents," he said. "An orphan, with nobody to look after him."

"So? How do you live? On fresh air?"

"I would like to have a job," I said.

"It's no good, young man. There's nothing doing if you are without parental care."

"But I must get a job. I could make myself useful. I know something about astronomy and aeronautics."

"Are you acquainted with nochmology?"

Alas, I did not know what nochmology was, so I was silent and stared at the ladies who were so busy typing.

"You know, Brush, he looks all right," Pale Niko interceded hesitantly on my behalf.

"I don't know," said Brush. "What do you need the money for, young man? Have you heard of the comet?"

"But suppose the comet misses us?"

"Will you treat us with your first paycheck?"

"Of course I will, sir."

"That's generous of you. Well, we'll show you to Mr. Hare."

Mr. Hare was the producer. He was lounging in a very uncomfortable chair, trying to look like an American. He barely glanced at me with his pale, colorless eyes.

"It's against the regulations," he said. "Have you fellows got nothing better to do?"

"But take another look at him, sir," said Brush, who was now becoming ambitious on my behalf. "He's a smart lad. You can tell at once."

"Have you ever been in the nick?"

"Where, sir?"

"In prison, young man."

"No, but I have been in a reformatory for two months."

Brush was obviously proud of me. He looked at me like a

[84]

criminal who has fathered an image of himself.

"Shall I show him to Duckbill?"

Mr. Hare, the producer, simply made a very uncooperative grimace, and we went into another room, where a gentleman wearing spectacles and with a very peculiar complexion was looking at himself in a mirror.

"Here's another lad for you," said Brush, depositing himself heavily on a box marked DO NOT SIT.

Duckbill examined me for a while and then, again looking into the mirror, asked: "Do you like the cinema?"

"Very much," I said, with assumed fervor.

"Which actors do you specially like?"

"All kinds." I was feeling rather hot, because I was not expecting these questions.

"Which actor, for example?"

I searched my memory desperately for names. Mr. Duckbill was nodding his head at his image in the mirror.

"And you, sir, remind me rather of Trevor Howard," I said finally.

Duckbill was motionless. "Do you think so?" he asked slowly.

"Certainly I do, sir."

He was silent for a while and then he sighed. "He looks all right," he said.

"Well then, shall we show him to Baldy?" asked Brush, brightening.

He took me to the room marked MAKE-UP. Some ladies dressed in white were bending over an armchair holding a discontented-looking blonde lady. An untidy man, bald, with the remains of graying hair, was studying the effect of various wigs that were being tried on her head. For some reason he reminded me of the tramps who feasted by the dustbins in our courtyard.

"Excuse me, sir," said Duckbill cautiously, while Brush remained reverently silent. "I have a nice boy here, sir."

Baldy looked at me and began to shoot out his dry lips as if he were trying to spit out a thread about fifty yards long.

"Why do you bring me such gooks?" he said. "I need boys with character and personality."

"He's an interesting little fellow," said Duckbill, still more cautiously, "He has been in a reformatory for two years."

Baldy sputtered again for a while, staring at me with irritation. "I don't fancy him."

"We could try him, sir. Let's shoot a few takes," urged Duckbill, who was beginning to have ambitions for me.

"Stop tormenting the director," said the blonde. "Voytek, darling, do I have to wear this horrible thing all through the film?" She flung one of the wigs onto the little table.

The director shot out his dry lips and said absentmindedly: "Yes, you must, you must."

Duckbill took a deep breath and asked: "Shall I try, sir?"

The director snorted. "You just mess about here. I have to do everything myself. You seem to think you're on holiday. Get out of my sight, or I'll kick you out altogether!"

Then he suddenly calmed down, blinking first one eye and then the other and silently chewing his lip. "What was I doing?" he asked.

"Voytek, darling, must I wear somebody else's ghastly hair?"

"Yes, you must. We have to get you looking more demonic."

"Do you agree then?" asked Duckbill, who seemed to be the director's assistant.

Baldy was silent, as another wig was tried on the blonde's head.

"Well, come along to the studio. He's given in," said Brush, taking me by my sore ear.

I sat for a long time in a big room full of children and grown-ups. A lady in a white overall had sponged my face and neck and hands with a damp, brick-red sponge. Something odd must have happened to my face, because all the grown-ups in the room looked at me rather unkindly. I soon realized that they were the parents of the children who were competing to appear in *Spaceflight to Andromeda*. They kept on fidgeting and adjusting the clothes and hair of their dressed-up offspring, who were behaving as if they were already actors in American westerns and looking haughtily at everyone else. Their parents eyed other parents' children as though they wondered how anyone had the nerve to bring along such miserable nonentities. Altogether the atmosphere in the big room was tense and unnatural. The only one who seemed to be at ease was a little girl of two or three years, whose dreary mother called her "Ducky."

She got into every nook and corner, pushing her way, looking into handbags and keeping up a running commentary all the time in a voice like Donald Duck's. People looked at her amiably enough, but with some consternation. Her proportions were those of a grown-up person who had forgotten to grow, and there was scarcely any hair on her small head. A tabby kitten, also quite a baby, was following her and trying to bite her. She would then hit out at the kitten, and both of them always missed. Nobody tried to chase the kitten away, maybe because he was also some kind of an actor.

Duckbill, who was the only one who looked like a real film director, brought me a sheet of paper on which were the words: "You mustn't never touch this barrier. Mind now what I've told you, you horrible brat."

"Does it mean that I've got the job, sir?" I asked.

His face assumed a vague expression and he said: "We can't be sure yet. You must do your best. Show me how you will say it."

"You mustn't never touch this barrier. Now mind what I've told you, you horrible brat."

"Wait, son. This is the cinema. You've got to put some expression into it. Your face must show horror and then anger. Watch me." And he acted the lines so well that a lady sitting nearby picked up her thirteen-year-old daughter in her arms and began to apologize to Duckbill.

Meanwhile little Ducky was snatching things out of the hands of various parents, screeching loudly: "I want that!" Then she began to yell to have the lid raised on the grand piano, but she called it "gran pino."

Brush found me and said: "Have you learned your part, Johnny? Come onto the set then!"

As soon as I was given the sheet of paper with my part, all the parents became annoyed and followed me with eyes full of real hatred.

The set was in a big, dark hall, gray, drab, and smelling of burned rubber. Some people grouped beside a camera were eating in silence from greasy paper bags. Behind them rose wooden walls with crooked windows. There was a huge white notice-board saying: NO SMOKING. Duckbill bustled about in the midst of all this, smoking a cigarette.

"Well, here is the art director."

I shook hands with a very fat gentleman in spectacles, who sat on a canvas chair. I felt at once, for some reason, that he did not like children.

"The art director also acts in the film," added Duckbill. The art director thereupon looked modest, but it was plain that he was pleased.

"This is a superb studio, my boy," he said. "Here we can recreate palaces, castles, big trees and mountains, and even a river, if we want to. Do you feel a mysterious thrill of adventure, coming into this factory of beautiful dreams?"

"No, sir," I said truthfully, but for what reason I do not know.

"The new, matter-of-fact generation," said the art director, laughing and patting me on the head with marked distaste. "And what part is this young fellow going to play?"

"I think it is to be Retep, the bad character," said Duckbill, examining me through a sort of magnifying glass or viewfinder.

"I visualized Retep rather differently," grunted the art director.

"But this is cinema," said Duckbill. "Hard work is what is wanted, not imagination." I realized that the art director could be disregarded.

A man with a beard came over, with a sandwich in one hand and a Thermos flask in the other. I took an instant liking to him. It was because of the way he looked at me and because a sort of sadness in his eyes reminded me slightly of Sebastian.

"Well, how are things? Are the plumbers ready?" asked Duckbill.

"The plumbers are always ready," said the bearded man, pouring out his tea and drinking it. Then he screwed the cup back on the flask and called, quite quietly: "Lights!"

In all corners of the studio voices echoed him: "Lights on! All lights on!"

I realized then that the man with the beard was the cameraman, and the "plumbers," as Duckbill called them, were his assistants.

[88]

But the plumbers, as it turned out, were not quite ready, because the cameraman spent a good part of an hour looking at the lights through a dark glass and shouting things that did not make much sense:"Track in! Tilt down! Put the scrim on! Bring the pup closer!"

Duckbill told me what I had to do. It was quite simple. After the words "You mustn't never touch this barrier," and before the words "Now mind what I told you," I was to slap my fellow actor, a little girl who turned out to be Ducky.

The kitten followed her onto the set and immediately forgot his part and began to play with the electricians. Duckbill told me that this kitten had a stand-in, which means a deputy who will take over in the more dangerous scenes. But he was the actor proper and his head was turned a little.

Everything suddenly became very bright, as all the lights were switched on. Everyone asked everyone else for silence. The only sound was the noise of hammering somewhere far to the back. Ducky and I were put in front of the camera. The back of a chair was supposed to be the mysterious barrier. Everybody began to call, with varying intonations: "Ready . . . ready? . . . ready!"

At last Duckbill called "Action!" A young lady clapped a blackboard in front of my eyes, calling out something at the same time in an atrocious tone of voice, and I said what I had to say. But when I was about to slap Ducky, she was looking at me so respectfully, with her eyes like blackberries, that I only stroked her shoulder.Anyhow, it was all over in about three seconds.

"Cut!" shouted Duckbill. "That's no good at all. You were supposed to hit her."

"But she will cry."

"Mind your own business. Do you want to be in the film?"

"Yes."

"Then don't just walk through your part. Do it properly!"

The shot was repeated. This time I gave Ducky a good hard smack. She began to howl and ran off somewhere into a dark corner of the studio.

"Cut!" said Duckbill. "That was a good take."

The girl who clapped the blackboard crawled out from under the camera, very angry.

"Why have you altered your lines?"

"I haven't altered them."

"You have. Instead of saying 'You mustn't never touch this barrier,' you said 'You must never touch this barrier.' "

"But that is the correct way to say it."

"Sir!" she called to the art director. The fat gentleman hurried to the scene and listened to her complaint. He was very annoyed.

"I will not allow the words to be altered. The pay is bad enough and on top of that our work is not respected."

"But sir," I said, "using a double negative is bad grammar. The typist must have made a mistake."

The art director shut his eyes and repeated the line to himself in a whisper. Then, with a forced laugh, he said: "You are right. Well done! Studio typists are a race apart. Speak your lines as you think they should be."

Again he made as if to pat me on the head, but refrained. He began telling the continuity girl how they had messed up the text of his books, including those that had been published abroad, and then he mentioned various prizes that he had received.

I must have been satisfactory in the third take, because Duckbill called cheerfully: "Thank you. That's OK. What do you think?"

"Everything is OK by the plumbers," said the bearded cameraman calmly as he reached for his flask.

Then I noticed that the director, Baldy, was standing between some pieces of scenery beside the blonde lady, who was seated on a chair, wearing a sort of plastic see-through costume.

He said: "That's no good. He's hopeless. He doesn't know how to act."

Duckbill, who was now championing me wholeheartedly, said: "I don't agree, sir. He has an expressive face, and he is the spitting image of Retep."

"You don't know what you're talking about," said the director. "A bunch of amateurs! I have to do your jobs as well as my own."

"Voytek," said the blonde lady in a languid voice, "you mustn't get excited."

"I'll stop the shooting altogether. I've no proper team, actors, or script. I have had enough of these constant improvisations."

"I beg your pardon, but what is wrong with the script?" asked the fat scenario writer, in an injured voice. "You yourself have altered it constantly, until I can't recognize my own book."

"The book is just drivel for kids."

"I object to that!"

"There's something I'm after. I don't quite know what it is . . . something with depth, something modern. I can't do anything with such old-fashioned stuff. I'm going to stop shooting. I've had enough."

He was about to walk away, spluttering, when the author and scriptwriter caught hold of his sweater and wouldn't let go.

"But, sir, we can work something out. Perhaps we can put bits in. You said yourself that a film is in the making until the day it is first shown."

Brush appeared silently, like a ghost, and took me by the ear.

"Come away, son. This is not a scene for children." And he took me out into a dark passage.

"It was all for nothing," I said, feeling very depressed. "Such a lot of excitement, and it all came to nothing."

"Don't worry. He will carry on with the shooting. His wife picked the book. She wanted to play the good fairy. So, whatever happens, Baldy will be making the film."

"But what about me?"

"You? We'll see. The screen tests will decide for us. Come to the cashier's office."

A man who was telling jokes went on telling jokes while he paid me sixty zlotys. The producer came in at that moment. He looked out of the window at something, with his colorless eyes, and said unpleasantly:

"It won't do. He has got no parents and no guardian."

"Look here, Hare," said Brush, "never mind the rules. I am his guardian."

Duckbill caught me in the corridor.

"Where can we find you, in case we want you?"

"So you think, sir . . . "

"I think nothing. But just in case."

"For the time being I am staying with some friends. They are on the phone."

As I went downstairs I looked at the photographs of actors

and actresses on the walls, and suddenly I heard a sharp tapping of heels. There was somebody coming up, and I almost collided on the landing with the girl in jeans. But this time she was wearing a very smart dress and a coat that may have been foreign. Our shoulders touched slightly. She jumped aside and said "Sorry," but it was rather my fault than hers.

I stopped and looked at her and she, too, stopped for a moment, glancing at me through the metal leaves on the ornamental banisters, and then she hurried on upstairs. But her glance may have been something that I imagined.

It was snowing again when I reached the street, as heavily as if it were January. Perhaps at any other time nobody would have thought such weather remarkable. But now everyone was wondering at it. Salesgirls watched the snow through big, dusty windows and passersby were looking up at the low clouds. A policeman, who was about to blow his whistle to stop a driver from taking a wrong turn, waved his hand instead and stared at the big flakes falling as if they were being picked from a huge wad of cotton wool. I thought of the angry film director, waiting for the comet like everyone else.

Our town does not look its best in such weather. It was quite gray, as if worn by long use, and the houses had become slightly eroded by rain and wind and frosts. The cars rushed past covered with mud and splashing up the water in the gutters. People huddled in their clothes against the cold and wet are not particularly attractive, either. One would have felt that life was not worth living if it were not for the thought that the real spring was just around the corner. But would it come this year?

When I reached our block I met Buffalo. He was running joyfully through all the big puddles in his new rubber boots. He had just come from a meal at a friend's house, and seemed to have eaten so much that he had stopped feeling hungry. But on second thought, he said, this may have been a slight exaggeration, because he still had room for a bit more pudding. He half closed his eyes, with their pale golden eyelashes, and went through a list of all that he had eaten. His friend, he said, never ate much, and his parents worried about him.

"Why do you stuff yourself so much?" I asked with disgust.

"Oh, I've joined a club where I am training to be a weight lifter."

I thought to myself that this must be one more excuse for eating nonstop.

"Have you given up thinking about the comet coming?"

"Pooh, the papers say that it isn't true. It will pass a long way from the earth."

"If the papers say that it *isn't* true, it means that it *must* be true."

Buffalo blinked, not quite understanding.

"They don't want a panic," I said, "and so they try to reassure us. That journalist who lives on the fourth floor keeps his light on all night. He knows the truth and he can't sleep."

"Huh! The truth is that you are abnormal. My parents even tell me not to play with you."

"So what? Aren't you still thinking that you are going to die?"

"I'm not so daft. This summer we are going to the lakes. There are all sorts of berries and mushrooms there, so I'll have plenty to eat. And anyhow, I would rather have lower marks and a peaceful life."

"You're lucky," I said, sighing.

"Of course. It stands to reason. I don't read any books except the ones I have to, and I hope I never shall. That's why I enjoy life. There's nothing wrong with my health, and on the whole everything's OK. What do you get out of life? You know the whole encyclopedia by heart, but what of it? My old man says that the whole lot of you are lazy, and that's why you're all fed up with life. What does your mother do? Just makes things from time to time to hang on the wall. And your father has been kicked out of his job ... "

"My father held different views from his boss on scientific matters," I said.

"Huh," said Buffalo, "he's work-shy. Imagine what would

happen if everybody could lie about on a sofa talking philosophy."

"Do you know, Buffalo, you are utterly primitive."

"I may be primitive, but I'm happy. I can put you on the floor with one arm tied behind my back."

That was really the end. It shows the intellectual level of boys my own age, and so you should not be surprised that I don't tell you anything about my school or about my schoolmates and their activities. Buffalo is by no means the worst of them. He actually gets good marks for his work. I suppose he works to annoy the others, because he is very unpopular in his class. He often comes home from school covered in mud and with his shirt torn because they have been roughing him up. His mother complains about it but I think that she is not popular either, because nobody does anything to stop it. Perhaps the fact that they are unpopular acts as the spur that keeps them going.

"Do you know," I said to Buffalo, "whenever I want to, I go on long journeys." But as soon as I had said that I regretted it.

"Huh-huh! I see you in our yard every day of your life."

"I know a secret. I can move backwards and forwards in time quite freely."

"I used to play that game, but the craze passed."

"This is not a game, Buffalo. It is the absolute truth."

"Well, prove it!"

I showed him the ticket that Sebastian had tried to get from me.

"So what?" asked Buffalo.

"I brought it back from there."

"It's an ordinary railway ticket. You must be collecting them."

"No, I'm not, honestly. When I want to, I travel to a valley with a river and a big, old house ... "

" ... And there is a little girl there with a white umbrella. She is very wretched and unhappy, and there is a wicked boy who is unkind to her," finished Buffalo, splashing into a puddle that was rainbowed with oil.

"How do you know?" I asked in surprise.

"I must have read it somewhere—I don't know where."

[94]

"I suppose you think that I am a sickly sort of dropout, who lives in a dream world?"

"What do I care? It's your affair," said Buffalo shortly. "Come on, we'll let the air out of the tires on my old man's car."

"Do you think that I'm trying to be funny? Just you wait. I'll prove it to you."

"Leave me alone, I'm normal. On the first of the month I made myself a card index—you know, those cards with column headings. I like keeping a record of everything: How I feel, work, amusements, dreams, and even the size of my turds. I give marks for them all, like in school. One must live with one's feet on the ground, not all up in the clouds."

I wanted to kick him, and then I seemed to lose interest in everything, and felt strangely awkward. At the same time, too, I began to doubt whether it was true that the Investigator Dog came to see me. It all appeared to be idiotic and absurd.

"All right, let's go," I said, feeling utterly depressed. "We'll let down your old man's tires."

I cannot explain it, but the more those tires hissed and sagged, the better and more normal I felt.

When I got home I began to read, but it was difficult to read while Cecilia was talking to my parents. It was actually a monologue rather than a conversation, and Cecilia's voice filled the whole place. My father listened with one eye on the television screen, which was showing some dull spinning operation.

I looked through the window at our little street. Snow was falling, covering the pavements, part of the road, and even the branches of trees that were already beginning to show green. My acacia, too, was covered with snow. And there was something uncanny about this snow, because of the live and vigorous green that showed through it. I was sure that the look of it made many

[95]

people think of the comet that was rushing toward us, and of the inevitable encounter.

My parents were listening to Cecilia in rather depressed silence, because it is not pleasant to hear that someone else is prospering. And today Cecilia had come, very excited, with sparkling eyes and noisier than usual, because she had received an invitation from an American university and was going to be in America for a long time, perhaps forever. My father and mother admired her very much and made a pretense of friendly envy, but I think that the envy they felt was the usual kind. Cecilia was trying to brush aside their admiration, and calling them stupid. She was worried about her Oxford accent, for she had studied at the most famous English university and now she feared that her pronunciation might get spoiled by life in America. She was friendly with a real, and very charming, English lord. I sometimes think that this lord might have been a relation of Sebastian's, although I have never mentioned it, because Cecilia would have been furious.

A neighbor of our was walking along the snow-covered street, or rather he was not walking so much as pushing himself along with convulsive movements on metal crutches. He seldom went out, and when he did it was mostly in summer, and an ambulance often came to his place. He lived alone and was quite old and afflicted with some dreadful paralysis, or perhaps shell shock from the war. He was jerking his whole body along, his stiff legs thrown out in all directions. It was as if a mournful procession of pain, despair, and human misery was moving along the street.

"Don't forget us, Cecilia," said my father, sounding slightly insincere, "let's have news, here in our out-of-the-way corner, of your life in the fashionable world."

"You are an idiot," said Cecilia, straightening her already very straight shoulders. "It hasn't yet been decided whether I shall go at all. I don't know what terms they will offer, or how I shall manage among all those Yanks. It isn't as simple as that. Remember that I am not in my first youth."

"Oh, Cecilia!" said my mother, "you don't need to talk about age. Just look at yourself in the mirror."

"Ah, yes," sighed my father, "it will not be long before you forget us altogether and stop answering our letters. That's life."

"Don't be a fool!" said Cecilia. "You don't know me at all. Neither of you know me."

"Perhaps you will marry a millionaire," said my mother, giving rein to her imagination, "and live in a big house on the Pacific coast, among palm trees and enormous cactus bushes."

"Marry?" said Cecilia. "Never! Intelligent people are doomed to solitude."

"Have pity on us poor souls, who will have to go on with our provincial lives." My father smiled with pretended humility. "But when you get out in the wide world you will change your mind."

"I never forget my friends. I can promise you quite seriously that if I go I'll invite Peter for the holidays. Do you hear, Peter? What are you dawdling about at over there by the window? Would you like to stay with me in America?"

"Who wouldn't like to?" said my mother softly.

"Be quiet. I am asking him. Are you deaf, Peter?"

"I am listening," I said.

"Would you like to spend your holidays with me?"

I could not really tell at that moment whether I would like to go to California or not. Our crippled neighbor was making his way, skidding and slipping, toward our gate, through the big puddle of slush.

Cecilia became red in the face and looked at me like an angry bird, so I said that I would, trying to manage the hoarseness in my throat.

"I see that you are not very keen."

"I would very much like to go to California," I said. I could distinctly hear my parents' sigh of relief.

"If the comet does not hit us," added my father under his breath.

Cecilia left then, because she wanted to get some forms that urgently needed to be completed. She was still shouting something as she went downstairs, and it must have been when she reached the entrance door that we heard her pitching into the caretaker for not sweeping up the snow. She finally appeared in

[97]

the street, waving frantically at every passing car because she wanted a taxi, and alarming the drivers into braking sharply and skidding all over the place.

We all remained silent. The television went chattering on about some abstruse modern agricultural problem.

"So there you are," said my father at last, in a flat voice. He and my mother had dropped their artificial gaiety. "Everyone gets the thing he wants, in the end."

He was silent for a long time, while my mother cleared the cups and saucers from the table.

"I'm losing the will to live," he said at last, angrily. "It's easy for her to go, she's not married and has no children. She can afford to take risks . . . . You know, I feel as if I had been pushed out of life. You can't imagine what it's like."

"Don't think like that," said my mother. "Why should you worry unnecessarily? Everything comes to an end, and so will this spell of bad luck."

"I am already afraid of meeting people. Everybody has interests and plans and prospects, and what have I got?"

"You'll find a job, you'll see—maybe even a better one."

"No, something has gone wrong with my life. You mustn't forget that we are no longer in our prime. You know, there is always the thought in my mind that everything good in our life is over, and that all that we have to look forward to is the downhill road."

"It's because you just sit here moaning. Go out and meet people. It will refresh your spirits and change your mood."

There was a heavy silence again, and then my father said: "When I think of the years ahead of me, I am afraid."

"Oh, these gloomy moods of yours!" sighed my mother.

My father flew into a rage. "Don't you understand anything? What have I got out of all this? Maybe I didn't do my best, but didn't I go short of sleep and sometimes even of food? And what is the result?"

"There are others who work even harder. And many who are lonely and unhappy. And they manage somehow."

"A fine lot of comfort that is!" snorted my father.

"Peter," said my mother, "go to Sophie's room and look out to see what's going on in the yard. There may be some children there. You must get some fresh air."

I still did not know what to do with my sixty zlotys. It wasn't at all easy to decide. And then I had to keep watch on the telephone, because the people at the film studio might ring me after all. My father was right about bad luck. As Cecilia would say—intelligent people should expect to have bad luck. I thought that I would keep the money for the time being. It looked as though my father was not expecting the comet, which was strang_, because it would have been a way out for him.

I pulled Miss Sophie's diary from under the mattress in her room without any particular sense of curiosity. It was not worthwhile going out into the courtyard. Buffalo's father was wringing his hands over his car, which was jacked up in the snow. Gagatek was kicking his football against the wall for practice, as usual. A few brats were making a snowman, which melted as fast as they made it. So I opened the diary at the last entry, on a page adorned with drawings of flowers:

"I went to the theater with Ziuta [something here had been carefully crossed out]. We sat in one of the front rows, because her father works in the municipal offices. Some boys from the 13th Street School, who were in the balcony, kept on throwing sweet wrappings down on us. Ziuta must have encouraged them with her idiotic giggle. She giggles all the time. She even giggled when she received her certificate at the end of the summer term, in spite of the fact that she would not be moving up into the next form.

"Then there came the most important moment in my life—the turning point of my existence. Who would have believed it possible? After all, I had not been keen on going to the theater, which is a bore compared with the cinema or television. The purple light that shone on the curtain faded, just as my life, up to that moment, had been fading . . . . And then I saw Him on the stage!

"I had never seen Him before, but I felt a sudden pain in my heart and even wanted to cry out, although I pressed Ziuta's hand instead. She was still giggling and would not stop.

"He began to speak in a resonant, manly voice, throwing back His head with its long, golden hair. There was so much strength and firmness in His whole appearance. The ill-natured actress who played opposite Him was pretending not to listen to Him. Now that I know all about Him I am not surprised, because Grazyna says that she is His wife in real life, and an awful shrew. All the people who work at the theater hate her. And Grazyna does not repeat gossip. It was her uncle, who makes the props at the theater, who said so. So He (not Grazyna's uncle) is apparently very unhappy.

"I have already bought the record He has made of the works of various poets. When I feel blue, I play it and listen to that vibrant voice, which reflects a whole range of emotions. And then I feel that He is speaking to me alone and I want to comfort Him and stroke His hair, which is slightly wavy and unruly like a boy's. I find myself talking aloud, and last night I woke up and began to cry for no reason at all. . . . "

The door opened. I managed to put the diary back into place just in time. Miss Sophie stood in the doorway, in her very short dress. Her face, under her mass of hair, was deathly pale.

"You rat!" she shouted. "You're looking at my things!"

Before I had time to explain that I had no ill intentions and that I sympathized with her and understood the weakness of human nature, she kicked me so hard that I fell out into the passage.

When she had banged the door shut—it was already damaged from her attacks of fury—I got up from the floor, and as I did so the thought crossed my mind that Miss Sophie was no longer expecting the comet.

The streetlights came on. Nearly all the snow had melted. The crippled old man was again making his way along the street in awful jerks. Perhaps he was going to the chemist for medicine, or maybe to friends for help.

You do not know what my father is really like. You probably think that he sits all the time in front of the television set, complaining about life and admonishing his children, and that he is an ordinary, overworked, tired, and rather dull father.

In fact, my father is tall, perhaps about half a head taller than most other people, and that is why one can so easily spot him in the street. I can always tell by his eyes when he is joking, however seriously he may be speaking. He has a funny mouth that seems to move about all over his face, not at all ugly, but rather gay and amusing. When his mouth looks one-sided my mother kisses him and laughs, because it is a sign of anger. But he is never really angry. Everyone admires his looks and says that he is handsome—even Cecilia, who usually finds everyone and everything repulsive.

My father is good at a lot of things. Before the war he almost finished at the Conservatory and he was Polish junior swimming champion. Perhaps he was not exactly a champion, but his name was mentioned in the sporting press. Later, thanks to the war, which no one can forget, everything became mixed up and Father got himself stuck with computers, which I believe he does not like.

I say "Father" on purpose, and not "Dad" or "Daddy" or "Papa," in order to avoid sounding sissy. My father feels the same way. He never kisses me or calls me pet names, and he usually pretends not to notice me.

But all the same, I remember everything very well—how he carried me on his back, and how at night he rubbed some violet-colored ointment inside my mouth with his finger, because I had caught some bug, and how he cried a little when it turned out that I would be all right, and that I wasn't badly hurt after being knocked down by a car. It is surprising how well I remember everything. You may disbelieve me if you like, but I even remember the moment when I came into the world—when I was born. And more than that, I have an impression that I existed before I was born and have retained some vague memories of that time. But this may be in some way due to Sebastian's influence.

My father is very nervous—even when he is watching television he fidgets in his chair as if something is biting him, and he walks so quickly that even my mother cannot keep up with him. He is always reading newspapers, watching football matches, and going out to meet somebody. But I know that he is so active because there is something that drives him through life, some thought or premonition that he keeps to himself, or a fear that seized him somewhere in the past.

I like to make drawings of my father. I show him in all sorts of roles—as a medieval knight, pirate, Red Indian, and even as an astronaut. My mother pins up my drawings on the wall, but my father does not recognize himself, although my mother may know who it is.

An icy wind began to buffet the balcony, snatching at clotheslines and flowerpots and old toys that had been left out. It froze the rivulets of rain on the window and their shadows moved about on the wall like spiders. The thought of the cripple was constantly in my mind, and a kind of premonition of long suffering kept on waking me up from a light sleep.

At last I fell asleep and dreamed that Retep stood by my side on a sand dune covered with silvery grass as sharp as a razor, and the two girls, Eva and the one in jeans, were wading together farther and farther into the sea. At last their hands separated as huge breakers reared up, as high as a wall. Retep and I rushed to rescue them, and then everything changed—how, and at what point, I do not remember. Perhaps in the moment of change I even dreamed of other trivial, fragmentary, and commonplace things.

We were now in a huge foreign city, with neon lights ablaze and headlights of cars flashing along a wide avenue. The flood of light streaming toward and away from us was shaping itself into a sort of endless red and white carpet, which we watched from above, as though from a high terrace or tower.

"We must make peace, once and for all," Retep was saying. "After all you are my only brother." I was about to tell him that I was quite sure that I had no brother, and he must have sensed what I was going to say, because he laid an arm on my shoulder. "You know, I searched for you all over the world, but you had gone into hiding."

"I didn't hide at all. It was Miss Sophie who would not let me go out. She is in love with the actor who has a shrewish wife."

"That will all end now, and we shall be together always."

"What about Eva, the little girl in white?"

"Oh, she never really existed. That idiotic Great Dane invented everything. Great Danes are the stupidest of all breeds of dogs."

"You have found me too late," I said, "I am going to die. We shall never see each other again."

Retep was laughing. There was no trace of anger or hostility on his face. "I will always be where you are," he said.

It was only then that what I had thought was the roar of the sea became the voices of the inhabitants of the huge city, who were shouting something and chanting a lament. I turned my eyes in the direction in which they were all looking and saw the whole western horizon glowing with light like an aurora borealis, which was flickering weirdly and moving toward us.

"It is the asteroid—it is the comet that we have been waiting for," I said. And I think that was the end of the dream.

It was the gray light before dawn. The whole block was still asleep, except for our neighbors in the flat above, who were rampaging about, shifting furniture, sawing wood, and banging the walls. It took me some time to shake off the dream, and then I thought about my past life, and it was not until I heard the rattle of milk bottles that I felt normal again.

I certainly do not believe in dreams. Of course I believe that they occur, for how can one not believe in the occurrence of something that one experiences almost every night? What I do not believe is that they have meaning, or that there is some kind of mystery about them. I have read several long books about dreams, but I must say—between ourselves—that there is something odd somewhere. Where do I get to in my dreams?—for I quite palpably and intensely get somewhere. From what place does Retep come to me, and by what road does he return? For, after all, I can recognize every flicker in his face or twinkle in his eye, every smile—all peculiar to him, and always the same, and yet I never see him in the flesh.

Somebody knocked at the door and my heart began to beat rapidly, for I knew at once that some new episode of my strange adventure was afoot. I put on some clothes without paying attention to what I was doing, and before any member of the family could awaken I went to the door.

Sebastian stood there, trembling intensely, either from cold or from emotion.

"Have you got that ticket, my friend?"

"Yes, I have. But why?"

"Let me have it at once. I didn't sleep a wink all night."

I took the piece of yellowed card from my pocket and he snatched it from my hand, fidgeting with it until he held it where the dim light from the window fell on it.

"That's it!" he said in a stifled voice. "We must go there at once."

"But there's nothing on the ticket. Even the date has got rubbed off. Have you been taking valerian drops again?"

He looked at me penetratingly. It was only then that I noticed the white or rather gray hairs around his black muzzle. Sebastian was no longer in his prime.

"Let us waste no time. Every minute is precious. But if you don't want to come . . ."

"Do you know, Sebastian, what I think?"

"What do you think?" he asked, shifting his weight from one pair of feet to the other.

"That all this is some kind of trickery. There is in reality no green valley or honey-colored house, and no Retep or little Eva."

"But you have been there yourself!"

"Perhaps I only seemed to. Perhaps it was some kind of autosuggestion or hypnosis. Maybe I am just a delicate, precocious boy, with a vivid imagination."

"Look, my friend, I know you well. I let you specially into the secret because you are the only reasonable boy among a crowd of children. I am no longer young and it is not a hobby of mine to tell fairy tales."

"But when I think about it all, there seems to be something wrong. After all, I am a member of the Theoretical Physics Society."

"Haven't I already explained to you what it is all about? Others will find it out in time. But, after all, I am not trying to persuade you! You are free to please yourself."

He seemed not at all proud or self-assured. He looked at me with humble dog's eyes, and he seemed to be normal. So I said, hesitatingly:

"OK, Sebastian, let's go."

"Thank you," he answered briefly, with visible relief.

"But where shall we hide ourselves for the takeoff?"

"Why should we hide? It's a waste of time. What's wrong with this place?"

He fixed his eyes upon mine. But I was rather annoyed with him and there was probably some sort of resistance in me,

[105]

because for a long time I could hear the wind, the squeaking of a door, the roar of the first cars in the early morning traffic, and a baby's cry, muffled by the wall.

I felt grass wet with dew under my feet. Somebody was moving away toward the lawn and I thought it was Sebastian, but this person was clearing his throat a great deal and muttering or humming to himself in a singsong voice. It could only be old Konstanty who awaited the return of Vincent, his arrogant grandson.

"Quick, follow me!" growled Sebastian nervously, in a voice so hollow that it sounded as if it came from the bottom of a well. He set off rapidly, following a path that he seemed to know. I ran behind him, lashed by twigs that shook cold droplets over me. We soon stopped by a ledge. I thought that Sebastian wanted to get his breath back, but he was looking around keenly and listening, with his tongue lolling almost to the ground. My eyes must have become used to the darkness, because I recognized that there was still some light—not much, but enough to distinguish the outlines of single trees and shrubs and even large stones.

Somewhere nearby there were sounds of laughter and shouting and a sound like dipped oars. Beneath the ledge was a steep precipice, its walls full of dark holes that were swallows' nests. Far below something flickered and I saw monsters emerging and then disappearing in the water. A white leg or arm or even a backside would appear from time to time. And I knew at once, as if I had seen them before, that these were boys who had brought horses to swim in the river. Their shouting and laughter were so exaggerated because some girls were bathing, not far away, around the river bend. I could even make out their silhouettes because some of them still modestly retained their white underclothes.

Sebastian suddenly began to bark dismally, in a penetrating

bass voice like an ordinary watchdog, and it came to me that he was not my Investigator Dog with perfect manners but an unknown wild creature.

"Sebastian," I said softly, filled with apprehension.

He stopped barking and asked impatiently: "What do you want?"

"Nothing. This is a rather strange place."

"I am here," said somebody in a small voice. It was Eva. She stood behind us in her white dress, holding her white shoes in her hand and breathing as though she had been running hard.

"At last you are here. Thank goodness!" said Sebastian, his whole body trembling. "Are you ready?"

"I am not sure," she said hesitatingly. "It may be an unwise thing for me to do."

"Run away—run away, while there is still time," growled Sebastian. Then he added gently: "Have you not suffered enough? How long can one endure captivity?"

"Psst! Be careful!" I hissed, for I could hear strange noises.

"They are leading the horses out of the river," said Sebastian, moving his ears as he listened. We soon heard the rhythmic noise of horses' hooves, like the sound made by the rocking of a big wooden cradle.

"Off we go, then," said Sebastian, "because the nights are short now. You can walk behind and take care of the lady."

"But where are we going?" whispered Eva. "I am afraid of the darkness. I am altogether afraid."

"Toward the town. When we get there we'll manage somehow."

We set off down the rounded slope with Sebastian stopping now and again to wait for us when we got entangled in the bushes or weeds.

"Can he be trusted?" Eva asked me.

"Who?"

"The dog. His appearance is not reassuring."

"He was a lord in his previous incarnation and a great traveler. He has very good manners. Don't you know him?"

"There are so many different animals about here."

[107]

"He has known you for a long time. It was he who arranged this escape."

She looked more attentively at Sebastian's great form moving ahead of us. He walked carefully and pulled the wet branches aside with his teeth to prevent them from catching Eva.

"If only Papa could be with us," she sighed. "Papa is an astronomer. I was born in the South Sea Islands. My mother was a native of the islands. You must have noticed my eyes, they are typical of those parts. Mama died when I was still a baby, because the climate did not suit her. So now we are alone in the world. . . . But this does not interest you."

Something came over me, and almost without knowing what I was saying, I asked: "What is the global mass of your sun?"

"Why *our* sun? After all, it shines for you too."

"I'm sorry, I asked without thinking."

"I don't know the answer. Papa would know. But at this very moment he is somewhere very far away—very near the North Pole—observing the sun's corona."

We almost collided with Sebastian, who was standing with outstretched neck beneath the remains of a rotted fence.

"Be careful," he said under his breath.

There were low-branching trees ahead of us that looked as though they were wearing spats. But it was only a big old orchard, with trees that had had their trunks washed with lime against pests. A regular knocking noise came from the dark depths.

"They are night watchmen hitting the trees with sticks to warn off thieves," said Sebastian, still farther under his breath.

Eva felt for my hand. Her thin fingers trembled against my palm. "How I hate this awful valley!" she said.

"Why? It is a beautiful place. I used to dream of this valley."

"What is your name?"

"Peter."

She was silent for a while and Sebastian watched us with some disquiet.

"That's odd," she said.

"Why odd?"

"Because Peter is Retep spelled the other way around."

"Never mind that," said Sebastian. "Don't waste time talking. Get a move on." He began to sniff very carefully at the stalks of what may have been nettles. "A stranger is following us," he said, more to himself than to us. Then he dropped close to the ground and began to crawl slowly into the depths of the orchard.

Eva gripped my hand more tightly. We moved silently behind Sebastian, holding our breath, past the watchmen's shelter, and emerged from the orchard onto an unplowed ridge forming a path through a tall growth of what may have been beans or peas. Mosquitoes whined and fretted over our heads like insomniacs.

"At last!" said Sebastian hoarsely. "Nobody can see us here. You needn't hold hands."

"But it makes me feel safer," said Eva.

Sebastian reflected, staring sourly at the rough, ridged path. "It hinders our movements," he said.

"I know best what hinders my movements," said Eva.

Sebastian tried to scratch behind his ear (it was a sign of embarrassment with him), but his awkward hind leg only scraped the ground. Then he moved onward without a word.

"I always thought about you," Eva whispered, as we followed Sebastian.

I found it difficult to breathe. "I thought too," I said.

"Is that true?" She pressed my hand. "Oh, how glad I am!"

Again Sebastian barred our way. "For heaven's sake, didn't I ask you not to talk?" he said with animosity.

"Nobody's giving *me* orders," I said.

"I am sorry I said something wrong, but our lives depend on our being careful."

"I don't care about my life."

Sebastian breathed a ponderous sigh, but as he moved forward again he struck me a painful blow with his haunch. He seemed not to notice that something flopped heavily to the ground in the midst of the tall-growing crop or to hear the sounds of muffled swearing.

We went on for some time in silence, with falling stars flaring and dying over our heads.

"I was very ill for a long time," Eva whispered suddenly. I

[109]

could see the two faint gleams that were her eyes. "They say that that is why they watch over me! I couldn't say which of them is the worse."

"Don't think about it. The important thing is to reach the town safely."

"You will take me with you? I can trust you both?" Again she pressed my hand.

"Yes, you can trust both of us."

"Where do you live?"

I was not quite sure how I should answer. Some beetles began to fly around, bumping into us and falling to the ground, buzzing helplessly.

"I live in Warsaw," I said. "Have you heard of it?"

"Ah, in Warsaw!" said Eva delightedly. "That's marvelous!" I was not at all sure that she had ever heard of such a place.

"Would you like a piece of apple?"

"Of apple?"

"Yes, I picked it in the orchard."

Sebastian had stopped and was waiting for us. He did not grumble this time, but only lifted his paw as a warning signal. We stopped obediently. Something screeched nearby like a rusty hinge and there was a loud snorting noise.

"Horses and carts on their way to town," said Sebastian. "Probably peasants with corn, or maybe merchants."

"Let us keep to the road, then," I said cautiously, "we shall reach the town sooner."

"Oh, no!" protested Eva. "Retep is bound to look for us on the road."

"I have a feeling that we are being watched," I said.

Sebastian stood silent, pricking his ears. A voice from the road growled "Blast you!" in nasal tones that somehow sounded familiar to me. But Sebastian seemed not to notice it and slowly moved into the cover of the tall-standing crop.

"Do you feel tired? Wouldn't it be better to rest a while?" he asked, without turning his head.

"Oh, no," said Eva, "I am very tough. I can do things that no one else can do, such as holding my breath for fifteen minutes. Look, you can see for yourself."

She placed my hand on her mouth—it must have looked rather as though I was leading a blind person. I could feel with my fingers the warmth of her face, and the warmth slowly spread over my hand. I had the impression that her heartbeat was getting faster and faster. Sebastian began to look around nervously and stumbled on a stone.

I moved my hand a little from her mouth, moist and sweating with her warmth. "I think we must be careful now," I said. We entered a tall forest, dismal with the soughing of wind in the treetops and the scent of pine resin and wet vegetation. Sebastian sniffed the strong odor several times and then kept his muzzle to the ground.

"On the whole," said Eva suddenly, "I am not like anybody else. Do you know, I often see my mother. We talk a lot and she caresses me and plaits my hair. Once she plaited it so tightly that no one could undo it."

An owl called mournfully, somewhere above us. Sebastian slowed down a little.

"But your mother has been dead a long time."

"That is true," said Eva, but her answer sounded like a question.

I thought to myself that there were duties in other directions that I must think about. I had slackened off in my schoolwork, and then they could be ringing up from the studio about the *Spaceflight to Andromeda* film. But the warmth of Eva's hand dissolved my feelings of anxiety.

We made our way through some undergrowth, wet, prickly, and full of cobwebs and spiders that struck all over my face and hair. Something started up from under our feet and fled into the depths of the forest, which rustled like a huge river. "Sebastian, do you know where we are?" I asked in a low voice. He looked up, but the stars could no longer be seen, and without a word he pressed on.

We saw a light, or rather a vague, wavering glow that continually disappeared and reappeared. This light gradually grew stronger each time that it came into view, and sparks flew up, but only once, rather high above the ground, as if a devil had brushed his tail against a branch. Sebastian sniffed with great concentration. We, too, caught the sharp smell of turpentine. At last we crouched behind a big pile of uprooted treestumps that looked like a mass of petrified octopuses. Through the twisted roots we could see a squat building and in front of it, a dozen paces from us, men sitting around a fire, above which hung a pot suspended on a stick.

One of the men, half-reclining against a pile of brushwood, was humming a tune, another was breaking up the brands in the fire with a stick.

"What do you see up there?" asked the man who was stirring the logs.

"I can't see anything. I am only wondering what could be there in the other place."

"They say that the angels are there, and the saints and the souls of the saved."

"Where's hell then?"

"Why worry about it? Hell must be there as well, perhaps in the top layer of the sky, or maybe in the lowest."

The man who leaned against the brushwood was silent for a while, and then he said: "Tonight there were stars falling all the time, one after the other. Perhaps the end of the world is near?"

"They're always falling at this time of year."

"But there must come a time when there aren't any more left."

"You'd better go and look at the fires."

"I don't feel like it. The forest feels peculiar tonight. The animals are hiding and the night birds are silent, as if there was some dumb soul wandering about seeking to be saved. Aren't you afraid of the end of the world?"

The man who was making up the fire did not reply, but struck the red-hot wood so hard that huge sparks flew up and died.

"Well, let us waste no more time," said Sebastian rising.

We went on through the dense, hostile forest. I imagined all the time that I could hear twigs breaking under some stranger's feet. We came to a jungle of ferns, so tall that they closed in over our heads.

"You know," said Eva, trying again to take my hand, "this year I found the crock of gold."

"Nobody has ever found the crock of gold."

"No, I have. But they took it from me. His mother took it."

I rather liked her, but I was also apprehensive. I could see neither her face nor her mouth nor her forehead, but only the occasional gleam of her eyes when she turned to look at me. I tried to visualize her appearance as I had seen her before. I was tormented by my effort to remember her smile and her look of fear, but I could only hear her slightly husky but very penetrating voice.

The forest became increasingly dense. We moved very slowly, avoiding the big tree stumps, so old and cracked that not even moss would grow on them. The ground was getting boggy and squelched horribly under our feet. Sebastian slowed his pace and sniffed irresolutely, turning his great head this way and that.

"How much farther is it?" I asked. He muttered something unintelligible and slackened his pace still more.

"Do you know where we are going?" I insisted. The Investigator Dog stopped and dropped his head. "We have lost our way, my friend," he said quietly. "In such a dark night it is impossible to see a thing."

"What will happen then? They are sure to catch us!" Eva almost shouted.

"How can I get my bearings?" murmured Sebastian miserably.

"What about your wonderful nose?" I asked ironically.

"I used to have a good nose, but who can keep his senses fresh, living in a town?"

A large fir cone dropped wet and heavy at our feet.

"I've forgotten it!" cried Eva, turning to rush back in the direction from which we had come.

"What have you forgotten?" asked Sebastian, blocking her path.

"The stone! The miraculous stone from my island, that I had from my mother."

"We would be better off with a compass," said Sebastian.

[113]

"That is exactly what it is. How could I forget it? We have lost our way as a punishment. I have been thinking all the time that it was anxiety that so tormented me—but it was the stone! We must go back at once!"

There was a sound barely perceptible like the soft note of a flute or the limpid noise of water poured from one bottle into another.

"What shall we gain from going back?" sighed Sebastian. "We have already wasted so much time."

"I cannot leave the stone behind. It is my most precious possession."

"It's useless to talk like that," said Sebastian, still more gloomily. "I am responsible for you."

"Try to persuade him," said Eva, wringing my hand violently.

"Sebastian," I whispered, "do you hear that bubbling sound?"

"I do. Happily my hearing is still good."

"It is a river flowing somewhere not far away."

"Maybe it is."

"If we follow it upstream, we shall come to the house and we can start out again from there."

"Yes, yes!" cried Eva, sinking her nails into my palm. "That is the best thing to do. We are saved!"

"Don't halloo till you are out of the wood!"

"Shall we go back, then?" I said.

"As you wish," said Sebastian, and he set off halfheartedly in the direction of the murmur that came from beyond a thick wall of alder trees.

The way back seemed interminable, of course. We battled through thickets of alders that whipped our faces with their wet, springy twigs. Eva whimpered all the time—although that is not the right word. Every now and again a spasm of despair seized her, because she had left the stone behind and because our mishaps were all a punishment for her forgetfulness.

In the end the vegetation grew so thick that it became impossible to go any farther and we had to slither down the cold bank to the river. We could not see the water but it was tepid, like cooled tea—we could only feel it on our legs and sometimes our thighs because it tickled our goose-pimpled skin.

"What about trying to find our bearings by the stars?" I asked once.

"Where will you find any stars?"

I looked at the sky, seen through the black tunnel of trees. There were no stars. Maybe they had all set, or night clouds may have blown up and covered them.

Eva was wading ahead of me, with her dress gathered up in one hand. Sebastian plodded in front like an old soldier, but sometimes he rushed forward, beating the water with his paws in a very odd sort of way. At first I thought that the former lord and seasoned traveler had gone slightly mad. Later I learned that, feeling fish swimming under him, he was simply making instinctive efforts to catch them. Sebastian had the mind of a rational human being, but he could not resist his canine instincts. This clash of instincts must have been very humiliating for him and he could not be blamed for it.

The banks of the river eventually started to rise sharply and the river flowed in a ravine, one side of which was extremely steep. Sebastian looked around carefully to climb the side with a clay bank, scratching desperately with his hind feet to get a hold. I could see it embarrassed him that Eva should see him scrabbling like this, but there was nothing else he could do.

We saw a field, or rather the outline of a field, ahead of us. There were horses hobbled nearby, snorting and stamping their hooves on the peaty ground. The boys who were guarding them were singing sleepily and the tiny glow of their cigarettes flickered in the darkness.

We moved on to still higher ground, passing several trees.

"There is somebody following us," I said. "He has been following us all the time."

"You are imagining things," said Sebastian, panting heavily.

"I heard someone wading in the river."

"That was the water running over loose stones on the riverbed."

We came to the beginning of the fence and climbed over at the familiar place.

"Oh, God," whispered Eva, "I am afraid."

"Perhaps we should give up the idea of getting the stone," I said.

"Never!" she cried—so that I had to put my hand over her mouth—"No! I beg you!" She kissed my little finger in a sort of despair and I felt rather embarrassed.

"Can we get into the house from the back?" I asked.

"Mm," murmured Sebastian, as he moved toward the black mass of the house, unrelieved by a single lighted window. I brushed some of the cobwebs, twigs, and caterpillars from my clothes.

"If only we do not waken Retep," said Eva. "Please give me your hand. I am so scared that I could die."

She clung to my hand, and then I saw a light swinging to and fro among the elder bushes, and slowed down. Sebastian, who was already squatting in the cover of some weeds, ordered us to take cover too.

Huddled together behind a scanty clump of weeds, we watched a lantern bobbing toward us from behind a corner of the house. It was one of those lanterns, blackened with smoke, that was used in stables in the old days. A pair of very white feet, illuminated by the lantern, made me think of corpses and I felt rather queasy.

Something flopped down heavily behind us, making the brushwood crackle, and I heard a scuffing noise as if the invisible newcomer were rubbing a stick against the bark of a tree. Before I had time to wonder who could be spying on us, the lantern swung closer to our hiding place and we heard the pleasant, singsong voice of old Konstanty:

"What are you doing, eh?—skulking about at night."

Silently we shrank back deeper into our cover.

"Don't try to hide, you rascals. I saw you from the shed."

"It wasn't us," said Eva in a silly, squeaking voice.

"Heaven help us," said Konstanty, "she is romping and

playing with God knows who—probably just common rogues."

"You had better mind what you are saying," said Sebastian angrily, lifting himself up from the ground. "We were here on holiday."

"That's right," I added. "We wanted to say good-bye because we are leaving now, for good."

"But it isn't right to be here at night. It is very wrong. The young lady is very young."

"Konstanty, you won't tell anybody, not a single soul, will you?" Eva pleaded, choking. "You won't betray us, Konstanty? They only saw me home from a walk."

The old man turned down the wick in his lantern. In its yellow light he looked more than anything like a kind old grandad about to tell a fairy tale.

"But they promised to find Vincent and bring me a letter from him," he said.

"We have found him," I lied—although I hate lying—"we know now who he is."

"That's interesting news. Is he doing well?"

"He is employed as a manager by my master, who is also a very important manager," added Sebastian, to back me up.

"What a crafty rascal he is!" said Konstanty with emotion.

"He is doing very well. Sometimes he even still maltreats people."

"I shouldn't think he maltreats them out of wickedness or ill will," said Konstanty uncertainly. "If he torments them it must be out of kindness of heart. He wishes everyone well, and so sometimes he will force them to be good even if it is against their will. So you say that he is an important manager?"

"Very important indeed. As soon as he has settled his most urgent affairs he will be coming home to see you," I said with fervent conviction.

"Well then maybe I won't tell the young master that you are gadding about at night."

"Goodnight, sir. We are leaving for good now. We'll just take the young lady to the door."

"But the dog mustn't bark, on no account, because they are all asleep."

"We'll be as quiet as mice. Goodnight!"

"Goodnight." And he went somewhere in the direction of the farm buildings, perhaps to the brewery, which we had never seen. The lamp swayed rhythmically, shining for brief moments on tussocks of grass, twigs wet with dew, and Konstanty's bare feet.

"It's a waste of time," said Sebastian, for the second time that night. "Do you remember which room we want?"

"Of course. I know the whole house like the palm of my hand. When I was ill I couldn't sleep and I wandered about for nights on end."

We ran as fast as we could around the back of the house to the porch with the broken panes. The sort of beetle, or big fly, that one usually finds on a dunghill was buzzing with transparent wings on the remains of the windowpanes. The rotten floorboards creaked under our feet. Something like a streak of shadow ran over the wet grass from the thicket to the corner of the house. As we stood dismayed, Sebastian signaled us to wait with a movement of his head and went over alone to the broken veranda railing.

It was Fela. She was feverishly tearing at the turf with her paws and whining. Sebastian listened for a while to her mumbled story.

"She advises us not to enter the house," he said.

"She has been following us all the time," I said.

"She is on our side."

"Don't listen to her, I beg, I implore you!" said Eva. "She is a stupid animal. Retep's father took her in out of pity, when the circus threw her out because nobody was any longer afraid of her. She hasn't got a single tooth in her head. She is a complete nonentity."

Eva clasped me convulsively as she spoke. I could see her eyes now—almond eyes that were wide open, giving her a strange unearthly look.

"Sebastian," I said as softly as I could, "seeing that we have already decided. . . ."

"I'm not so sure about it," he said hesitantly.

Nevertheless, I pressed down the big, rusty door handle, which looked like a skeleton bird's wing. The door gave way with a sigh, and we were met by a smell like the warm smell of corn in a granary or the pleasant aroma of a pantry.

"I will lead the way," Eva whispered. She moved ahead, making a blur of whiteness in the dark, and I followed, unsure of my footing. Sebastian growled at something that sprang up and fled, almost from under our feet. It must have been the cat that liked to lie on the piano.

Eva opened a door and we found ourselves in the room where we had seen her before. The air was still filled with the scents of a hot summer evening, of apples ripening on a windowsill, grapevines, and country warmth.

As Eva ran to the little table by the window there was suddenly a violent sound of banging and scraping at another window—not in Eva's room but somewhere near. I hissed a warning. Sebastian slid on the polished wooden floor on his stiff legs in an effort to bring himself to a standstill, and swore under his breath with embarrassment.

I advised him to lick his paws, and he was doing this when the window opened noisily.

"Who's there?" We recognized Retep's voice.

"It's me, Chippy," a harsh bird's voice answered.

"What do you want?"

"The die is lost!" said Chippy, getting his clichés mixed up. "They've kidnapped the young lady."

Retep did not ask who, or where, and silence reigned for a while. He was probably considering what to do.

"Have you seen them?"

"Yes. They were running toward the town, across the orchards and through the forest by the distillery. They dodged about a lot, to deceive pursuers."

"It's a good thing you were around."

"I'll do anything I can for you. As for them—I'll do for them!" and there was a rickety flapping of ferocious wings.

"Wait. You can show the way," said Retep, and he seemed to go away, probably to his room. We heard the click of a gun being loaded.

"My God!" Eva almost cried aloud. "He will kill us. He won't let us go!" She began to search desperately among the things on the table, until she found the little wooden house like a Swiss chalet, lifted its roof, and took something out—it must have been the stone.

But at that very moment the musical box began to play, sounding all the louder because the house was asleep. The tune was half gay, half sad. I felt for the lid, to shut off the mechanism, but as I fingered the crocheted tablecloth something fell to the floor—books or sheet music, to judge by the sound, and the sad, gay tune continued, so loud that one felt that it filled the whole valley and echoed across the river to the town.

At last my hand found the little carved house in the darkness. I snapped down the roof and the music stopped dead, but the echoes of it still seemed to sound through the big house, only slowly dying away.

Doors started to bang one by one. There was a loud stamping of feet, as if to scare something away. We ran to the door, which gave way at the impact of Sebastian's bulk, so that he slithered out into the hall and stopped just about at the foot of the stairs, as Retep's mother was descending.

She held a paraffin lamp with a white shade, shielding it with her hand against drafts.

"Eva, my dear, are you ill? Are you wandering about again in the night? Go to bed, my child. We will call a doctor in the morning. You will always be our dearest little Eva. Come and give me your hand, child."

Eva retreated to my side and Sebastian scrambled to his feet and stood protectively in front of us.

"Who came?" asked Retep's mother, raising the lamp above her head, which was covered in white curl papers. "Have they brought a telegram from my husband? Is there some news at last?"

"Oh, heavens! Let us get away," said Eva. "I know the way."

We fled through the hall and down a rickety spiral staircase that smelled of mold and earth, stumbling at every step. Sebastian tumbled down last of all and slammed a heavy door, pushed home the rusty bolt, and sneezed heavily.

It was completely dark here. I could not see a glimmer of either Sebastian or Eva. I heard only Sebastian's tired panting. A repeated scraping noise quite close to me seemed to conjure into life a small red insect glowing in a pinkish mist that, as it grew brighter, showed up Eva's white hand. Eva was squeezing something, and, when the light grew stronger still, we could see Sebastian's eyes staring in surprise.

"We are safe," said Eva. "I would like something to eat— something sweet and sour."

But we continued to stare at her hand that held the source of the faint light. "It is a torch with a dynamo," she said, "you have to keep on pressing the lever to make it shine. It is a new invention. Papa brought it home for me from his last trip. Would you like to see it?"

"I have seen them before," I said, "we have one like it among our old junk at home. Somebody gave it to my father before the war. . . . Where are we now?"

"In the old cellar. I will show you the way out. I used to play at soldiers here. I only like boys' games. Haven't you got any food?"

I patted my pockets. "No, I haven't."

"Pity, but I'll survive until we get into town."

"The town is quite a distance away," said Sebastian gloomily.

"But we are safe, at last. I have my miraculous stone and I had time to pick up this torch at the last moment. It's a good sign, isn't it?"

We were silent, looking around at the rough walls sparkling with crystals that looked like silver dust.

"Well, you must admit that I am brave," said Eva.

"You are brave," I said, and she cuddled up to me as if she had seen a lot of westerns with heroes and heroines cuddling up to each other while emotional music gets more and more intense in the background.

"Do you love me?" she whispered.

Sebastian cleared his throat and looked at me with pained eyes.

"Yes, we do," I answered.

"Well, let us go. We could treat ourselves to ice cream when we get to town, couldn't we?"

"Yes, we could."

"I love you too—very much—enormously," she said.

She worked her dynamo furiously and we saw a passage to the next chamber, where squat barrels were ranged with their lids weighted with big stones, and earthenware crocks covered with dust and cobwebs. Eva lifted the edge of the cover on one of the barrels. "Ah, pickled cucumbers!" she said, and from among the stalks of dill herb she pulled out a big cucumber and began to bite at it with relish, squirting the juice over her nose as she bit.

"Let's get on. There is no need to waste time," said Sebastian, shaking spatterings of juice off his back. "He knows that we are in the cellar."

"He can't do anything to us now," said Eva, savoring her cucumber, "we shall come out from here a long way outside the park."

There were wooden boxes in the next room, tripods, odd-looking skis rounded at each end, coils of rope with snap hooks, tropical helmets full of holes and backened with age, bales of canvas, and square glass plates scattered over the floor. I picked up one of the plates and saw that it was a negative of a tropical landscape, with white palm trees against a black sky and white animals grazing on black grass. Other plates had white mountains with black peaks and gray figures of climbers hanging on to white ropes.

Eva worked her torch dynamo while I looked at these souvenirs of long-ago travels, with their powerful atmosphere of nostalgia.

"What constellations of stars do you know?" I asked Eva.

"I don't remember. I like looking at stars without knowing their names."

"What about the moon? Do you like moonlight?" I asked, with an odd feeling of anxiety.

"No," she said emphatically, "I loathe the moon."

"How long a cycle does your moon have?"

"What do you mean?"

"How many days are there between the moon's waxing and waning?" I asked, with a kind of nagging hope.

"How many days? I don't know. A month, I should think."

"You don't know? You, an astronomer's daughter?"

"Oh, you see I am going to be a ballet dancer. I am mad about dancing, like my mother."

Sebastian quietly stuck his head between us. "What do you want to know, friend?" he asked. "Why do you ask so many questions?"

"Never mind. It's OK. It's only that I have some feelings of foreboding."

"This is not the time for forebodings."

We went along a passage that began to drop steeply. The smell here was really dungeon-like—a smell of cold and damp and old bricks. We kept on for a very long time, hugging the slippery wall, until our path was crossed by a small stream or some kind of gutter that ran from one side of the passage to the other. The smell of the place became more sour. In the light of the torch I could see a kind of foam or suds on the surface of the water. Eva threw the tail end of her cucumber into it and jumped across. "We shall soon reach the castle cellars," she said.

"What castle?"

"The one that was a hospital during the last war."

"When was the last war?"

"Why do you ask questions all the time? You ought to know yourself."

We passed through a sort of hall with a vaulted roof and derelict ironware on the walls, almost eaten through with rust. Sebastian stopped and waited for me to catch up.

"What is it making that noise?" he asked.

"Where?"

"Behind us. Can you hear?"

I held my breath and listened. There was a rumbling, confused noise, like a distant waterfall.

"It could be rain. After all, we couldn't see the stars because the sky was clouded over."

"Look." He lifted a paw. A few soggy grains stuck to the hair. "Do you understand?" he said.

"You mean it comes from the brewery?"

"I know nothing about that. But this water is not the underground stream."

We pressed on. Sebastian looked back constantly, because the sound of water did not recede at all. A few minutes later he halted again.

"I'll go and find out what it is," he said.

"It isn't worthwhile. We may be near the exit."

But he had already turned and disappeared into the darkness behind us.

"Show me the miraculous stone," I said to Eva.

She raised her hand in a defensive gesture. "I can't."

"Just for a moment. I'll give it back."

"No," she said, and then hesitated. "Oh, all right, I'll show it to you, but you mustn't touch it."

She dropped on one knee on the uneven brick floor and placed the dark stone—which looked like an oblong boat—on a drier spot. It wobbled as if it were standing on a single, pointed leg, rotated for a while, and then came to rest, reflecting at its darker end the darkness of the passage ahead of us.

I could see indistinct, raised marks on its surface. It could have been a primitive sundial carved on a lump of ironstone.

"You know, when I was ill I was still on the island where my mother was born. I was born there too."

"But you said that you were born here!"

"No, you don't understand. I was there really. I can remember everything—the plants, the trees, and the sea. I could tell you everything that happened, day by day and hour by hour. But nobody believes me."

She was silent for a while, frowning, and then she said: "That was where I got the stone."

I wanted to remind her that she got it here from her mother before she died, but just then Sebastian came back with head hanging, licking something from his black lips.

[124]

"The flood—"he said, controlling his voice. "Somebody has let loose an awful lot of water. We must try to get away while there is still time."

"Oh, it must come from the brewery," said Eva indifferently. "Nothing will happen to us. We do not have far to go now."

We quickened our pace instinctively nevertheless, and passed through several vaults and some winding passages, and then we had to stop.

"Just a minute," said Eva, "I can't see the exit."

We stared blankly at the trailing springs and skeletons of old bunks.

"Why can't you find the exit?"

"Because I can't see it. But there used to be one here."

"Where?"

"It must have been in the left-hand wall."

Sebastian crawled under the beds and carefully sniffed along the wall.

"You must have made a mistake. We shall have to go back."

But when we retraced our steps we could find no alternative passages. The noise of the water grew louder.

"I could swear that the exit is in the wall where the beds are," said Eva, her voice still cheerful.

"But I have checked," said Sebastian.

"Then perhaps it is in the right-hand wall. I am sure that there is one."

We went back again as fast as we could, the more so because a small pool had formed at our feet. We rushed into the vault with the beds, and Sebastian began to sniff along the other walls. He must have been losing his composure a little, because he knocked the piles of old beds about, and one of them almost fell on his back. Eva caught my hand in hers and I felt the perspiration on it as her fingers worked between mine, as if trying to find something.

"There is no exit here," said Sebastian hoarsely, and I could feel that he was losing his nerve. He inspected the floor and tried to move some projections on the wall, at first with his teeth and then with his jaws. When he had gone all around the place feverishly, he came back to us.

[125]

"The water is coming," he said.

Eva ran to the left-hand wall and began to pound it with her fists. "It's not true! There is an exit. I remember it very well. Let us run. Why are you standing there like posts?"

She must have forgotten to keep her torch alive, because the light started to fade as if it were being swallowed up by everlasting darkness. I could just see her dark head shining for a moment, her long neck, her sloping shoulders under the silk dress, and her thin legs in their bedraggled white socks.

"There is no way out," I said heavily, for I had rather stopped caring about anything. There was a remote fear nagging at me that I would get bad marks, that my father would never find any more work, and that I would die a lingering death.

"You're right. Nobody will ever get out of there." The voice was barely audible, as if heard through several walls.

"Did you say that?" I asked Sebastian.

"No, I thought you did."

We remained silent for a time, listening to the sound of approaching water.

"It's him! It's Retep!" said Eva.

Suddenly the beds jangled, there was a dull thud, and we heard a sound like weeping.

"Dearest Retep," Eva called hysterically. "Let us out of here. I don't want to die!"

Retep's voice came muffled through the walls: "It's too late!"

"That's not true! I love you. You are the only one in the world I love."

"You are lying again. I don't believe you, I don't, I don't—I don't. . . ." He repeated the words many times, or perhaps we imagined that he did.

"Retep, I am already soaked and my hands are stiff and my fingers blue with cold. I am shivering as if I were going to have a fit. . . . Retep! I know you love me."

"You were unfaithful to me," cried Retep passionately.

Eva started to pound the wall again with her fists. "No, no!" she said. "It was only that I could not bear being guarded any longer. I wanted some freedom for a while. . . . Retep! Can you hear me? I don't care about freedom now. Let us out, I beg you!"

"It's too late," came the reply indistinctly.

Eva stopped her useless attack upon the wall. All was silent again for a while, except for a nearby lapping of water like the sound of a cold mountain stream. Eva revived the light in her torch, sitting on the edge of a rusty bed with her hair hanging in damp strands over her face. Some centipedes ran across my feet and I stamped to shake them off. Sebastian crawled over to Eva and began gently to lick the hand that held the torch.

"No, don't." She stirred and hid her hand behind her back. Sebastian stood stock-still with his tongue hanging out, swallowing unhappily. Then he began to wrinkle his nose. A loud buzzing came from a big grey bag with dark ridges on it that hung from the ceiling. It was the nest of some wasps that had found a hiding place here.

Quite suddenly I felt the approach of a threatening presence and for a moment I was suffocating with terror. I wanted to throw myself at the walls and crush the old bricks to powder, or smash myself. For that short space of time I did not wish to exist. But I managed to control myself and put my feelings into some sort of order, for I already knew this aggressor and I knew how to fight him—or at least, how to prolong the hopeless struggle.

There are still many questions about him that I am unable to answer. Is there a universal Anthropos-Specter-Beast? Or does each one of us have his own personal Anthropos-Specter-Beast, like having a guardian angel? And if each has his own, do they differ from one another: some better, some worse, some more efficient than others? Are they allocated by choice, or is it merely chance?

Some intelligent human being in the care of a very inept Anthropos-Specter-Beast might ask why, at some time over the centuries and ages, the human race did not unmask this horrible menace. It seems to me that those who believe in God and the Devil have ascribed the activities of the Anthropos-Specter-Beast wholly to divine and satanic powers, to various demons, to souls in purgatory, to the embittered dead, and to ordinary rank-and-file devils. Thus allocated, the problem receded and anxiety was overcome by prayers. Rationalists—among whom I am privileged to count myself—dismissed the problem from the beginning by turning their backs on it, especially as science was able to solve so many previously unaccountable riddles. This must have discouraged genuine thinking intellectuals, or even rather taken the wind out of their sails.

It must also be noted that the Anthropos-Specter-Beast makes his cruelest attacks upon children and old people. This fact, by the way, provides a very good explanation of my theory of the faculties or senses. The faculties of children are not yet fully developed or efficient, and old people's faculties are already impaired, even if they have not deteriorated altogether. And then too, who is there who really takes seriously the worries and woes of children and old people? As for the rest, duped and bound up by their own senses and instincts, they do not want to hear about the threat, and pretend that it does not concern them. They are deadened by their pursuit of ambitions and pleasures, and watch with cruel unconcern their neighbors' struggles with the enemy.

The Anthropos-Specter-Beast lives in the unconscious part of all of us. Many of our desperate aspirations and laborious endeavors are no more than a hopeless attempt to escape from him. I even suspect that humanity's dream of journeying out beyond the solar system is only a desire to attain the uttermost bounds of being. The dreams of legendary paradises are all an attempt to escape. If I were to achieve a position of importance, my first action would be to give all my fortune to founding a prize for the scholar who can explain the nature and operations of the Anthropos-Specter-Beast, for we need to know whether his task is to torment men during their short lives and lure them into the terrifying unknown, or to oppress them forever.

And now, as I overcame my mad fear in the cellar, the memory of a midwinter night came into my mind. I could see the broken glass in the crippled man's window. His neighbor, with hair on end, holds him down on his bed and the cripple shouts in a terrible, non-human voice: "He is here! He has come to fetch me!"

"Who has come? What are you talking about?" asks the neighbor.

"*He* came! The dreaded one."

Every one of the neighbors knows that the crippled man cannot name him, so they cross themselves and bury their heads under the pillow and pray for the man to be silent, and to stop reminding them.

We heard a muffled, rasping noise, as if the brick wall was being brushed with a birch broom. We looked at each other. "That's Fela," said Sebastian, without much interest.

"Does it mean that there's hope for us?"

"My dear friend, how can she help? The wall is not very thick here but, even so, one would need a pickax."

"Maybe it's Konstanty? Or Chippy?"

"Chippy?" said Eva, from under her veil of dark hair. "He is an utter degenerate. His mother, a hideous, clucking hen, is a household favorite, and so her son can do anything he likes. He hardly ever leaves the brewery. And he will always go along with the stronger side."

Fela started to scratch the wall again with her broken old claws, but we did not take any notice of her useless efforts.

It came to me that, far away, everyday life was still going on, that I was always outstripped and left behind, that nobody cared for me—that I had wasted my time, had no aims or prospects, no chances. I was being seized by the fear of loneliness and of being isolated from everything that made up daily life. I know that this may be rather difficult for you to understand and that you cannot see the reason of my fear but, after all, you too get scared in the middle of the night, when you are wakened by the strong autumn wind or a summer thunderstorm. It was this fear that made me feel a desire to return to our town, to my parents, my school, and even to that half-witted Buffalo.

"Sebastian," I said suddenly, "shouldn't we go back *there* and get some help?"

He was silent for a while, and then he said: "I guess, or maybe rather I feel, that we mustn't. That's one plane and this is another."

"But, Sebastian, only for a while—an instant, a second!"

"Don't press me to go—and you, too, you must not think about it."

"Is it because you don't want to leave her alone?"

He took a long time and a great deal of care in shaking off a black beetle. "We mustn't, my friend. It was part of the agreement."

"I have never made any agreement with you!"

"In any case it's too late now."

"Sebastian," I pleaded, trying to look into his eyes. But he lowered his head, lest it should happen that accidentally, and against his will, we should set off on our way back.

But I knew the secret and could try it by myself. So I concentrated and went through all the motions which would enable me to see once more our street, our apartment, the little square with the acacia tree and the monument to the educationalist. I cannot reveal the secret to you, because I must not and also because I learned it by accident, thanks to the Investigator Dog. And if there is no one besides me who can pass into this other world, then no harm can come of it. But if all of you started to travel backward and forward whenever you wished there would be traffic jams and confusion, and perhaps the real end of the world. For who would care about learning the business of living, working, suffering and dying? The world is not yet sufficiently mature to understand my secret, so I hope that you will forgive me for not revealing it to you. I may, of course, change my mind and let you know the whole truth later, in my memoirs.

Sebastian, hiding his eyes from mine, talked insistently, without stopping, trying to break my concentration. He did not trust me, and suspected, not without reason, that I wanted to make the return journey alone, if need be.

"I forbid you," he said, "do you hear me? Something terrible will happen. Turn your thoughts back, while there is yet time." He would probably have leaped at me and held me down but I was already moving away, with his terrified voice growing fainter in my ears. I had forgotten the cellars and the threatening waters and was simply entering into my own life again.

When I regained consciousness I was standing in the middle of the little square in front of Mr. Josef's workshop, among the horde of cars in the yard. The bright spring sunshine shone blindingly on windows and radiators and I had to screw up my eyes in order to see anything.

I had drifted a good bit, almost to the end of our street. It may have been because Sebastian was trying to hold me back, or because it was the first time I had made use of the secret. Besides, Sebastian drifted too, whenever he was nervous or not in form.

I had no time to gather my thoughts, for Mr. Josef saw me at once. He was still shifting cars around, and pulled so hard on the handbrake of the car he was in that its tail jumped.

"Stop him! That's the one!" he shouted to his young assistants, pointing his finger at me but unable to move.

Several mechanics of my own age, or maybe a little older, all of them dirty and oily, made a dash for me, brandishing huge spanners. But I did not wait for them. Without thinking, I ran toward the ruined house, with its miserable birch trees and rabbit warren of hiding places. The pack of mechanics climbed after me over the piles of rubble.

"Stop him! He's the one who smashes the cars," yelled Mr. Josef, directing the pursuit from the rear.

"Hit him in the sump, lads! Smash his carburetor!" cried Mr. Josef. Then, just as I was really in a corner, something strange happened. A very large gentleman, red in the face with rage, stormed into the yard, went over to Mr. Josef, grabbed him by the collar, and pulled him out of the car. I could hear a ripping of overalls, grunts, and then a terrifying yelp. The young mechanics stopped chasing me, and I too stood still on top of a pile of debris, transfixed by the incomprehensible scene.

"You rotter!" howled the red-faced man, pulling Mr. Josef about relentlessly. "You've spoiled my car, you've ruined the engine!"

"Just a minute, please! Let's be calm!" Mr. Josef tried to regain his breath. "What has happened, sir?"

"I'll see you in jail, I'll ruin you, I'll tear you to pieces!"

"Let go, or I'll call the police!"

"The police!" roared the red-faced man. "I'm the one who's going to call the police!"

He drew a deep breath, shook Mr. Josef even more vigorously, and started yelling "Police! Police!"

Mr. Josef, terror-stricken, tried to kneel at the feet of his enraged customer, but only remained hanging on his arms. "For heaven's sake, what is the matter?" he croaked weakly, looking around piteously for help.

"What is the matter?" cried the big man, "you are asking me what is the matter? You are the owner of this swindler's setup. They didn't put any oil in the engine."

"Have the pistons seized up?" asked Mr. Josef warily.

"Yes, yes, yes!" shouted the customer, dropping him on the ground.

At that point another customer, who until then had stood aside from the row, came over and joined in. "Do you know what they did to me? They stole my spare wheel. Brand new it was."

Mr. Josef struggled to his feet, somewhat regaining his composure. "Frank, did you put any oil in the gentleman's car?"

One of my pursuers, who was holding a big sheet of greasy tarpaulin, spat and said: "Of course. As much as was needed—up to the mark."

"Then it all drained away after a few miles," said the customer.

Mr. Josef brightened. "Ah, now I know what it was, my dear sir. The boy forgot to turn off the drain plug."

The big man roared and again threw himself upon Mr. Josef, who ducked expertly and ran out into the street where he had more freedom of movement, calling "Keep an eye on the till!" to his mechanics.

I reached home quite safely. The only person I met on the stairs was the old woman who usually sat with the others by the rubbish bins. Her purplish face relaxed into a smile and she said in quite a friendly way, "Good morning, young man!"

"Good morning," I replied.

"Remember us, my child, if you have anything nice in your bucket." The color of her face reminded me of the color of the liquid in the bottles from which she and her companions drank.

My mother opened the door to me. "Where have you been? Everyone came home from school a long time ago."

"I was helping a chap with his homework," I lied with some feeling of disquiet.

"We are just going to Cecilia's."

"Why? What has happened?"

My mother looked mysterious and did not answer. The radio was raving away in Miss Sophie's room. Someone was gulping as though being strangled, but it was only the singer in her favorite pop group.

My father was sitting in front of the television set, gloomily watching a program on land drainage. He was still wearing his striped dressing gown, which usually meant that he was especially put out about something. My mother always reacted on such occasions by becoming intensely busy and sighing heavily, in order to make him feel that he was lazy and never did anything to help in the home. My father then usually said gruffly, "I am thinking." But today my mother was not putting on her act.

"There were two phone calls for you," said my father, "somebody wanted to speak to you. He rang twice."

My heart started to beat fast, because I had already guessed who it was.

"For me?"

"I told you it was for you. Somebody wanted you."

"It must have been one of the fellows at school."

"No, it wasn't a school friend. It was a grown-up with a strange accent. Do you know any taxi drivers or lorry drivers?"

"It must have been the father of someone I know. He never knows what he is supposed to do for homework."

I put my hand instinctively on the receiver to stop anyone else from answering it, for no school friend ever rings me—absolutely nobody does, although they tried to at first. It is because I am, for some reason, afraid to use the telephone; I would rather go out and find the person I want to talk to. I do not know how to carry on telephone conversations. The most tiresome thing about them is the silence when the person at the other end is waiting for you to say something to keep the conversation going.

"We have lived all our lives like people sitting on suitcases," said my father, presumably to my mother. "Hardships uncertainties, failures—never anything but stopgaps and makeshifts—living from hand to mouth. When shall we begin to really live? We are getting on. What hope have we now of really living?"

"It is better not to philosophize so much and to get on with some work," said my mother, who was busy mending a chair with a shaky leg.

"What's got into you now?" my father exclaimed.

"Well, look at other people who manage to live without complaining."

"All right then! Tomorrow I will go to the labor exchange and I will take any job with a shovel or a pickax that's going."

My mother did not say any more, and I wondered whether my father had not fallen out with his boss about sport at all, but about some matter more crucial to a man. It is not funny when a man as old as my father thinks that he has wasted his life.

"Everybody has got ahead of me," he went on quietly. "They've left me a long way behind, and no matter how fast I run, I could never catch up with them. If it wasn't for the children. . . ."

But he did not finish, because just then the telephone rang. I picked up the receiver in a flash.

"Is that you, Johnny?" It was Brush's awful voice. "Where were you when you weren't there?"

"I have a lot of homework to do," I said cautiously, to put my father off.

"You can start saving cash for the binge you're going to treat us to."

"What did you say?" I pretended that the line was bad.

"The Spitter has approved. Don't forget to be in the make-up room at half-past seven tomorrow morning."

"All right, I'll remember."

"What's the matter with you, Johnny? Are you ill? You seem to be talking nonsense."

"I'm reading a book."

"Hello, hello!" Brush began to shout, thinking that someone else had got onto the line by mistake. "See you tomorrow morning, Johnny. Mind you're there on time."

"Bye till tomorrow," I said, in a trailing sort of voice, to make it sound as if I were bored. But my heart beat fast and for some reason I was filled with an absurd sort of joy. I even began to help my mother, but before I could be of any real help, I suddenly remembered that somewhere out in the universe Sebastian and Eva were waiting for me, up to their middles in water that stank of outflow from a brewery. I began to search in drawers for some tool that would help me to free them. I could find nothing except some rusty nails, an old file, a broken electric switch, gas and electricity bills, and some faded snapshots in which my father, looking very thin and with a mop of hair, was embracing my young and very girlish mother.

"What is he rummaging about after?" asked my father. "It gets on my nerves."

So I abandoned my search and took from the bookshelf a thick volume entitled *Man—The Perfect Creature*. I put aside my anxieties and tried to turn my attention to the thoughts of the French scientist Pierre de Duparaise, although it was not easy to concentrate on such childish stuff. The learned professor went into raptures over man—an organism so complex that much of him is still not understood—such marvelous structure, such beauty, such purpose—and so on. But I know, of course—only don't tell anybody—that there is nothing to rave about. It is only our old-fashioned upbringing that has made us admire ourselves, just like babies who are delighted with themselves when they manage to get a door open on their own.

We are only a little more developed, in some respects, than other creatures. We know nothing of our origin or our end. We grope along, almost without moving forward, pushed—but not too much—by the will to live. This instinct is not at all divine, and there is nothing marvelous about it. It is simply the characteristic that made it possible for the first living organism to survive. The thing is that we want to enrich and improve our existence, and that is why we invented so many beautiful ideas, images, and words. But if any of you could ascend a few hundred miles into the sky and look at men through a telescope, you would see swarms of little creatures scurrying in all directions, without rhyme or reason—helpless little creatures being killed on roads, perishing at sea or underground, flying into rages, mad with joy, sunk in stupor. You would also see that there is no boundary between life and death.

But you may not be particularly interested in all this, and, as a matter of fact, you are probably right. The moon seems to be much more beautiful and marvelous if one knows absolutely nothing about it. To tell the truth, I regret to some extent that I have turned out to be a fellow who knows a lot and has thought things over. For what do I get from it? Nothing but despair.

My father and mother dressed for the visit to Cecilia's, and my mother knocked cautiously at Miss Sophie's door. There was no answer. The radio was more or less shaking the walls and windows. When my mother ventured to open the door, Miss Sophie was lying on her stomach, staring at the wall hung with strings of dried rowanberries.

"Sophie, dear, are you asleep?"

"No!" Miss Sophie screamed the word like a cat—she really caterwauled, for her "no" was full of lamentation, anger, peevishness, and pain—a desire to hide from the world, a sense of superiority, contempt for others, the sadness of self-imposed isolation, and many other feelings all rolled up into a single sound.

"Sophie, we are going to the charming monster's. Are you coming with us?"

"No!" Miss Sophie yowled again.

"Come with us, my child."

"No."

"But you'll suffocate, lying like that for days on end."

"No."

My mother stood for a while, quite helpless, and then we went off to the Old Town to Cecilia's.

As we passed through our courtyard I noticed that various curious things were happening. First of all, Buffalo's parents' car. It was parked untidily, with the doors open, and a strange dog was romping around inside, tugging at the fringes of the carefully folded rugs. The crippled man was sitting on a little folding chair, seemingly basking in the unusual spring sunlight, but he was actually watching both the car and Mr. Josef, who every now and again looked warily out of the entrance door and then disappeared again while, somewhere at the end of our street, his outraged customer was still shouting.

Buffalo ran out with a string shopping bag in his hand. He took no notice of me, but rushed headlong in the direction of the self-service store with a wild look in his eye and around his mouth the remains of some creamy food.

The leaves of the acacia tree by the monument stirred rather pathetically as we passed it. I felt a bit uneasy because I had quite forgotten it and could not imagine now how one could love a tree, however beautiful.

My father as usual was ahead of us, walking so quickly, with his shoulders heavily hunched, that my mother and I could not keep pace with him. He couldn't even guess, of course, that he would soon be seeing me in films and would perhaps be able to boast to his friends that the fame that surrounded our name would open up new prospects for the family. Actually I did not care so much about the fame. Money was more important in our situation.

We saw a warehouse besieged by an agitated crowd, and there were queues outside some of the shops. Everybody in the street seemed rather excited and there was a feeling of vitality and spring in the air. We passed a big new roundabout that was under construction. Pneumatic drills vibrated, bulldozers roared, and the jaws of mechanical excavators opened and shut with a bang. Workmen in helmets moved feverishly about among stacked-up tramlines, piles of sand, and caldrons bubbling with asphalt.

A jet plane flew low, circling over the city center as though it had lost its way and was looking desperately for the airfield. Cars seemed to be moving faster than usual. A loudspeaker buzzed as though there was some sheet metal loose in its works, so that it seemed either to be jerking out hysterical warnings or uttering some sort of spasmodic supplication.

In Cecilia's Old Town area everything was perfectly peaceful. Pigeons swarmed on the cobblestones, some tourists were taking snapshots of small dark-walled houses with faded paintings on their façades. It all looked like the quiet end of a city summer evening.

Cecilia opened the door. Her eyes glittered. "It's all settled!"she cried—so loudly that a window slammed somewhere behind her in the apartment—"I've burned my bridges!"

"Congratulations, my dear!" said my mother, and kissed her on the cheek. Cecilia stiffened and pulled her face away slightly, because she was always afraid of germs.

"I have got rid of the apartment and sold my belongings. So now I am homeless."

"I hope that the future millionairess will not spurn our humble hospitality," said my father, with a forced smile.

"I don't want to impose on you, my dears. If you could give me a corner for a few days it would be very nice; if not, I will go to a hotel. I am due to leave by air in a week. . . . I know I'm mad, but I can't help it. I have enjoyed taking risks all my life."

"I wish you would let me have the pictures," my mother said and then added modestly: "I have the chance of a one-man exhibition, to be entitled 'Portraits of My Friends.'"

"I suppose so—after all, I'm going to take these daubs of yours across the sea with me," said Cecilia, quite unaware that she was hurting my mother's feelings.

There were a number of my mother's portraits of Cecilia on the walls of the apartment. It must be admitted that Cecilia did not always look her best in them, but they were very lifelike, especially those which showed her with her famous eyes flashing with rage or intelligence or with the eyes of a visionary or even a downright witch. Any portrait painter would concentrate without hesitation on Cecilia's eyes. He would have no choice, because Cecilia made every new acquaintance look her straight in the eyes. Each of them was a different color and both were flecked with varying colors, and added to this there was the magnetism that Cecilia had put to much use in her stormy life.

I went over to the window and looked at the steep slope below, at the faded grass verges, the young, leafless trees, and the vast expanse of the huge river brimming with the spring floods. Behind me my parents were talking to Cecilia, and suddenly I felt that my mother was crying, and I was seized at the same instant with a pang of fear and a wish to return to Eva and Sebastian.

"Peter, are you deaf?" shouted Cecilia—and a big Gothic tile fell from the roof and broke into pieces—"I've been talking to you for a whole hour!"

"But we only arrived here five minutes ago!"

"Don't try to be smart, I don't like it."

"Cecilia has a present for you," said my mother, trying to smooth things over, "thank her politely."

"Here you are, you little idiot. It's an old shell from the Polynesian islands. Do you know where Polynesia is?"

"Of course. In the southern hemisphere."

"Listen to the sound the shell makes. It is the most beautiful sound in the world. It was my grandfather—who passed that way escaping from exile—who brought it home for my mother."

"At one time shells like that were fashionable," said my father. "There were big, spiky shells on the shelves in every home, and children listened to the sea in them on winter evenings . . . shells or musical boxes in little Swiss chalets. Aren't you sorry to leave this one behind, Cecilia?"

"She will find more beautiful ones there," sighed my mother.

"People who were not destined to travel were the ones who listened to shells," said Cecilia.

My father took the shell from me and held it to his ear. He listened for a long time, as if to confirm that Cecilia had spoken the truth, and I thought what a pity it was that my father could never be young again and that he had spent all his youth sitting on suitcases.

Cecilia turned off taps, pulled out plugs, and checked the window catches. As we left her darkened house, bells began to ring in the belfries of the old churches that had been reconstructed after the war.

We took a taxi and went home, listening to all the instructions that Cecilia rained on the driver.

Buffalo caught me outside our block. He was just returning yet again from the shop, with his string bag full of packages and bottles.

"We are having a glorious binge!" he stuttered, gasping for breath. "Grand stuff! My folks are having a big blowout!"

"Have you won in the lottery?"

"No, we are drinking our savings. The comet will smash into us tomorrow. End of the world."

He opened a bottle of beer and started to drink, choking with hiccups.

"Grand stuff! Lord, what grand stuff!" He put the bottle back into the shopping bag. "Come to our place. You'll have the time of your life."

"Perhaps it would be better to play at partisans?"

"That doesn't matter now, mate. The spread is waiting for us," and he pulled me toward the staircase. Just then the door onto their balcony opened and Buffalo's diminutive, haggard father appeared, with spectacles hanging from one ear, his thin hair on end, and his narrow chest heaving under a cherry-red sweater.

Buffalo's father looked at his ruined car, at the cripple, who was folding up his little chair because it had unexpectedly started to hail, at the windows being closed in haste all around the block—everything swaying a little, as if rocked by some unnatural force.

"Hey, you shabby lot, you scum!" he yelled in a high-pitched voice. "You screwed every penny you could. You gave short weight, stole purses, starved your own children—and what now? What have you gained by it? Tomorrow the ground will open, fire from heaven will burn your stinking houses, your rotten furniture, your filthy cars. Go to hell!"

He put two fingers in his mouth as if he were going to whistle, but he probably felt sick, because he suddenly slumped over the railings and hung there inert, still making rude gestures at our block and everyone in it. His little wife ran out to help him, but he pushed her away and fell into the room behind him, only to reappear a few moments later dragging a big sofa and trying to push it over the railings into the yard.

"I'll show you lot!" he cried again. "I'll teach you a lesson!"

"Stop it, Dad!" shouted Buffalo, alarmed, and he ran toward the stairs. "Dad, don't spoil the furniture! They won't understand anyway."

My father tossed in his bed for a long time that night, unable to sleep. I slept with him in the room with the television set, because Cecilia was sleeping in my mother's room. He turned over noisily and murmured to himself, and this kept me awake. So I began to think about the girl in jeans and about Eva. I saw the valley that was more like a wide, deep ravine, the fast-flowing river, and the house that I described to myself as "golden," although it was simply yellowed with age. And I saw Eva on the riverbank, all in bright shining white. But there was nothing unusual or symbolic about this whiteness; I have read somewhere that children were dressed like this in the past. Eva stood on the bank, with her arms raised frenziedly, bending sideways a little, as if pulling away from something that held her, and saying, with anguish in her voice, "I love you, I love you madly." I saw the restless, rather wild eyes, the full lips, and her pale hands with the thin fingers. It couldn't have been a dream, because Eva rose before my eyes in whichever direction I looked.

To tell the truth, now that nobody can hear us, I prefer the girl in jeans. I cannot explain why, but there must be some reason for it. The one in jeans is an ordinary little girl, rosy-faced, with blonde hair that she is always pushing behind her ears, and a generally well-scrubbed look about her. I simply fancy her. I think I even fancy her a lot, although I am ashamed of my feelings and even repress them. In order to put her out of my mind I began to tell myself that when I grew up I would marry Eva. I have no particular wish to grow up, but things have gone so far that it seems proper that I should marry Eva,

As I was thinking of this the thought suddenly sprang into my mind that both Eva and Sebastian were there in the icy water, numb with cold, beating against the wall and calling for help, as the flood rose to their middles and then to their necks. It came to me also that whenever I went to the valley it was always the same early evening or the beginning of the same night. In other words, time stood still in the valley when I was not there and started to move on only when I returned. Or is this only my impression?

I felt an urge to go out "there," if only for a while, just to "cast an eye," as Sebastian would have said. So, pressing my fists against my ears, I tried. I repeated everything that the Investigator Dog had taught me. But nothing changed. I still lay in my bed, hearing the wind blustering on the balcony, the creaking of furniture, and my father's sighs. I felt suddenly hot, because I realized that I could not remember something which was essential, and that I might never be able to return to the crazy Eva, imprisoned by Retep, or to the Investigator Dog.

"Father," I said.

"What is it?"

"Wake me up tomorrow at six."

"All right. Now go to sleep, it's already late."

I was in the make-up room at seven o'clock next morning, one of the first to arrive. My hands were trembling and my teeth were chattering and I was unable to speak a single straightforward sentence. It was not because I had stage fright. It was simply the events of the previous night that had shattered me, and my fear of not being able to return to Eva and Sebastian. Something had snapped: I seemed to be suspended over a precipice, and at any moment something dreadful might happen.

Ladies in white overalls trimmed my hair, patted stuff on my face and dabbed at my cheeks. People were constantly dropping into the make-up room because it was rather a cozy place, like most places where women are in charge. There was a teakettle singing on the electric stove. The firstcomer was Brush, looking like a burglar who has been on the job all night.

"Don't speak to me, little ones," he said to the make-up girls, pulling an awful face, "I've got a splitting headache, a real hangover! Can you give me some tea?"

Pale Niko put his head around the door, but did not enter. The last visitor was Hare, the producer, in person. He stood by the window staring straight in front of him, seeming not to notice anything, but the whole roomful of people immediately became uneasy.

"Their make-up will not be finished in time," he said dourly.

"Oh no, sir! We've nearly finished, sir," the ladies protested, hastily putting finishing touches to some other boys, who were looking derisively at each other and at me.

Duckbill came in, in a suede jacket and very dark spectacles, and admired his profile in the triple mirrors.

"Well, boys," he said, "now to the dressing room." And he led us to the next room, full of rough wooden racks, where we were given our costumes—a kind of shiny colored space suit and dome-like helmet. Anyone could have seen that we were to be astronauts. The costumes were made of poor stuff and soon began to split on some of the boys. My suit and the suit of a rather plump boy in spectacles seemed to be stronger than the rest, and the others tried to persuade us to swap, but Duckbill would not allow it. "Everyone," he said, "keeps his own suit, and it's going to be like that throughout." Then he gave us an outline of the story.

I was to play a bad character and the boy in spectacles a good character. The good fairy (she was the blonde actress whom everyone called "the Boss's wife") was to take us on an interplanetary journey, like a class on a school trip. Why we were being taken, and to what end, was not important because, according to the shooting schedule, that would be shot last of all. I was to be a solitary, over-clever boy, impossible to please and contemptuous of other children my own age—therefore I wore a black space suit. The boy in spectacles would be my opponent at every turn, righting all the wrongs I did and finally becoming leader of the expedition and bringing it to a successful conclusion.

This boy was called Dorian (his parents must have searched for a long time to find a saint of that name in the calendar). Dorian, who was very conceited, was getting red in the face and correcting Duckbill about the story, which he seems to have altered in the film script.

"It doesn't matter," Duckbill was saying. "After all, when we have finished shooting we shall be putting the story together in a different way."

"No, you must not do that," argued Dorian, "it must follow the book, because everybody has read the book and remembers the story."

When we were ready they packed us into a big bus. I found a place and sat, rather dazed, watching Dorian's pranks. He continually changed his place and touched and handled everything within reach. When he found a dusty microphone he pretended to be a guide with a load of foreign tourists. The driver was not pleased, but for some reason he tolerated his unruly behavior. Eventually Dorian held up his two forefingers behind the driver's head, to represent donkey's ears or horns. All the boys watched him enviously because he had obviously established himself beyond all doubt as an amusing rascal.

The small girl, Ducky—whose mother, accompanying her, was in a state of visible irritation—got in Dorian's way. A tabby kitten, called Bubbles, was with her, but he was under the care of an elderly gentleman who kept constant watch over his pet.

I turned to look out of the window, because we were already approaching the airfield, and my eyes met the eyes of the girl in jeans. She was sitting next to me, touching my side with her elbow and smiling like a summer morning. My heart began to beat so fast that I thought that she would hear it. It would not have been polite to turn away from her, so I looked at her with my mouth and throat dry. My heart beat still faster and I thought, without any sense of fear, that I was going to die.

She gave me her very warm hand and said, "I am Mayka. We shall be acting together."

I saw then that she was wearing a sort of plastic space suit or rather a kind of plastic tunic. On her knees she held a helmet that looked like a derby hat. And on top of the helmet lay a leash plaited from several thongs of leather. But again, there was no dog with her.

"My name is Peter," I stammered. "I am very pleased to make your acquaintance."

"I know you by sight. I suppose we live not far from each other."

"Yes, possibly."

"You are friends with that ridiculous Buffalo, aren't you?"

"Well, we are not really great friends," I replied cautiously. "We know each other because we live in the same courtyard."

"It is my birthday tomorrow. Could you come to my party?"

"Yes"—my parched lips could manage no more than the barest whisper.

She looked out of the window, because we were passing some earth-moving machines that were working on the road, and I had a chance to gather my wits. To have met with her now, on this coach, was the last thing that I would have thought possible. But now here she was, inviting me to her party as if we had known each other for years. I was quite unprepared for that. I had never had any luck with girls. No pretty, pleasant girl had ever spoken to me first or wanted to play with me. Somehow it always happened that they chose someone else, usually a fellow whom I despised. But any girl who was cross-eyed or stupid or rough or just ordinary would fall for me immediately, and I had to endure her endless declarations of love and date her simply out of politeness.

Now, surprised by my good fortune, I looked Mayka over. I felt pleasure in the sight of her smooth cheeks and golden hair tucked back behind her ears, and her lips that moved slightly as I watched her. I even reproached myself for ignoring her until now.

She smiled at me again. "Shall we stay together? Would you like to?"

"Very much," I said, covering my feelings with an ordinary tone of voice.

She watched Dorian for a while as he larked about, and then asked, with a scornful look on her face, "Do you know who he is?"

"No. I only know that he is to play a good character."

"I don't like 'goodies'," she said.

"I am playing a 'baddie'," I said hastily.

She looked at me with the sort of respect that Cecilia showed when she looked at the portrait of Oscar Wilde. I felt lighthearted and filled with the certainty that we would get by, even without my father's salary, and that we would survive even the asteroid that everyone was calling "the comet."

"You used to go out with a Hungarian or Peruvian, didn't you?" I asked.

"With who? I don't remember."

"A dark chap. You were eating ice cream together in the street once in the autumn."

"Oh, it must have been our neighbor. He used to plague me but he has left now, thank goodness."

I leapt slightly in my seat. "Is that true?" I asked. Luckily the coach leapt too, as it entered the airfield gate, and covered my exultation.

"Is what true?"

"That he stayed such a short time in our country," I replied evasively.

"I don't even want to think of him." She struck her helmet contemptuously with the leash as she spoke.

"What are you going to do with the money?"

"The money I earn from the film?"

"Yes. I shall use mine for the holidays."

"I am thinking of hitchhiking."

"As a matter of fact," I said, "I don't much care about money. I applied to get into the film because I was bored."

"Don't exaggerate. Money is important too. What does your father do?"

"He is an expert on computers," I answered casually.

"That's interesting, because my father is the director of an institute where they have computers."

"I'm not particularly interested in that kind of thing, myself," I said hastily. "Look! We have arrived."

Our bus passed several large aircraft, which were not (at all) the silvery color that one would have expected them to be. Some had black patches of soot and oil stains, and on one of them I even saw ordinary mud, as though it had been taxiing over muddy fields.

"Peter," said Mayka softly, holding out her hand, "shall we be friends?"

"Of course," I answered. I wanted to kiss her hand, but I was embarrassed and pulled my own hand back too quickly, knocking her helmet off her knees.

On the huge concrete apron there was an assortment of packing cases, cables, and scaffolding, and in the middle stood a camera with straddled legs, covered with a black cloth, looking as though the cameramen had blindfolded it to stop it from seeing anything. A lot of people were milling about among all this equipment, some of whom I already knew—Brush, Pale Niko, Duckbill, and the mysterious Hare. The cameraman with the beard, whom everyone called "the Commando," was eating something out of wrapping paper and drinking tea. Baldy, or "the Spitter" as Brush called him, was standing nearby. He stood with his arms folded across his chest, shooting out his lips and staring across the concrete at the faded grass beyond. Through the doors

[147]

of a van I saw the blonde actress who was the Boss's wife. She wore her transparent plastic costume, covered by the sort of sheepskin coat that lorry drivers wear, and was greedily unwrapping and eating sweets.

"Don't wander away, troops, keep together!" Brush called to us. "I will familiarize you with the situation." We sat by the doors of a huge hangar, watching the mechanics, who had stopped working on their aircraft to stare at us with equal interest.

"There is our rocket, just as it was in the book!" said Dorian excitedly.

Some distance away, in the empty expanse of the airfield, a big painted rocket stood on end, with steps leading up to its open doorway. It was actually a rather shoddy model. It reminded me of the rocket I had recently seen in a feverish dream. But in the light of common day it was rather disenchanting.

Mayka, close beside me, was whispering to herself *"Je suis, tu es, il est . . ."*

"What are you doing?" I asked.

"Nothing. I was saying French verbs. What a bore it all is."

I, too, had expected something different. But then everything burst into enormous activity. The cover was taken off the camera. Somebody got too close to it and was ordered away by the director, who hid himself under a black cloth with a sort of viewfinder. Duckbill, aided by Brush and Pale Niko, took us in hand and formed us into a procession. Mounting the steps, we entered the rocket, which had no inside. We simply had to hide on the other side of it, behind a plywood board carrying printed German inscriptions from the last war. Brush headed the procession, taking the place of the Boss's wife, who did not think it worth her while to get familiarized. Brush, who was rather good at impersonating her, explained to us that films in which animals and children are taking part can take longer to make, and the budget allows for a reduction of the daily shooting schedule. We did not know whether to feel pleased or offended by this information. When Pale Niko entered through the rocket door the space was so tightly packed that he immediately fell out, head over heels, on the other side.

"They wouldn't have props like this in the West," he said bitterly, brushing off the dust. "Do you remember the set they had in *The Martians' Revenge?*"

But Brush was already forming the procession anew, and we marched up the steps into the rocket and out again about fifteen times. The director, Baldy, kept on having the camera moved from one place to another, and roughly ordered us about and changed our marching formation. He eventually ordered the Boss's wife onto the scene and she marched with us, still wearing the sheepskin coat. I tried to keep close to Mayka, but the director shouted: "The black one there—what's his name? Why is he shoving to the front? His place is at the end."

Brust pushed me to the tail of the procession. "Johnny, remember you are the villain. *Capito?*"

"This is a poor setup," said Peal Niko, scornfully. "A decent company would provide soft drinks."

Meanwhile Duckbill began to give us orders through a large megaphone. In the end everything got into a muddle. Ducky did not want to go up the steps again, the kitten was scared by the roar of a jet aircraft and disappeared into the landscape, and the rocket tilted sideways. Little girls were falling against the signboard and screaming their heads off. The director sat down beside the camera, holding his head in his hands, and completely stopped spitting.

The scriptwriter approached him timidly. "It looks very good," he said. "The rocket is exactly as I imagined the spaceship."

"You are the only one who likes it," growled the director. "You've finished and got your money. Now I have to make some sense out of your filthy rubbish." The scriptwriter grew pale.

"I hope you are not referring to me," he said. The director jumped to his feet.

"Who else do you think I was talking about? Who wrote the script, pray? Was it Shakespeare or Edison or Vasco da Gama?"

"I got the publishers' prize for the book," said the scriptwriter icily. "And I have a telegram from Hollywood here in my pocket. I could go there any time I wanted to and earn good money."

The director clasped his head in his hands again. "Will somebody tell me what I am doing here?"

Nobody answered his question. There was a sound of terrific explosions in the neighborhood of the rocket, which disappeared from view behind clouds of smoke.

"Stop! Stop!" howled the director. "What fool is doing that?"

Duckbill ran up panting to report like a sergeant. "Special effects are trying out the firing for takeoff."

The director stamped with rage. "What for? Who told them to? The children could get hurt."

"I was thinking, sir . . ."

"For goodness' sake don't think, I beg of you."

Meanwhile, the fireworks expert, a fair, slightly bald man with an ambiguous smile, ran through our ranks and hid behind us, sorting out his equipment. I saw that there were shining detonators and gold-colored cables in his wooden box. The detonators were big. They could easily have blown up a cubic yard of earth or destroyed a wall of average thickness. Then I had an idea.

I moved imperceptibly closer and closer, dropped to my knees in pretended weariness, and dipped my hand into the box among the slippery cartridges.

"Aha, my dear fellow," said the fireworks expert, "your fingers are itching?"

I quickly pulled my hand out while he stood over me with an unpleasant smile on his face and said in a drawling voice: "One of those sweet little things could blow your dear little arm off up to the elbow."

"You should be ashamed to talk like that to a child," chided the owner of the kitten.

"I know what I am talking about, my dear sir. When we were filming *Shell Shock*, in one of the forest scenes I poured a little too much gunpowder . . ."

"Be quiet," growled the old man.

Still smiling, the effects man fastened his box with a huge padlock.

"*Nous sommes, vous êtes, ils sont . . .*" Mayka started whispering to herself again.

"What are you doing?" I asked.

"I am conjugating verbs," she answered. "Sit down next to me, because that Dorian is staring at me all the time."

So I sat down and watched her, while she recited her French verbs as though she was murmuring prayers. As I watched her I felt that all things were passing, and then I thought that there was no point, therefore, in getting involved in imaginary troubles. I began to regret that I had for so long refused to utter Mayka's name, and that I had wasted time waiting for the comet and in pretended devotion to that wretched acacia tree.

"Johnny! Johnny, where are you? Stick up your horns so that I can see you." Brush's voice reached me faintly. "The director wants you."

I jumped to my feet, full of foreboding. "That damned comet is heading straight for us, everybody's got problems, and the whole show's a madhouse," growled Brush as he led me to the director, who was glaring at the pale-faced scriptwriter.

"Are you Rodriquez?" he asked me curtly.

"It's Retep, sir," a lady holding a thick book corrected him.

"It's all the same. Well, are you?"

"Yes, sir."

"Do you know the story of the film?"

"Yes," I said, rather uncertainly.

"And what do you think of it?" His gaze was so intimidating and he spat so hard as he spoke that I put my hand to my face and then pretended that I was brushing dust or something from my eyelashes.

"It is rather naïve," I said. "The rocket looks as if it was fueled with saltpeter or sour milk. For a journey like this, ionic engines would be needed."

The director brightened up, but the scriptwriter grew paler, as if he had already had a dose of radiation, so I hastened to add: "But I think, sir, that all these science-fiction ideas are a bit naïve, so it can't be helped."

"You see," said the director, "even a child knows what's wanted."

"The reverse is true," said the scriptwriter. "The child understands that scientific accuracy would kill the poetry."

[151]

"That's just the trouble!" The director got annoyed again. "Poetry! In my job you can't just film things like naïve scientific fantasies, hackneyed psychological drama, or moral tales from the provinces. The story should be in the form of a fairy tale or a philosophical tale, a metaphor for today's world, some new generalization."

He suddenly became lost in thought and began to spit desperately, and it was obvious to everybody that he was greatly moved and striving to express something so profound that society would be shattered by it.

"One cannot do the impossible," said the scriptwriter faintly.

The director pounced on him. "Indeed one can!" he said. "We'll both do it, or I'll fire everybody."

"Voytek, darling, how much longer do I have to freeze here?" the blonde actress asked in a bored voice.

"Until you're dead," shouted the director, "you're the cause of all the trouble. You wanted to play a good fairy, a blonde goddess! You are sabotaging everything!"

The actress stiffened like a wildcat. Her blonde hair stood on end like angry fur, her bright eyes narrowed with hatred and her teeth actually became fang-like.

"You cad!" she spat, and disappeared into her dressing quarters, the sheet-metal door banging behind her like the crack of doom. There was silence for a while, broken only by Ducky screeching "Come here!" at the kitten, because she could not understand that it was a cat and not a dog.

There was a sudden commotion behind us and a horde of people poured through the gate in the perimeter fence onto the concrete apron. There was somebody trying to control them, but with little success. Duckbill, holding a megaphone, was moving about energetically in the throng, pulling all kinds of faces, serious and gay, official and raffish, almost in the same breath. A crowd of brightly dressed schoolgirls on an excursion poured onto the airfield.

A huge jet was starting its takeoff run a short distance away, right behind our rocket, and the girls began to scream when the jet stream blew their skirts up.

Everyone watched the foreign aircraft take off, except the director, and his gaze was fixed on the ground. His eyes looked sunken, his back was hunched, and his hair even looked slightly grayer.

"Please sir," I said, when the hubbub had died down a little, "don't worry too much. It is difficult nowadays to think of something new for children. In my case a dog comes to see me, who was an English explorer in his previous incarnation, and we go off on trips together. But there is nothing new about that either. I really think it is not worth worrying over."

I felt something touch my hair. It was the scriptwriter, who put his hand lightly on my head.

"We could make improvements here and there," he said hesitantly, "we've only just started shooting."

"Yes, we could make a few alterations," muttered the director, as if talking to himself, and he continued to stare at the ground without moving.

So I went back to my comrades. They were numb with cold in their split spacesuits, and stared miserably at Bubbles who was frantically trying to escape from the harness in which he was restrained by his owner. I started to look for Mayka who was nowhere to be seen. I finally found her sitting in the cabin with the Boss's wife, chattering gaily and combing the actress's long hair, which flowed like a sheaf of corn over her plastic-covered shoulders; and it occurred to me that they resembled each other like two sisters.

The director and the scriptwriter were still standing together, each with his own worries. The cameraman finished his sandwiches, screwed his cup back on his Thermos flask, and gave his orders in a quiet voice:

"Lights! Generator!"

"Move the tenner closer," called the plumbers.

Then they filmed a board with colored rectangles, which was held up by a plumber in a sheepskin coat.

Mayka came running from the van, with glowing cheeks.

"She is marvelous," she said passionately, "she is absolutely wonderful. I have got her autograph and she gave me this for luck." She lifted a lock of her golden hair and showed me a red hairclip, like a large drop of blood. The schoolgirls were squeezing through the exit gate, giggling. Duckbill, hovering around them like a guarddog, increased their giggles to a gale. My own spirits, however, were invaded by a strange sadness.

"Where is the special-effects man?" I asked Mayka.

"Oh, the 'bangs' man? He went off a long time ago. He is afraid of the director."

Brush came over to us, stiff with cold and his dreadful nose quite blue.

"The familiarizing session is over, troops. Hop into the bus."

"Will the effects man be here tomorrow?" I ventured to ask him.

"Yes, he will. Have you some business with him?"

"No, I was just asking."

We went over to the bus. All the others were in their seats, even Ducky and her irritable mother, but Mayka still lingered.

"Shall we sit together?" I asked.

"I have to go with Dorian. His father is taking us in his car."

I felt very annoyed, and Mayka must have noticed it.

"Don't be cross," she said, "it somehow got arranged like that. Good-bye."

She made a move to give my hair a friendly tug but did not succeed and only hit the back of my head. I shrank away from her, but she was already running along the road on the other side of the airport fence, waving to somebody with both arms. I saw a car with the scriptwriter sitting at the wheel and Dorian holding a door open, waiting. He was holding Sebastian on a thick leather leash.

I made a desperate rush toward them, pushing aside stragglers from the crowd of schoolgirls. When I reached them they were all seated inside the car and trying to pull the great dog in after them.

"Sebastian! It's splendid to find you!" I cried, breathless.

The Great Dane looked at me with the eyes of the bearded cameraman but showed neither surprise nor joy nor any kind of feeling. He looked at me with complete indifference as they tugged him into the car.

"Sebastian, don't pretend that you don't recognize me! At least say something."

A fleck of saliva dropped from his black lip.

"I cannot come back to you," I said. "Help me, because I have forgotten everything."

But his front legs were already inside the car. The engine started up, there was a grinding of gears, and Dorian clucked to the apathetic dog, as though he were calling a chicken: "Cheep, cheep, cheep, come on then, come on, old fellow!"

The great beast struggled meekly into the car, his muscles rippling under the thin coat.

"Sebastian, what's the matter? I don't understand. Sebastian, save us! Sebastian!"

But the car had already started. The door closed, and for a moment it seemed to me that I could see in the rear window the empty, impassive eyes of Mayka's dog.

In that moment I lost all sense of life and feeling. Confused, I climbed into the bus and must somehow have blacked out during the journey back, because the next thing I knew was that I was signing a paper. Hare was staring at me with his morose and colorless eyes, Brush patted my arm, and I was given some money, which I stuffed into my pocket. Then I wandered through alien streets and somebody spoke to me—maybe it was Buffalo. Later, at home, I was aware of my mother shouting to make my father hear her while he was watching a program on garden flowers. Cecilia was taking a cold shower and calling out something about iodine. People outside in the street were gazing up at the sky, while the wind tugged at their clothes. As for me, my head was now in a turmoil. When I had calmed down a little I wanted to go straight to Mayka's place and sort things out. But what was it that had to be sorted out? Wasn't everything over between us and hadn't she just left me flat? Even Sebastian had broken off relations with me.

A crowd was assembling in our courtyard because someone was being carried out to a waiting ambulance. It was not the cripple. I could just see part of a deathly white face, and suddenly our apartment seemed to fill with a smell of sickness and pain. To dispel the depression that weighed upon me I took the diary from under the mattress in Miss Sophie's room and began to read a passage that was heavily surrounded with decorations, but for some reason I had to read the same sentence several times because the neat, uniform writing jumped and dazzled under my eyes.

"What a fool I have been. I have wasted so much time—an eternity—nearly two weeks, running like a silly schoolgirl to the theater and the cinema, and spending a fortune on dull records. And for whom? For a woman chaser with a nasal voice. Besides, Lucina has told me the sort of fellow he is. Apparently he carries on with all the young actresses. It would be an insult to compare this comedian, this Don Juan, with Him—my ideal and only love. I decided to get top marks at school in the subject He teaches. I answered two questions, and He was embarrassed, poor man, and made a slight mistake and gave me 'average' for the first one, but I will cherish that wrong mark until my dying day—although I shall probably die young. I am sure that He suspects my feelings for Him. Our eyes meet all the time over the heads of my classmates. I could swear that He blushes slightly—in any case He buries his head quickly in a book. He must be mine! He must!"

I give only the bare words of the passage, but it was ornamented with dots, dashes, and flourishes, and at the bottom of the page there was a heart pierced by an arrow, in a pool of blood, marks left by kisses—a riot of symbols signifying the love that burned in our taciturn Miss Sophie, so silent that she might have been a lodger instead of a member of the family.

I looked out of the window again and saw Gagatek—the flesh-and-blood, everyday Gagetek—kicking his football with precision and dedication, unaware of the storm of passion that had gathered over his head.

But you do not really know Miss Sophie. You know that she is haughty and unpleasant at home and sentimental in her diary, but that does not explain her to you.

Miss Sophie is actually a beautiful girl. I can swear to that, although I am her brother. Her beauty is slightly exotic, as though she had spent a long time in Asia, or still farther east—which is strange, because our parents are normal Europeans. Her hair is dark brown, long, and slightly wavy (but she is trying to straighten it). Her face is oval, her nose is long and finely molded and she has just a few freckles. Her mouth is small, and on the whole she looks like the child Jesus—which may sound like blasphemy, but it is the truth and cannot be helped.

Although she is slimming, she is already so slender that a strong gust of wind could snap her like a flower stem. Her only defect is the ring finger of her left hand, which is slightly longer than the same finger on the other hand. This worries me, and she is always pulling the shorter finger, although she must know that it does not help. She is very concerned about justice and fair play. She has been like that from early childhood. When Father sometimes swore at an announcer or speaker on television, Miss Sophie would go into fits and everything that had been said had to be taken back and apologies made to the image on the screen. As a small child she was incapable of telling a lie—she just did not answer. She may have learned later to lie, but I rather think that she did not.

Sometimes Miss Sophie likes to hit me, but never too hard— just enough to punish me. She is almost grown up now, and if she writes rather sentimentally in her diary, it is because her life is hard. It is no fun being a girl.

I am very sorry about reading her diary. I wish that I did not do it, but I cannot resist the urge. Anyhow, I understand everything and am capable of sympathizing with her. It is not really wrong of me to read the diary—in fact it is quite the reverse. If I could, I would drag those idealized loves by their ears and force them to their knees at Miss Sophie's feet.

As I was thinking this, the doorbell rang. I went to open it, my heart beating with all sorts of expectations, but it was Miss Sophie who entered.

"What's the news about the film?" she asked, with rather a nasty smile.

"What film?"

"Don't pretend you don't know."

"I'm not pretending. I just don't know what you mean."

"Secret lover!" she said, and locked herself in the bathroom. I stifled my pride and hung around waiting for her to come out. At last she reappeared, with her hair freshly arranged, and went to the kitchen to look for some low-calorie food. I followed her and pretended to look for something on the table.

"I really don't understand why you were asking about films," I said.

"It's nothing," she said indifferently, but I was not satisfied.

"But why did you mention the film?" I asked. "I have nothing to do with it."

"Stop being a nuisance. Anyone would think that you really had offered yourself to act in a film."

As though she had no further concern, she started to rummage about looking for some of last season's apples, which by this time of year had lost all nutritional value. She seemed absorbed in what she was doing, but the odd smile was still hovering about the corners of her mouth.

As a precaution, I hid the money that I had been paid that day inside the television set, but was immediately seized with fear that the notes might get burned or that something might go wrong with the set. So I began to look for another hiding place but none seemed safe. In the end I pushed all the money into the shell that Cecilia had given me, and when I held it to my ear it no longer sang, as if choked by money.

Later that night it was I who tossed in my bed and my father who was disturbed by my creakings and turnings. I tried to make contact with Sebastian and Eva, but without any result. At last I began to wonder if this was not some kind of illusion, a collection of dreams, a trick of the imagination, the sort of thing that clever, precocious, ultra-sensitive boys are prone to experience.

Then I had a dream. I saw a city teeming with people, and a tower that could have been the Eiffel Tower. Retep and I were sitting or standing on one of its platforms, watching the lights of the aurora borealis, which grew gradually brighter and brighter and became very hot. The huge city below us receded and became unreal, and I felt as though we were slowly ascending in a lift.

"They set us at variance with each other," Retep was saying, and he hugged me closely. I thought that he was scared of something and afraid that I would leave him, and that was why he gripped me so tightly. And then I noticed that there was nothing fearful or hostile in his face. It was a face that I remembered well from long ago, as though known from the time of my earliest conscious memory.

"I am your brother," Retep said, "and I am your father too, and maybe also your future son."

I tried to tell him that this sounded rather complicated, and that it did not seem to make much sense, but then I saw that we were standing in deep snow up to our waists, facing a window aglow with lights. There were wolves howling somewhere, and over our heads a thousand million stars were shining like glowworms. We looked through a gap in the curtain into the room behind and saw our families sitting at a table in the yellow glow of a paraffin lamp, drinking tea and eating jam from small plates. "I cannot go away," I said, "I must go back at once." "Don't be afraid," said Retep, "we shall meet them all there." And I saw myself, in a long coat, reaching to the ground, in somebody's else's clothes, and with a kerchief tied under my chin, like a peasant girl. I was tending some goats and there were boys pointing their fingers at me mockingly. "I am not feeling well, Retep," I said, "I must go back." And then I was lying in a strange bed, which I somehow remembered well. Behind the bed was a wall made of thick logs, plugged with decayed moss, and I could distinctly hear the deathwatch beetle eating at the wood. I heard it clearly because blood was pouring from my mouth in a thin stream that ran through the bedclothes onto the floor in a big pool. Cecilia, with trembling fingers, was lighting a thick candle ornamented with figures of angels and flowers. There was no ground beneath us. I think there was nothing at all.

I started to release myself from Retep's grip, and as I did so he said, in a slow, penetrating voice: "Don't be afraid. It is the same everywhere. They are only reflections of our thoughts, our aspirations, and our dreams."

Next morning I had no time to think about my dream, except that it was strange that Retep haunted me at night, as though returning the visits that I had paid him. He appeared at moments when I felt defenseless, overcome by weakness and the mysterious power of dreams.

Although I was in a great hurry, I had time to hide the shell deep in a closet among some old clothes. I pulled out the wad of notes, out of curiosity, and the empty shell began to sing again. And I thought that it is difficult to understand why people in the distant South Sea Islands find so much magic, poetry, and mystery in these shells. I, for my part, find Iceland, for instance, much more interesting and mysterious—a strange country, formed by volcanoes, treeless, bare, black, terrifying, melancholy—full of spirits and ghosts, ruled by the old Viking gods, Wotan and Thor. I do not much like the people of the South, who are supposed to be all life and energy, with a cheerful belief in human wisdom. I prefer the gloomy Scandinavians, who worry without cause. I may be wrong about the South, but I cannot help being irritated by people who enjoy life and are full of enthusiasm. What is there so enjoyable about life?

While I was hurrying to the film studio, I bumped into the optimistic Buffalo, who, although it was still too early for school, was sitting under the acacia by the monument.

"The comet is going to hit us today," he moaned. "There's no escape. And I've got a splitting headache."

"So early in the day?"

"It's the end of the world at home—the Last Judgment—I can't tell you what it's like." He licked his dry lips with the tip of his tongue. "I would exchange my promotion to the next form for a swig of beer."

"You shouldn't drink alcohol at your age. It weakens the memory, restricts growth, and causes degeneration of the nervous system."

He wanted to kick me, but he did not have enough strength. He fell back on the wall with a loud groan and dozed off, tousled by the spring wind.

I sat on the bus in the same seat as the day before, and after a while the sound of quick footsteps filled me with excitement. Someone sat beside me without a word. Out of the corner of my eye I saw that she was playing with the dog leash and watching the bustle through the window. She looked so pretty that my heart bounced. I tried to breathe slowly and carefully in and out to quell the commotion that I felt. She did not look at me at all.

"Where is the dog?" I asked.

"Rameses? He is in the next bus with Mr. Brush. It's because of this wretched Bubbles, or whatever his name is."

I felt a pang of resentment that God had given her looks that attracted me so much. Then it was borne in upon me with great intensity that in any case it all made no sense, that it was too late, and that the comet was almost upon us.

"Are you cross with me?" she asked unexpectedly, and her voice made me feel faint.

""No," I said, "why should I be cross with you?"

"It's all right then. I cannot bear it if anyone is cross with me. Shall we go back together?"

"What about Dorian?"

"I give up! Are you jealous too?"

I wanted to explode and demand answers to a lot of questions—about this "jealous *too*" business, among other things— but I was overcome by a feeling of hopelessness, so I just shut my mouth and sat with my eyes fastened blankly on Bubbles, who was playing with the ends of the driver's untied shoelace.

"Why are you so quiet? It bores me," Mayka said after a while.

"Everything bores you," I said.

She leaned her arm on my shoulder. "Don't be silly."

"All right. I won't be silly."

"Then we are friends again?"

"Yes."

"Give me your hand."

"What for?"

"Give it to me. Please."

"Girls and their whims!"

"It may be a whim, but I very much want it."

"Everybody is watching us," I said.

"What do I care? I am asking you for the last time."

A thin rain was falling on the airfield like a sort of persistent mist. The camera crew opened a big umbrella over the camera, as though it were royalty. The bearded Commando was eating a belated breakfast and watching workmen lay rails for a sort of narrow-gauge railway, energetically aided by the assistant direc- tor. The scriptwriter was smiling and busily drawing in the thick scenario book, and announcing that there would be some fresh dialogue of a rather more profound and philosophical kind.

Hare, the producer, watched, but took no part in the bustle that was going on around the rocket, which had been repaired and somewhat modernized during the previous night, and which stood there creaking in every breath of wind. I was looking for somebody other than any of the people I could see.

At last I saw him. Bent over a wooden chest, hidden from the director's eyes, behind the body of the spacecraft, he was fastening long cables to a cluster of detonators, with an animated smile upon his face. Eventually he took a few cartridges, hid them under his coat, and began to creep in a roundabout way toward the model. He was so absorbed in this operation that it was easy for me to get at the open box. I picked out the three detonators with the longest cables and was about to hide them in my pocket when I felt someone's eyes upon me.

A drenched dog stood in front of me, gazing at me with eyes misted blue with sickness or weariness.

"Sebastian, is it you?" I asked.

"You betrayed us," he answered harshly.

"It is *your* behavior that is strange. Did you not pretend yesterday not to recognize me?"

"We have been waiting for you so long, and you have played traitor."

"Sebastian, I swear that I wanted to go back!"

"Then why did you not go?"

"Because I forgot everything. Simply that. I tried to go back many times, but without success."

"Did I not tell you?" He swayed slightly, striking his bony haunch against the metal side of the van. "I have been looking for you all over the town."

"Sebastian, have you been drinking valerian drops again?"

"A thimbleful—hardly anything."

"Could you return in the state you are in?"

"I could—I must. Let us get behind this hut."

He sat heavily in the middle of a puddle and opened wide his big eyes, full of wisdom and stupidity, nostalgia and plain kindheartedness.

"You love Eva," I whispered.

He blinked his eyes, with their long, scanty lashes.

"Let us not waste time," he said, "the place there is already full of water."

"Peter! Where are you? Peter!" Mayka's voice was close at hand.

"Hurry up!" I said under my breath. "I want to hurry too."

[163]

"Peter, come here!" called Mayka. "Where are you hiding?"

"I cannot concentrate. Why did you say what you did?" asked Sebastian.

"Because now I understand everything."

"You don't understand anything, my friend. And maybe you never will."

"Peter! You must come here at once. Do you hear me?" cried Mayka.

"Sebastian, the comet will strike in a few hours' time!"

"The asteroid."

"I mean the asteroid!"

"Don't talk now; it's a waste of time. Let us go."

We were about breast-high in water. It was pitch-black and very cold, and there was a smell of acid and alcohol. After a few moments I heard the sound of Eva's dynamo torch and the outlines of the big castle cellar began to appear, with the skeletons of the hospital beds. The surface of the water flickered with myriads of small eddies. From beyond the wall came the loud cries and twitterings of swallows.

"Oh, Peter! Peter!" cried Eva.

I heard a splashing noise and the torch went out. It was Eva plunging desperately toward me. I felt her cold, slippery hand on my head and my face.

"How good," she sobbed, "how good to have you with us."

"It's all right, don't cry." I tried to free myself from her trembling hands. "I'll never leave you again. Let me go, or you will choke me."

"No, I won't let you go. I am terribly scared. Peter, Peter, must we die?"

"I will save you, but give me a quarter of an hour."

"You won't disappear again?"

"I swear I won't."

I pushed her away as hard as I could and made for the wall behind which we had heard Fela scratching. Eva frantically pressed the button on her torch and a shaft of reddish light flickered across the wall and fell on me.

"Don't be afraid. I am not going away," I said, but she was already pushing her way toward me through water thick as oil. I pressed myself against the wall and began to examine its surface. Again Eva clutched my arms and then my neck with the desperation of someone drowning, and wailed monotonously in a strange, hoarse voice, pressing my neck with her hands. I twisted so that her hands parted, and slapped her face. She uttered a piercing shriek, holding her cheek, and immediately became quiet. I felt with my fingers along the uneven surface of the wall and soon found a crack, or hollow, filled with crumbling mortar.

"Shine the light here," I ordered. Whimpering, she began to operate her torch and I could clearly see the face of the wall before me. It looked as if it had been built much later than the other walls. With my fingers I picked out as much mortar as I could from the hollow between the bricks, then I felt for the detonators in the breast pocket of my shirt where they were above the water level and so had kept dry. As I carefully straightened the ends of the leads, I heard a whine on the other side of the wall.

"Keep away, Fela!" I shouted. "Get as far away from the wall as you can!" I pushed the charge between the bricks. "Do you hear me, Fela? Run down the passage." The tigress moved away from the wall with a plaintive whine.

"Take hold of my hand," I said to Eva, "and keep the torch on all the time."

I pulled her behind the pile of iron bedsteads, as far as the cable would stretch. Eva did not speak any more, but her whole body shook, and her shaking imparted itself to me and I began to tremble too.

"Give me the torch," I said. She gave it to me obediently.

"It will be dark in a moment, but don't be afraid," I said, with as much composure as I could muster. "You had better hang on to my overalls."

She started to cry again, this time quietly and submissively.

[165]

She pushed one hand inside my spacesuit, and her hand felt like a wet and terrified little animal. I unscrewed the glass of the torch and it slipped from my fingers and fell into the filthy water.

"What has happened?" Eva's teeth chattered and she tightened her hold about my ribs.

"Nothing. I only splashed the water."

She did not believe me, and I felt that she was listening to my movements. I took the little glass bulb from the reflector very carefully, but my stiff fingers would not hold it.

"We'll use our head instead, if we can't have the light," I muttered to myself.

"What are you doing?" whispered Eva.

"I'm saying that it's going to be all right."

"But what are you *doing* there?"

"Stand still. You are making my hand unsteady."

"Oh Mama, Mama! Come and save us, Mama."

I felt as though my hair were standing on end, although it was wet and matted. With enormous effort I connected the cable to the batteries.

"Crouch behind me in the water, as low as you can duck," I said.

"What's the use? I am already half dead. I can't stand any more."

"Duck down quickly! We shall soon be free."

She moved back and sat down in the horrible water, and I got behind an iron bedstead. I was about to press the button of the dynamo when a sudden fear crossed my mind.

"Sebastian!" I shouted.

"Sebastian!" Eva called behind my back.

But there was no answer.

"He stayed behind," I whispered.

"Where? I saw him."

"When?"

"Just a little while ago, when I shone the torch. He was sitting on a top bunk."

"Sebastian!" I called still louder. There was silence for a while, except for the swallows, who had nests behind the wall.

We heard a clanging sound. "I'm here. What do you want?" We recognized Sebastian's voice.

"Take shelter behind the beds. In the water—as low as you can."

"Damnation! My head is swimming."

"Don't waste time." I repeated his favorite admonition. "Ready?"

He dropped into the water with a splash and blundered about for a while, rattling the beds, and then he was quiet.

"Are you ready?" I asked.

"Ready," he replied indistinctly.

I pressed the dynamo button. It creaked and I pressed harder and harder, until the grinding of the mechanism became a penetrating hum.

A dull force struck us heavily and in a second we were submerged in the water. I struck out with my legs and arms in an effort to lift myself clear of the water, but something spun me around and drove me under and beat my head against the brick floor. I thought that I would never get my breath again, but I managed to push with my feet against the flow and, lifting my whole body, emerged in the nick of time, spluttering and choking with my first breath. Beds were still tumbling from the tops of the piles. There seemed to be clamps on my ribs, but they were only Eva's arms.

"Are you all right?" I asked, still half-choking.

"I am not sure," she answered.

There was the sound of a train to the right of us, and there was something cold on my cheek, but the cold immediately lessened.

"Sebastian!" I called.

The water began to stir and he nearly knocked me down with his big heavy head.

"What was it?" he asked. "Was it the asteroid?"

"Have you forgotten which world we are in? I blew up the wall."

"With what?"

"With the effects man's detonators."

"Did you bring them from there?"

"Yes."

"That was wrong. I warned you."

"Did you want us to perish in this filthy water?"

"Nothing must be brought from there."

"Who told you so?"

"I feel that it is so," he said heavily . "I am afraid, my friend."

"Don't talk like that. Can't you feel the fresh air?"

But he was silent. He was definitely concerned.

"Let's go," I said.

We made our way in the direction from which the fresh air was coming. I saw that the level of the water was dropping and its sound was no longer ominous. Eva still clung to me. "It's because we have the stone," she said.

"So you didn't lose it?"

"I hid it inside my dress. I will never lose it."

Sebastian, who was in front of us, suddenly stumbled. "Damn!" he said. "Mind the bricks."

We climbed a heap of rubble and slithered down on the other side. The water was very shallow here. Sebastian began to sniff the air.

"What's the matter?" I asked.

"I can smell straw. Not the straw in the old mattresses, but fresh straw. It's as strong as the smell of tobacco."

We pressed on, feeling our way and keeping to the rough walls. Occasionally something that smelled like leaves clung to our feet. I picked a slimy scrap out of the shallow water and could just make out that it was part of a patient's bedside chart. The temperature graph climbed in a zigzag and broke suddenly near the margin.

"I can see your back now," Eva said.

"We are wading out of our slough of despond," I said.

"There used to be a military hospital in this castle," said Sebastian. "They thought nothing of bombing military hospitals."

"Where does this light come from?" I asked. I felt grass or moss underfoot. Swallows were calling shrilly over our heads and their voices came to us, not through the wall, but directly, as if we were walking along the nave of a big church with swallows' nests in its roof.

Sebastian stopped and took a deep, hoarse breath and shook himself hard, splashing water in all directions. "We are free," he said quietly.

"But when will this passage come to an end?" I asked.

He was silent for a while, scratching his ear.

"It has come to an end. Look behind you. Day is breaking."

I looked back. There was a sky of an intense willow green, and an aqueous redness was pouring upward from behind the horizon. We could see one another, but we could not perfectly distinguish one another's features. A cool, faint light lay upon our backs and arms. Never before had I been awake at such an early hour, and I gazed with some awe at this morning twilight which was like the light when there is an eclipse of the sun.

The swallows continued to circle over our heads, startled and thrilled by the dawn-burst. I could see well enough now to follow their flight under the green-blue sky.

"It rained in the night," said Sebastian slowly, "that's why the cellars were flooded."

"No, it was Retep," said Eva, and bit her tongue, looking at me with terror. "We must get away as fast as we can."

"To the town?" I asked.

"Yes. He could no longer harm us there."

She crouched suddenly, and I saw something flickering on the ground like a bird with a broken wing. It was her miraculous stone, the keepsake that her mother had brought from the Southern Seas.

"There is the town." She pointed to a gap in the wall.

Something rustled in the nearby bushes and an object that looked like a large boulder or bundle came hurtling at us and stopped in front of Sebastian. A big tongue emerged from this object and started rapturously licking Sebastian's nose. The Investigator Dog raised a paw in self-defense and backed away awkwardly.

"Go away, Fela. Beat it!"

But the tigress could not contain her joy. She circled around Sebastian, yelping and rubbing her head against his side, and snatching at his stub tail with her toothless gums. Sebastian wiped his black lips and said disgustedly: "That's carrying friendship too far."

I touched Fela's shabby wet back and asked: "Do you know the way to the town?"

She dropped onto her front paws and nodded her poor old head.

"Then lead us," I said.

She ran joyfully ahead of us and then began to whimper and draw up her hind leg, which must recently have been hurt. Limping awkwardly, she kept looking back to see if we were following. As soon as we passed the orchard we took the sandy road, pitted by the raindrops that had fallen during the night.

"Walk on the grass," said Sebastian, "don't leave footprints."

"Retep went back home," said Eva, jumping a deep rut, "he suffers from difficulty in breathing in the morning and mustn't go out."

I felt a faint warmth on my back. It was the rising sun, driving the last of the darkness from the ravine-like valley which, in cross section, was not at all like the letter V, but was like a capital L. We were walking at the base of the L, along a wide slope ridged with furrows and scattered with clumps of hawthorn and wild pear or cherry trees. From the far edge of this slope came the slow tolling of a bell for angelus. Partridges flew up from under our feet and sought cover among thistles covered with spiky balls. High above our heads an invisible bird twittered furiously. It could have been a lark, although I am not sure whether larks still sing in the early autumn, for some trees were undoubtedly turning color, and red and brown leaves lay curled in the furrows alongside the road—the sign of the premature end of summer or the beginning of autumn. We passed the hamlet by the railway balt, hidden by a veil of smoke from a train that had just passed through. We crossed the railway line and stood on the top of a hill that was littered with stones. From below came the deep murmur of the river bordered with alder bushes, while beyond the

[170]

river, at the end of the valley, lay the town with its stone buildings. The town spread over seven hills, like Rome, and in the clear
air we could distinctly see towers of churches, domes of syna-
gogues, and minarets of mosques. I exaggerate about the mosques
because there was only one, which stood modestly apart, almost
on the outskirts of the town. Just at that moment the bells of all
the Roman Catholic and Orthodox churches began to toll, one
after the other. We stood, with our hearts bursting with emotion,
looking at this town, not at all romantic but very ordinary and
somehow familiar, perhaps because of memories of past holidays
or association with some historic story, or just from some of my
father's reminiscences.

Eva cupped her hands about her mouth and shouted at the
clear sky:

"I am free!"

We listened to the echoes which lingered for some time on the
other side of the river in a big grove of oaks.

"We are free!"

But suddenly she took her hands from her mouth, and we
followed her gaze. In the midst of a crowd of red stones which
someone at some time had broken up into pieces, stood Retep, in
knickerbockers, holding a gun. Chippy stood beside him, rubbing
his dirty beak against the edge of a stone.

"You will never be free," said Retep in a weary voice. "There
is no way of escape from this place."

"I want to get to the town. I cannot bear it any longer," said
Eva, bursting into tears.

Sebastian moved to her side, trembling throughout his great
body, and baring his teeth. Retep took several steps toward us,
and the marks of his sweating fingers showed on the lock of the
gun.

"She is ill," he said quietly. "She is mad. A poor, demented
girl. She only imagines that her father is an astronomer who
studies the sun's corona. Let us go home, Eva. Mama had a
sleepless night and everybody is looking for you."

"Don't believe what he says!" cried Eva. "He is lying. I'll never
go back!"

[171]

Fela sat apart from us, scratching and biting her fleas and pretending not to know us.

"Don't let him put it over on you, friend," growled Sebastian. "I will explain it all to you later."

Retep came still closer, hesitantly, and touched the girl's shoulder, saying sternly, without looking at us:

"Don't make a fool of yourself in front of strangers. Our affairs are no one else's business. Let us go home and not waste any more time."

A big hawk was circling over our heads without moving its wings, watching us and seeming to be waiting for something.

"You are wet through, your lips are blue with cold. Dear Eva, what are you doing?"

She jerked away from him in irritation and Sebastian growled.

"You wanted to kill us during the night," I said.

He looked at me as if he had only just noticed me. The old man Konstanty was coming up from below us, still carrying his now useless stable lantern, and smiling his kind smile under his white whiskers.

"I wanted to kill you?" Retep's eyes were red from lack of sleep. "The holiday season is over now. You had better go home. There's nothing here for you."

"Look out!" growled Sebastian. "His gun is cocked."

"Are you scared?" Retep sneered. "Or would you rather fight? I owe you an opportunity to get your revenge."

Chippy, behind us, tore the turf with his claws as if limbering up for the fray.

"I will take my opportunity," I said, and rolled up my sleeves.

"Hold it, Konstanty!" Retep threw the gun at him. "You are in a funny sort of getup for boxing. What is it? A brownie's outfit?"

It was only then that I realized that I was wearing that stupid spacesuit. Chippy hiccuped and started to sing: "The wolf was out to kill and sup/Until the pigeon ate him up—You won't scare me with your black pants."

"Keep him at arm's length and wait your chance to hit him," muttered Sebastian. "Do you remember what I taught you?"

"Sebastian, Eva, run!" I said. "I'll hold him back."

"No, we will not leave you alone with him. We will all resist him together or all three run away together," whispered Eva. "Tell me again that you like me."

"Can we start?" asked Retep.

A big stork alighted in the meadow below, and jerking its head paced watchfully in the tall grass.

"We can start." I said this with my mind elsewhere, trying to catch at something—I do not know what—that eluded me.

"I am keeping my fingers crossed for you," said Eva. "Oh heavens, where is my stone? . . . I've got it! Thank you Mama. If we come out of this alive I swear that I will never tell a lie again."

Somewhere behind us I heard the lurching clatter of a train and then, on the other side of the river, a penetrating shriek. But it was only the echo of the piercing whistle of one of those old-fashioned engines with a tall funnel.

"What a to-do!" Konstanty beamed in anticipation of the fight.

"Just wait until he comes at you," said Sebastian, out of the corner of his mouth.

The echo of the engine whistle floated over the river and beat backward and forward along the valley in the direction of the town, until it died away. Retep furtively crossed himself, or maybe he was only wiping away a hair or a lash that was getting in his eye.

We found a smooth piece of ground among the boulders glittering with specks of quartz.

I thought that Retep was trying to say something. I could see his half-open mouth and the tip of his tongue struggling to form a syllable. "Do you want to say anything?" I asked.

He swallowed as though his throat was dry. "You're never going to trouble me again," he said. "I am glad about that."

"But it's you who come to *me* in the night."

"Watch out, brother!" he said with an unpleasant smile, and then he retreated and began to dance on his toes with his knees flexed.

"Cock-a-doo . . ." Chippy started to shout a war cry but broke into a loud hiccup in the middle, as he ruffled his shabby feathers and flapped his miserable wings.

Retep fixed his eyes on mine, looking at me with such

[173]

intensity that I felt my eyelids burn, and began to blink. Taking advantage of this moment he came at me and landed a right-hand punch to the head near my ear.

He did not hit me hard, but it hurt, and the sting of the blow cleared my wits. I hit him in the pit of his stomach and was surprised that he made no attempt to protect himself with his elbow. He jumped back rather tardily, relaxing his muscles. Then I went for him, intending to deliver a few hard punches as fast as I could, but we clinched somewhat awkwardly in a short flurry of infighting.

"You will forget everything," I heard him say in a hoarse voice. "This is the only way out."

I wanted to say something in reply, but he butted me with his head. The blow landed between my eyes and I felt as if a whole syphon of soda water had spurted into my nose. I raised my hand to the spot, and at the same moment he fetched me a hard blow under the ribs.

"Cock-a-doodle-doo!" Chippy succeeded with his crow for the first time.

I stepped back, but Retep grabbed me by my spacesuit. The metal fastening clicked, and before I had time to protest that it was against the rules he was tearing the plastic and feeling for my throat, his mouth twisted into a stiff, lifeless sort of smile. I tried to push him away and free myself from his weight. I shoved against his chest, but he pulled me with him and, as our feet caught in the grasses between the stones we both rolled down the slope.

The old man was laughing with pleasure. "This is real sport," he said, "this is something worth watching!"

Retep pressed his weight upon me heavily and started to gather up the collar of my suit in his fist, so that I gasped for air. The loud thumping that I heard must have been my own heart beating. Somewhere, as if far away, Eva cried out desperately. Sebastian barked in a deep voice, like a bloodhound, the thin drunkard's voice still shrieked "Cock-a-doodle-doo," and beyond all these sounds the river rumbled like a huge flood.

I drew my legs up and kicked with all the strength I had, driving Retep off me so that he staggered and fell. He got up heavily, propping himself with his arms on the sharp edges of the granite rock, and looked at me with strangely protruding eyes that seemed unable to sink back into their sockets.

"Take a stone, master! Just take a stone!" called Konstanty.

Retep started to feel hurriedly over the surface of the rock, but before he could find anything I fell upon him with all the force of my body. He groaned and tried to protect himself with his knees, but I already had a grip on his throat. There was an ant running on his hair. Something dripped from me upon my hands, and Retep looked at me with his blue eyes staring like a pair of peeled pigeon's eggs, absolutely glassy and empty.

"Let go, let go!" Chippy pecked at my back in a haphazard sort of way. "Let go, you're killing a human being."

So I let go. I got up slowly from the ground, keeping my foot on Retep's arm as he lay there. Eva covered her face and her shoulders shivered convulsively. Sebastian patted her helplessly with his big, clumsy paw and the old man roared with laughter, wiping the tears from his face with the back of his hand.

"What a rough-and-tumble for you! These young ones are really good for a bit of fun."

Eva started to run frantically toward the river, flying along the hillside like a small piece of paper carried by the wind. A few birds scattered before her and then returned to their nests. Sebastian gave chase, running like a charging rhinoceros and growling like distant thunder. It was a moment in which everything seemed utterly given up to fear and foreboding.

I caught up with Sebastian and Eva by the riverbank, as they ran along the steep slope toward the water filled with reflections of sky and clouds.

"Let us keep together," I said, "it may be deep."

"You are right," said Sebastian, recovering his wits, "the river has overflowed its banks here."

I wanted to give Eva my hand, but she pushed me away violently. "I hate you!" she hissed.

The water carried us with it and we held on to Sebastian, who paddled valiantly to keep us all afloat.

"Wait, you rascals," Konstanty called to us from the bushes. "Where the devil are you going? You haven't told me where our Vincent lives now."

"The good people hanged your Vincent long ago," Sebastian shouted.

We drifted into midstream, where big dragonflies dipped and skimmed on the smooth surface of the water.

"How could it be so?" Konstanty whimpered, wandering in the alder grove, his voice getting fainter and fainter as the distance grew greater between us. "It's not that he didn't mean well. He acted out of kindness of heart."

Sebastian puffed and blew and paddled even faster, with panic in his dark eyes. We were already near the opposite bank, but we tried to stand up too soon and found ourselves submerged in deep water. I swallowed quite a pint of it. At last I caught some overhanging branches and, breathing heavily, we crawled out onto a sun-warmed meadow, with birds hopping about on their thin legs.

"The day is already far advanced," said Sebastian. I noticed with surprise that he deliberately avoided my eyes. "Let us get on, we still have a long way to go."

A moan or cry came from the opposite bank, and Eva instantly sat down in the tall grass that country folk call Our Lady's Tears. We heard branches cracking.

"Eva!" called Retep. "Dear Eva, don't go away. Let us play our game of hoop-la and gather honey from the bees and in the evening count the falling stars."

Eva rose from the ground in a strange panic and rushed hither and thither like someone trying to get out of a locked room.

"Eva, Eva! You will perish there without us."

There was a heavy splash and a commotion among the overhanging bushes.

"Help!" we heard Retep choking and sputtering. "Eva, give me your hand."

"He is drowning," cried Eva, turning back to the river brink. We ran after her and found her struggling helplessly, bogged down in greasy black mud.

"Help me, don't just stand there!"

The alder bushes hung motionless as the water ran smoothly toward the town, and a few shreds of white cobweb, or maybe of autumn gossamer, drifted in the hot mint-scented air.

"He is drowned and lost forever," Eva started to sob.

"He must have got out onto the bank again," said Sebastian in a low voice.

"He has drowned, I know it."

"Nobody knows anything until the end of his life."

"We must go back," she said hesitantly.

"To the manor?" I asked.

"No, home. You'll never forget his name—do you know why?"

"Yes," I said.

"You were strangling him so dreadfully."

"Let's not waste time," we heard Sebastian's usual reminder. "We have quite a slice of the journey still ahead of us."

"Wait a little longer," said Eva.

"Why?"

"I don't know myself—but wait."

We stood there without speaking for a long while. I raised my head slightly and saw, very high in the hot sky, a blue-and white striped balloon that hung over the ravine-like valley, or valley-like ravine, spying upon a lonely hawk, the marshy riverside fields, the briskly flowing river, and on us, each of us plunged deep in his own thoughts. There was nothing specially odd about the balloon. The balloonists must have been surveyors or map makers, measuring the earth scorched by the hot sun of the summer's end.

Sebastian gave Eva a gentle push and she started forward obediently. We reached the road, which was paved with rough stones, and as if moved by the same urge we all three turned to look at the place we were leaving behind, and then walked on with our faces toward the sun.

"I have lost my stone," Eva said in a low voice.

Sebastian sighed. "Where did you lose it?" he asked.

[177]

"It must have been on the other side of the river."

"Shall we go back?" he asked uncertainly.

"It doesn't matter any more."

"It doesn't matter *now*." Sebastian sighed again and turned his dark eyes upon me. "Didn't I tell you that you must not bring anything here from that other place?"

"But we were saved because of it."

He did not answer, and walked behind Eva, sniffing with adoration the stones that her feet had trod. I thought that perhaps he never had been an English lord or a famous explorer, but that in his previous incarnation he could have been a small, very ambitious and bad-tempered Pekinese, and that in his next incarnation he would simply be a gay sort of mongrel from a holiday resort—a bit of a scrounger, a bit of a buffoon, but on the whole a good-natured ruffian.

The road was rather tortuous, with a thick oak wood dropping steeply to it on one side. From time to time we passed a solitary cottage, its garden overgrown with weeds and the bluish panes of its small windows looking at us like eyes. We overtook big carts carrying corn to the mill, rattling noisily over the stones. To our left, on the other side of the river, boggy fields stretched along our way, with farmhouses under thatched roofs buried in vegetation, and great flocks of birds feeding by the waterside. I thought, although I may have imagined it, that Sebastian was constantly whispering in Eva's ear. She walked without turning her head, her full lips tightly compressed and her hands folded on her breast as though she was praying.

Our road was eventually joined by a smaller road, a dusty track that led eastward. A cross stood at the junction, decorated with faded flowers, and some boys sat at its foot, on the ground packed down hard as concrete, tracing lines with a stick.

"Are you going to the church fair, too?" one of them asked.

"No, we are going to visit relations," I said.

"My feet are sore from the stones," said Eva.

"Then we will rest for a while." I suggested that we should sit on a stone with cracks still filled with rainwater. Eva stretched out her dusty legs and I noticed for the first time that she had lost her white shoes.

"Have you got your inoculation certificates?" asked the same boy.

"What for?"

"You have to be inoculated because of the epidemic. They check on you there at the tollgate."

"Have you been inoculated?"

"No. That's why they didn't let us into the fair."

"What kind of epidemic is it?"

"How should we know? Just an epidemic."

"What are you doing here?"

"Playing shovelboard."

They had traced a deep line with a stick across the path, with a triangle midway along it, the line itself forming the base of the triangle. In this triangle they had placed a small pile of copper coins, head up. Then they moved back about five yards along the path and drew another line across it. From behind this line they began to throw into the triangle with the coins small lead discs, which they called *mauras*. The player whose *maura* finished up nearest the triangle had the next move. He tried to hit and scatter the pile of coppers by dropping the *maura* from above. The coins that scattered tails up were the prize. If no coins reversed, it was the turn of the next player, that is, the player whose *maura* fell next nearest to the triangle. When the bank ran out, they put a fresh pile of coins in the triangle and started again.

It was very quiet here. The river, which was now some distance away, branched into several arms. The heat haze quivered above the sandy road. We could hear a bumblebee humming anxiously as it flew backwards and forwards on the trail of a scent, the sound of the *mauras*, and the quiet oaths of the players.

The town was very near. Gray terraces of houses towered up

into the lowest clouds, swallowing up one of the arms of the river in a maze of black culverts and rickety little bridges.

"Shall we go on now?" asked Sebastian, putting his head on Eva's knee. "Have you rested enough?"

But she was looking at the crucifix with the rusted Christ.

"There is no need to hurry now," I said, licking the salt sweat from my upper lip, "this is one of the last hot days before the autumn comes, and then rain and snow and everlasting bad weather."

"But aren't you in a hurry to get back to the film?"

"I don't feel like going back now. Haven't you ever dreamed of something pleasant and wanted the dream to last as long as possible?"

"But this is not a dream. I am always afraid that something unpleasant may happen. We had better get on."

"But the town is closed because of the epidemic."

"We could try following the riverbank into town."

"Sebastian, why must we go into town? We could go back home from anywhere."

"We can't now. I will explain to you later."

"You are plotting something, Sebastian. Look me straight in the eye."

He blinked his eyes with their gray but very long eyelashes, and tried to meet my gaze.

"Please, my friend, let us go now."

The shovelboard players began to squabble and swear. The least successful of them was whimpering for sympathy.

"Very well then, let us go," I said.

We went down to the river and the weed-grown shallows and headed for the town. The dusty bushes were sparse here, but they provided some cover. Eva stumbled now and then on submerged stones. I offered my hand to help her, and she pressed it with her little hand, which was now warm again and pulsing with life.

"It isn't true," she whispered.

"What isn't true?"

"That my mother came from the islands in the South Seas, and that my father is studying the sun's corona."

Sebastian, who had been carried away by the current, swam nearer so that he could hear what we were saying.

"They brought me up," she whispered still more quietly.

"They? Who are they?"

"Well, they—" She turned her head for a moment in the direction of the valley, shrouded now in light mist.

"Do you want to go back?" I asked.

"No!" she cried, and burst into tears, hiding her face in her dark hair.

Sebastian looked with desperation, now at me and now at her, except that once or twice he looked down at the fat perch playing fearlessly in the shallow water.

We stole into the town without being stopped by anyone, and climbed up the near bank by a big baroque church, where the fair was being held. A multitude of market stalls were arranged there, piled with washtubs, buckets, wooden spoons and ladles, stacks of brooms, strings of garlic, rakes and scythes, cartwheels, new yellow harness, spinning wheels, rolls of rough cloth, sheepskin coats, herbs for curing every kind of ill, dried mushrooms, new honey, cracknel biscuits, *buza* (a white drink made with mare's milk), potato turnovers, large heart-shaped cakes, kaleidoscopes, butterflies on wooden wheels, popguns, pictures—all with the same landscape of brimming rivers and birch trees in a sunset, Kelim rugs with tiny blue and black checkered patterns, and many other curious objects, all smelling of pinewood and paint and human sweat.

People were in crowds around the stalls, among them Jews with a curl hanging beside each cheek, Orthodox priests in russset cassocks, men with thin moustaches and embroidered skullcaps, and boys dressed in white for their first communion. I think that I even saw a Turk in a red fez, but I am not sure, because there was such a crowd and the noise was so confused—

cries of stallkeepers, bursts of laughter, pipe music. Everyone looked happy and nobody pushed or swore. We went farther along a narrow street of very old houses until we came to a lopsided little square, or rather a meeting place of several roads, where horse-drawn cabs went by with the drivers cracking their whips, and people strolled in their holiday clothes, besieged by shopkeepers in their small booths along the walls. I saw, through the window of a café, boys eating unusual-looking ices and eyeing the schoolgirls who passed by in their long dresses, under the surveillance of nuns. News vendors called the names of their papers in several languages, and above our heads electric signs flashed advertising the newly arrived talkie films. Here too the people all smiled and treated each other politely. I know that this sounds unlikely, and that somebody might want to suggest that my description of it all is only symbolic, but the town really looked like that. My father often tells me about his childhood, and the town where he lived was almost exactly like this one.

"Well, friend," said Sebastian suddenly, "thank you for all that you have done for us." He licked my ear with his warm tongue and added "Good luck," in English. I could see the skin twitching nervously over his long back, although there were no flies or mosquitoes about.

"Why are you saying good-bye, Sebastian?"

He turned his eyes away and fixed them as dogs do when they catch sight of another dog.

"Because you must go back, my dear fellow."

"What about Eva?"

"She cannot."

"Why can't she?"

"Because she can't."

"What about you?"

"I am staying here."

"Sebastian, I don't understand at all."

He looked at me with cold eyes. "You'll understand one day. I may call on you at your place some time. Go on now, don't waste time."

"What if I don't want to?"

He stood on his hind legs and pressed me against the wall.

Some passersby made friendly remarks about us to each other. It was obvious that they liked children and handsome dogs.

"You have a reason for going back," Sebastian said.

"How do you know that I have?"

"I know all your secrets. You have been invited to a birthday party today."

"Let me go, Sebastian!"

"No, I won't let you go. Everything went wrong because of you. You are not to be trusted."

He brought his eyes closer and closer to mine, until I could see scarcely anything but his eyeballs, empty like the bottoms of dark tumblers. He was sending me on the long journey back.

"Everything here is unreal, my friend. You are going now to the airport. The spring rain is falling there. You will meet your friends and watch jet planes landing, as big as houses. In the evening you will watch a film on television about Zorro, the hero of children the world over, and at night you will dream about something that never was and never will be, and the next morning you will have forgotten everything and will wake up to the hum of the city and the sound of a piano playing through the wall."

"Nobody plays the piano in our place."

"Don't ever come back here to find us. Remember that. There is no need, and it is not worth it." Sebastian's voice dropped as he spoke, as if he were trying to lull me to sleep.

But I looked intently over his head for glimpses of the strange street. I thought that I could dimly see Eva's dress, like a white patch, but the patch dissolved in the sunlight and disappeared in the leisurely street traffic. I began to strain my eyes to see and Sebastian saw what I was doing and suddenly pushed me roughly so that my head hit the wall. Then he ran into the midst of the passersby, who moved out of his path. He threaded his way between the horse cabs, hid behind a billboard, and finally disappeared into a hedge.

I tried to chase him, running along narrow streets and looking inside porches that smelled of vegetables and dampness, rushing into shops and awakening profuse janglings of bells as I entered, and finally finding myself in the little lopsided square.

The cabs were hurrying by as before, the electric bulbs in the signs blinked, the newspaper sellers called out the names of strange newspapers, and a fat disabled man was playing a concertina. A chicken that a passerby carried by the legs looked at me with the white of its dead eye, just like Chippy. But I am sure that Chippy was alive and well, for it is a known thing that talebearers live longest.

The passersby were still pleasant and polite, but I felt the old fear slowly gripping me—a kind of panic, a dreadful feeling of loneliness and of not belonging to my surroundings. It was this fear that made me wish desperately to be home again, to see my father who does nothing, and Miss Sophie with her battle against overweight, to read her diary, to watch a horror play on television and wait for the comet that was heading for the earth like a missile.

What would I do if I had a magic wand and a cap of darkness to make me invisible? I would like to go straight to Mayka. I feel a bit shy with her, especially as I can do no more than just sit and look at her when I am with her. So I would go unseen to her room and stay there as long as I wanted to. I would look at her face, with its dignified expression, and at her slender shoulders and her rather short fingers—for that is what they are, though it does not matter. And I would know all her secrets—I am not ashamed of this, because all her secrets are beautiful.

But when I think about it, I begin to realize that the best thing of all would be to visit her without being invisible, if she invited me simply because she cared, for with magic I would do everything without the other person's wish, and everything would be gained by force, and shallow. Without real partners in life I would feel terribly lonely, wandering among people, using magic powers that gave no satisfaction.

It is just as well that magic wands and caps of darkness do not exist.

"Has the third section separated, Johnny?" Brush tugged my arm. "Have you gone into orbit?"

"Yes, I am orbiting a bit," I answered, rather indistinctly.

"We've been looking for you all over the airfield."

"But why? What has happened?"

"We are filming, Johnny. The Spitter feels inspired, and you just wander off somewhere!"

"Such a fuss we've had," said Mayka, "the Boss's wife, Sybill, would not come onto the set. Everybody begged her on bended knees, but I managed to persuade her in the end."

"Now everything's fine," said Brush, "everybody is on his toes. If only the sun would come out . . . Who has messed up your spacesuit, Johnny?"

"I don't know. It just tore by itself."

"Dresser! Where is the dresser?" Brush began to yell, "Bring a needle and thread, and come quickly!"

An old lady came running with her mouth full of pins and started to stitch up the splits, her fingers trembling with haste.

"J'aime," said Mayka.

"What did you say?"

"Nothing. I'm trying to memorize. J'aime, tu aimes, il aime."

"Stop! What are you doing? Stop!" shouted Baldy.

"Do I have to stop what I am doing?" asked the old lady, panic-stricken.

"Yes. What are you fiddling about there?"

"I'm sewing up the splits in his suit."

"Merciful heavens! I'll slaughter the lot of you. I can't stand it any longer!" The director beat at his temples with his fists. "Who told you to sew them up?"

"Mr. Brush. It was Mr. Brush who told me."

"Sir, the boy has ruined the suit completely," said Duckbill, smiling and competent-looking but timid underneath.

"The whole point is that he *ought* to be wearing a shabby spacesuit. The child has more sense than any of the rest of you!"

"Take your paraphernalia and beat it," said Brush, quite unabashed, giving the dresser a push.

"Sir! Sir!" called Duckbill. "The sun is coming out! As soon as that bit of cloud moves away!" He pointed at a cloud that covered half the sky.

"We're going to start shooting. Take up your positions!"

"Lights! Generator!" The plumbers sprang into action.

Duckbill came running, dressed in suede and nylon like a real Hollywood director. "Form a line, children! Be quick! You are at the end, remember," he said, holding me by the arm.

"Can I form a pair with him?" asked Mayka.

"You may. But don't talk too much."

She took my hand and a strand of her golden hair broke loose and lifted slightly in the wind.

"Retep—"she said, pressing my hand for emphasis, "did you know that the name is made up of the letters in your name?"

"Be quiet. No more talking," called Duckbill.

Mayka smiled at me, and at that moment I no longer had any regrets, either about leaving that silly Eva, or Sebastian—pretending to be a lord—or about those idiotic expeditions without purpose. Besides, my Mayka would soon grow up into a woman, and one had only to look at her to be pleased at the thought.

Sybill, in the role of our leader, appeared in the van doorway and threw off the sheepskin coat—disclosing herself encased in a tight, almost transparent costume—and came over to join us, followed by make-up girls and dressers, who were constantly adjusting something about her clothes and person.

When she had taken up her position at the head of our procession, the lights flashed and everybody began to run about like mad, while the camera rolled forward and back again "to stretch its legs." Then in the middle of all this stir the order came: "Cut!"

The "bit of cloud" had not only cleared away from the sun, but it had increased still more and become a huge stormcloud.

The cameraman unscrewed the top of his flask and began to eat a sandwich. They brought Sybill a pork chop the size of a discus at the Olympic Games from the airport restaurant, and again everything came to a standstill.

Mayka and I hid under a piece of tarpaulin, for it was hailing now. We held each other's hand and Mayka opened her mouth several times to say something and then stopped. So I began to play with her fingers, which made her smile, and we were very happy.

They summoned us to action stations several more times, but each time the cloud changed its mind and covered the sun again.

At last, toward lunchtime when everyone had lost hope and was dozing in corners, and even the electricians had begun to roll up the cables, the clouds disappeared when no one was looking and the sun shone out in a clear sky.

Pandemonium broke out immediately. Everybody started to shout at once, snatching various pieces of apparatus from one another's hands. They took the covers from the camera and tried to switch on the lights, but at that very moment they all failed. They formed the sleepy children into a procession. Sybill ran up as fast as her dress would allow her. Duckbill walked about among us, reminding us of the parts we had to play.

"Keep smiling, troops! Don't act stiff. You are setting out on a long and marvelous journey! You are going to be the first children to go out into the mysterious universe."

"We know the book very well, sir," said Dorian. "It's a set book in the school syllabus. You had better watch your lights."

"We're off at last." The scriptwriter, who hated children, rubbed his hands together with pleasure. "May the first day's shooting bring us luck!" And he smiled amiably at Pale Niko, who looked surprised at the thought that luck could have any place in it all.

"Silence! Keep quiet everybody!" shouted Duckbill.

"Is everybody set?" The director began to purse his lips and sat down between the legs of the camera.

Mayka released my hand.

"Retep," she said, "I have something to tell you."

My heart started to beat violently, but I replied with feigned indifference:

"I'm listening. What is it?"

"You know, I have to call off the birthday party. Dorian has invited me to a tea party to celebrate the first day's shooting. It is the custom in film studios, and I couldn't refuse."

I felt as if night had enfolded me. Dim shadows waved and shouted. I had a distinct physical feeling that my blood was running down into my feet, and that I was sinking deeper and deeper into the concrete. I felt very cold.

I heard Mayka speak: "Why don't you say something?"

"Oh well, I understand, of course," I answered in an almost soundless voice.

"You are not cross?"

"No. Why should I be?"

"I knew that you were a darling!"

At this moment the director shouted in a terrible voice:
"Camera!"

Somebody clapped the boards in front of the camera, and to the sound of the camera running, we set off toward the rocket, which looked rather shabby after its battering from the weather.

Duckbill urged us on: "Hurry up, hurry up! Don't waste film!"

As we approached the steps leading up to the rocket entrance, and as Sybill started to mount them, wriggling her almost bare hips, and a smile of satisfaction blossomed on the director's disgruntled face, a man broke from the crowd of spectators over by the hangar and began to run toward the rocket. Members of the film unit tried to bar his way and seize him but he dodged them and, leaping like a hare, raced over to us and seized me by the ear.

"Ow!" I cried, terrified.

"Cut! Cut!" shouted the director. "The fool has spoiled the shot! Who is he?"

He was my father.

"Off home with you!" he said in a dreadful voice.

"I can't. I must stay until they have finished shooting."

"I'll finish it for you at home! Off you go. No arguing!"

I had no choice, and allowed myself to be led, still by the ear.

Duckbill ran up. "What are you doing? We are making a film!"

"——your film!" My father uttered a few almost inarticulate syllables.

Everybody stood horror-stricken, and no one dared to interfere. I had never seen my father in such a state. Mr. Hare stood by the hangar, holding the dog on a lead. Hare looked at us with irony and the dog with indifference.

"Sebastian, don't pretend, I know it's you," I said. But he only yawned.

My father dragged me into a taxi, and the thought of this extra expense upset me still more.

"Playing truant all this time!" said my father grimly, as the taxi set off. "And I was foolish enough to think that my children would be different."

"I wanted to help you by earning some money."

"The best way you can help me is by getting through your schooling."

"But you are out of work, and I can't sleep at night because of it."

My father began to whisper to himself, or maybe it was just that his mouth was trembling. When we arrived, the crippled man was sitting under the acacia tree, watching the few signs of life in our street. Buffalo was trying to extort a buttered roll from a little girl, while his father despondently tidied up the inside of his car (which had been disorganized by children).

We entered our apartment in silence. Miss Sophie—the sneak—pretended not to see me and hid in her room.

They were showing a milk-bottling process on television. It must have been running for some time, because no one was watching. Cecilia was sitting bolt upright and my mother was rearranging some small objects.

"Have you brought him home?" she asked.

"I have," said my father gloomily. "Tomorrow I shall take him to school myself."

For a while nobody spoke. I opened the cupboard and took out the shell.

"I did earn some money," I said, "it's the truth."

"Tomorrow I will take the money back to them, together with

this one-piece goblin outfit from the department store."

My mother patted me as she passed. "It's one misfortune after another," she said quietly. "Did you know that Cecilia is not going to America?"

"Why not?" I asked, surprised.

"She had a telegram. The university has gone bankrupt."

"How can a university go bankrupt?"

"It was a private one, maintained by private funds."

"So it went bankrupt for good?"

"Completely. They even asked for the air tickets to be returned to them."

I could think of nothing to say. So we listened to the man who was enthusiastically describing the process of milk-bottling. But something was cutting across the sound of his voice. I went to the window. A band of itinerant musicians was playing in our street—by the monument to the educationalist—the old hit song "Don't Care About Me," which was popular when I was quite small.

"Perhaps the comet is going to hit us," I said.

"No fear," said my father, "it missed us quite a while—maybe three hours—ago, and by a good margin. They gave the news just before this program."

Cecilia's cheeks were flushed. She sat motionless, but her eyes began to blaze and spark.

"I'll show them!" she cried, and by a rather strange coincidence there was an immediate flash of lightning that seemed to strike somewhere nearby. My mother rushed to disconnect the television set.

"They'll get to know who I am, you'll see. I shall fly to America on my broom this very night and scare the wits out of them. I am not called the Monster for nothing." And she turned a terrifying look upon us. But it was the lightning that really scared us. It had already been hailing, it is true, and it could have been simply the first spring thunderstorm. But who was to know?

"Yes, it was really a mean trick," said my father with rather false sympathy, "a university is the last place that one would expect to behave like that." My father was obviously pleased, because nothing raises one's spirits so much as other people's misfortunes. And there is nothing wrong with that. My father was not really rejoicing, or feeling a wicked satisfaction, he was simply heartened and bolstered in his own self-confidence. He had realized now that everything is ruled by a fate that gives and takes away without justice or reason, and that it was useless to bear a grudge against others for what happened to one. He had also realized that he was not alone, but joined in a bond of brotherhood with millions of other unlucky people.

So he began to hum a tune and to commiserate even more with Cecilia. As if there was not enough misfortune, Miss Sophie's foot slipped on the scales in the bathroom and she twisted her ankle. It appeared that she had gained more than eight ounces. I looked out of the window at this thunderstorm that had been loosed by Cecilia, and could find no comfort. I was probably the most unfortunate of all. Eva had gone off with Sebastian and Mayka with that futile Dorian, my father had ruined my film career, the money I had earned would have to be paid back, and on top of everything, the clumsy, idiotic asteroid had missed—and the scientists had estimated that it would not be coming our way again for another two thousand years.

Why had everything come to such a sad and melancholy end? I was weary after all my adversities (and you must have had some fellow feeling for me in my worst moments). Nobody came out happily except, perhaps, our fat author and scriptwriter, who collects big prizes, and perhaps also, to some extent, the director, because he has been stirred by an ambition to do great things. But if you had a wife like Sybill, the world would appear to be as gloomy a place to you as it seemed to be for him—although I am not quite sure about that.

Let us go back again to the moment when the sun appeared unexpectedly from behind the clouds while everybody was dozing in corners, except for the electricians, who had begun to wind up the cables and dismantle the lights.

"The sun, sir!" shouted Duckbill, at the top of his voice. "Isn't that marvelous?"

"Lights! Generator!" The bearded cameraman gave the order, carefully screwing the top back on his Thermos flask.

Everything began to stir. The camera crew were running about and yelling, the director was spitting so much that the scriptwriter hid behind the big scriptbook. Even Sybill revived and moved at a trot in her plastic costume to take her place at the head of our procession.

"Attention, troops," Broom said, "put more life into it! The whole country will be watching you when this is shown in the cinemas."

"Don't forget that you are the first children to set off on an interplanetary journey, to investigate the mysteries of the cosmos," added Duckbill. "And remember to be quiet. No talking."

"I would like to walk at the rear with Retep," said Mayka.

"Yes, of course. That's a good idea. Only be quiet please."

Again the make-up girls ran along our ranks, dabbing at our faces with sponges, and the wardrobe girls adjusted our spacesuits, and again Sybill tucked her plump midriff into place under the transparent plastic, and Duckbill's yell resounded all over the airfield:

"Ready!"

Then Baldy shouted:

"Camera!"

At this signal we moved toward the rocket, which had been somewhat enlarged and restored.

Mayka stealthily took my hand, looking at me in a strange way, as if she wanted to stress that it was important to her that we should be filmed with our hands joined.

"Do you remember my birthday?" she whispered.

"Oh, yes. All the time."

Bubbles the kitten was clawing at somebody's spacesuit and darting sideways like a kid, but taking care to keep inside the frame of the picture. Everyone admired him, and Brush, somewhere behind us, said: "What an actor! He has a career in front of him."

Over the airfield could be heard the first lark of spring, and I felt that I was a real astronaut.

"I care a lot for you." Mayka's fingers tickled my hand. "You don't know how much I care for you."

"I was very anxious to meet you too."

"Is that true? Can you give me your word?"

"Yes, in capital letters, with an exclamation mark."

"I am so glad. This is going to be the most beautiful film the world has seen."

"Because you are in it."

"Because we are both in it."

I felt like leaping into the air and staying suspended above the airfield, calling out to the whole world, or at least to my town and Mr. Josef and Buffalo and Cecilia, to the director tormented by ambition, to our leading lady in her transparent suit, to the prizewinning scriptwriter, and to Miss Sophie who watches her weight. But I only sighed, and they all began to look at me.

Sybill was already mounting the steps to the rocket entrance, swinging her hips laboriously, the scriptwriter began to rub his hands together, and a smile of pleasure crept over the director's face, when somebody broke away from the crowd of spectators gathered by the hangar. The man caught up with our procession on the rocket steps and seized me roughly by the ear. I wanted to free myself, and jerked my head so violently that we all fell into the dark doorway.

"Cut!" shouted the director.

Duckbill ran up, pale with rage.

"Are you mad?" he shouted, catching my father by the lapels of his jacket. "To spoil a whole shot—two hundred feet of film— just like that! Who are you?"

"I am his father. He is playing truant from school."

"Father or not, we are making a film. You have ruined the work of a large number of people." Duckbill was still angry, but the information had shaken him a little.

"I don't care," said my father. "Peter, come home at once!"

Brush appeared. "Who's this barging in?" He looked at my father with his insomniac burglar eyes. My father began to lose some of his self-assurance.

"Gentlemen, it's a disgrace! The child hasn't been to school for a week."

"Now I see how much of an orphan you are, Johnny."

"You must have misunderstood me, sir," I said faintly.

"So that's what it was!" My father's face grew red again. "He pretended to be an orphan, did he, on top of everything else! Just wait until we get home."

The director came over at that point with the girl who clapped the boards and carried the script book running behind him.

"Shall we make a copy or not, sir?" she kept on asking monotonously.

"Copy of what?" asked the director absentmindedly.

"Well, all this footage. Because at the end some outsider got into the frame."

"It was Retep's father," said Brush in a slightly vindictive tone. "This is Johnny's father."

Baldy stood in front of my father and stared at him, pursing his lips. They stood like this for quite a while, for the director must have been making up his mind about whether to print or not. But my father, not used to such behavior, began to show signs of uneasiness. He looked down and shuffled his feet, and even sighed once or twice.

"I think that I have a certain right . . ." he said timidly, at last.

"Make a copy," said the director decisively. "We may find it interesting when we see the rushes."

Drops of sweat appeared on my father's forehead. He even began to smile inanely. And the director kept on pursing his lips, until we all began instinctively to purse our own lips—Duckbill, Brush, the children, Mayka, and I—and at last my father started to do the same, with the silly smile still on his face.

"This is Retep's father. He wants to break the contract," said Brush.

"Very well, I understand," said my father apologetically. "But I am concerned about his schoolwork."

"He acts well and he has talent. I need him," said Baldy.

"Yes, of course. But my wife—actually my wife doesn't like— or rather she has doubts—to be precise, she is worried . . ." and my father dried up, although he went on making mumbling noises.

"I'm pleased to have heard what you had to say," muttered the director, still deep in his own thoughts. "I'm pleased to have met you. Will you cooperate with us in a retake? Take up your positions, please, and stand by for shooting."

Still absentminded, he held out his hand to my father and went back to the camera. Brush slapped my father heavily on the back.

"Don't worry, old man. We'll find a tutor for Johnny. And now go back to your place in the crowd. You will run onto the scene only when the leading lady begins to climb the steps. *Compris?"*

Duckbill himself led my father—who was obviously scared—back to the hangar. When the camera started rolling he ran out too soon and hit Dorian quite unnecessarily. We repeated the shot several times, until at last the director decided that it was enough. But one could see that he was not satisfied. My father was sorry, because during these unsuccessful attempts he had already acquired a taste for acting.

"Can we do it once more?" he asked, following Baldy.

"No, that's enough. It's a waste of film."

"I will pay for it."

"The first shot was OK. That's enough."

Everyone started to disperse, but my father remained there alone, brooding silently over his fiasco.

"Why are you so downhearted?" I asked. "The first time it was very good."

"You don't mean that?"

"Why should I tell lies? It looked natural. It was an interesting piece of acting."

"Never mind," said my father, still pursing his lips. "Only don't tell your mother anything about it. There is no need to bother her."

"They pay good wages."

"They? Who?"

"The film people."

[195]

For the first time my father smiled a genuine smile, the way he used to do. "I've got a job. I've been accepted by the Meteorological Institute. It's something that interests me and nothing to do with those wretched computers that are always making adding mistakes. Shall we take a taxi? It's on me."

"I can pay part of it. But do you mind if I take somebody else too?"

"Not at all. Take all of them—the director, the cameraman, or whoever you like."

"It's just an actress—my colleague."

The taxi took us through the town. My father sat in front with the driver and did not even glance at the meter as it clicked away. Mayka and I sat in the back, furtively holding hands.

"You know, next term I will get myself transferred to your school," said Mayka.

"That would be marvelous."

"How nice it is that spring is already here!"

Her Great Dane sat beside us, holding his leash in his mouth. I may have been mistaken, but I thought that he winked at me.

Buffalo was crouched by the monument in the little square, guzzling something from a big box, and, almost without looking at me, he called out: "Grand stuff! They have given up saving, and now they are getting decent grub for me. I have no time now for games."

"Not even playing partisans?"

"No. Not even that."

My father looked at him with horror. It was lucky that we did not see Miss Sophie coming out from the entrance porch on extremely high heels and wearing a practically nonexistent skirt. She walked with a waddling movement, rather like the Boss's wife, and had chains and metal rings and pendants hanging from her waist, almost to her knees, because all this was the fashion. Even Ducky, who treated Bubbles as if he were a dog, was proud of a little metal disc pinned on her chest with the words "To hell with teachers" on it.

An elderly gentleman came out from behind a pillar. He was maybe a little older than my father, and he walked up to Miss

Sophie with a put-on, springy sort of step, and raised his hat and gave her a bouquet of flowers. She put her arm through his and they went off to town.

At home, Cecilia was packing suitcases and ordering my mother about. My mother gave me a long look. "Well, how is it?" she asked.

My father pursed his lips. "They are quite cultured people," he said. "I had a chat with the director. They are a hardworking lot, like everyone else. You cannot imagine the work that has to be put into even a few retakes."

"What refakes?"

"Not 'refakes'!—retakes. They are variations of the same scene or shot. There is always something that can go wrong, or somebody who might botch his part." My father stopped short, overcome by some unpleasant memory.

"I can see that they got around you," said my mother.

"No, not quite. Peter is doing well at school. It won't do him any harm. And he has a chance to meet some interesting people, and, well, generally . . ."

"Generally what?" asked my mother.

"I am taking Peter with me to America for the holidays. Do you hear?" called Cecilia so loudly that something clicked in the television set and the program changed to a show with chorus girls. My father did not have time to answer my mother's question. He settled hastily in front of the set and tried to sharpen the picture.

"I am not sure that I shall have time for America," I said firmly. "There's school, and my work in the film, and there are my scientific interests."

Cecilia stopped packing and her mouth dropped and she blinked her eyes. Then my mother, too, stopped helping her, and looked at Cecilia with new interest. She must have seen a quite different, more human face, which could be put on canvas and put in her exhibition.

"What a good thing it was that that damned comet missed us," said my father.

I went to the window and opened it halfway, because it was

hot outside. The last clouds had cleared away and a slight breeze held the not yet full-blown scent of spring. I thought how pleasant it was, and that there was no sense in worrying all the time about things that do not matter. Constant worrying, I decided, was a bore, and makes one old before one's time. Future troubles could be dealt with as they arose.

I already had my own girl friend, with golden hair and a face that looked as though she had just washed it with dew collected from forget-me-not flowers. Sebastian would call on me one day, I knew. He would surely visit me. It was nice to think that I could go off at any time to see Eva, for a change. She fills me with uneasiness, perhaps even fear, but I fancy her too. In fact I fancy her very much.

So, feeling rather pleased—so pleased, indeed, that I was beginning to fidget about by the window, which usually irritates my father—I looked at our little street in the spring sunshine, at the cheerful pigeon walking about on the bald head of the statue in the square, at Mr. Josef in front of his workshop revving engines, at passersby enjoying the fine weather, the band playing the old hit song. "It's a Lovely Day Tomorrow," at the men eyeing the girls more boldly, boys with their guitars, giggling girls in their short skirts, gay dogs hurtling about like torpedoes, at the huge jet plane circling over the city, carrying people to faraway lands and wonderful adventures.

But what of the Anthropos-Specter-Beast? I would rather you had not asked me that question. I would prefer my tale to have a pleasant ending. Besides, it is not very polite to be too curious. Everybody knows that curiosity killed the cat. . . . I advise you to close my book here and now. That is what I would do if I were in your place.

The worst thing is that soon I shall know all there is to know about the Anthropos-Specter-Beast, although I shall have to pay dearly for my knowledge, and when I do get this knowledge I shall never be able to pass it on. This is why I think it would be wiser for those of you who did not take my advice to choose any of the old, comfortable explanations for what I call the "Anthropos-Specter-Beast."

Give him the form of someone you know—some bore, some eccentric or malicious creature, an impudent fellow, an unpredictable crank, or a mad prophet—anyone who troubles our life. Let it be our everyday misfortunes, change—fate itself. Let it take the form of our nightmares, the anguish of the small hours, forebodings of pain, disaster, or death.

In fact I regret that I ever spoke of the Anthropos-Specter-Beast. It would be better for you never to have heard of him. It is possible that you could succeed in avoiding him altogether, but I am not sure.

As for me, I am no longer afraid of him. My fear has vanished, leaving me with a sense of relief. I imagine that all human beings cease to fear when their end is near. They begin waiting and longing for him to come and do his work with them.

The Anthropos-Specter-Beast is close to me now, all the time. By day he is somewhere behind my back, and from time to time I feel his breath in my hair. Sometimes his voice can be heard in the creak of a door, in the sound of the long fingers of the rain drumming on the windowsill, in the sudden stillness that waits like an eternity. I know that all these are not his real voice—that he has no need of these sounds to utter the things he has to say.

I no longer fear him. Every hour, every minute, every second, I am aware and waiting for this Anthropos-Specter-Beast of mine, who is probably the Anthropos-Specter-Beast of all mankind.

The door opens and the specialist, who is a woman, enters, followed by medical students. She looks cold. It must be freezing outside. She rubs her freckled, rather masculine hands together briskly. It occurs to me that she does this as an excuse for not looking at me. She asks her students something in a matter-of-fact voice and runs a quick eye over the chart at the foot of my bed, and the rocketing and plunging fever line of the graph. This graph fills me with terror. I know that this dreadful line breaks like a brittle wire every day, at its highest and lowest points, and then shoots straight down or up to its other extreme. The specialist looks at the analysis figures. Only eleven hundred white blood corpuscles are left. She puts it aside quite carefully.

"What dreadful weather!" she says. "One would not like a dog to be out in it."

"It seems that we are going to have the winter of the century," says one of the students, rubbing his spectacles.

"They keep the radiators going well," says the specialist. "No, I don't envy the people who have to be out today,"

"I do not envy anyone," says one of the students.

"Yes—well," says the specialist, brushing this remark aside, "perhaps we should move on toward three."

The students hasten to agree with her. They all seem to be in a hurry to leave, not because they do not like me or because they have more urgent things to attend to. There is simply nothing that they can say. My case has long since been exhausted as a topic of discussion. At one time there were jokes, laughter and banter, and appeals to patience and courage. They sometimes treated me as if I were an adult and explained that there are some difficult cases where medicine is rather helpless, but one must not lose hope, because medical knowledge is advancing by leaps and bounds and every day brings some new discovery. We live, they said, at a time of wonderful expansion of the human intellect.

"I would like to lie on my left side for a while," I say apologetically, because I do not want to be a nuisance.

They all turn back from the door. The specialist herself turns me over, so that I can see the window, the bare branches of the trees, and the smoke from the chimneys blown low over the rooftops. The others quickly rearrange my pillow and then they all go out.

Now I am alone again. I do not know what to do with myself, because I have no wish to go back again, in my imagination, to the street with the statue—a street that probably does not exist at all, or which, if it does exist, may be inhabited by quite different people. I do not want to go back to my home—to a mother who paints, to an irritable father, and Miss Sophie, with her slimming mania. If they had really existed they would not have left me here in this dreadful hospital. I do not want to see Sebastian, the

Investigator Dog, again, because nobody has ever actually met such a dog.

I ask you not to be angry with me for telling you such an unlikely tale. I would really like to be in love with a girl like Mayka or Eva, to play truant when I felt like it, to act in a film about space travel, fight with boys of my own age, read my sister's diary, even to be scolded and abused by an Aunt Cecilia. I would even like to get bored and fed up with life.

In fact, I invented this tale for myself, to free myself from pain and anguish and from my morbid thoughts. So do not take my fate too much to heart. Who knows? I may even get well, but if I do not, it is no matter—nothing will change. The comet will move again toward the earth. Trees will lose their leaves and bear fresh ones. Flowers will scent the air and produce their fruit. The young will fall madly in love, and the old will fear death. What matters is that, for a short while, I have enjoyed freedom. I wish you the same pleasure. If only one could enjoy good health. If only . . .